UNTANGLED PASSIONS

Jeanette was not prepared for the mind-numbing sensation of Julian's hands in her hair. Blinking in complete consternation, she did her best to steady her breathing.

Her eyes grew heavy as gooseflesh riffled her scalp, and shiver upon delightful shiver danced down her spine. The comb, like teasing fingertips, ran across her crown and around the tender tips of her ears. Julian's hands grazed the nape of her neck in gathering up the bulk of her hair. As the weight of her hair lifted, the breeze whispered against heated skin with sweet delicacy.

Jeanette closed her eyes. She was touched by his gentle consideration in not pulling too hard. She felt a definite sense of loss when he handed her back the comb, saying, "There, that's much better. Now you should be able to make it neat again."

"Thank you," she breathed unevenly. Her cheeks felt very hot, and her scalp tingled with the memory of his touch.

Jeannette had no idea of how beautifully pink-cheeked and alive she looked, or how much restraint it took in the man before her not to reach out to take her in his arms. . . .

SIGNET REGENCY ROMANCE
Coming in August 1995

Dawn Lindsey
An English Alliance

June Calvin
Miss Henderson's Secret

Martha Kirkland
The Marrying Season

Lord Endicott's Appetite

Elisabeth Fairchild

A SIGNET BOOK

To my English teachers
for fostering my appetite for words,
especially Doris Williamson.

SIGNET
Published by the Penguin Group
Penguin Books USA Inc., 375 Hudson Street,
New York, New York 10014, U.S.A.
Penguin Books Ltd, 27 Wrights Lane,
London W8 5TZ, England
Penguin Books Australia Ltd, Ringwood,
Victoria, Australia
Penguin Books Canada Ltd, 10 Alcorn Avenue,
Toronto, Ontario, Canada M4V 3B2
Penguin Books (N.Z.) Ltd, 182-190 Wairau Road,
Auckland 10, New Zealand

Penguin Books Ltd, Registered Offices:
Harmondsworth, Middlesex, England

First published by Signet, an imprint of Dutton Signet,
a division of Penguin Books USA Inc.

First Printing, July, 1995
10 9 8 7 6 5 4 3 2 1

Copyright © Donna Gimarc, 1995
All rights reserved.

Ⓟ REGISTERED TRADEMARK—MARCA REGISTRADA

Printed in the United States of America

Chapter One

~

Summer 1802

The wind blew fitfully out of the east, as the carrier let Jeannette down, hot, tired, and dusty, in front of the house, instead of at the rear as he should have. But it was the large, bedraggled mourning wreath, like a tear on the gray, ragstone face of the Elizabethan manor house, that drew Miss Saincoeur to the wrong door. That, and habit. She was not yet used to thinking of front doors as a piece of her past.

The wreath beckoned in the bright sunlight, a mute expression of a grief so deep it had been left hanging for all who passed to see. The black silk ribbons were wind-tattered and gray with dust, the paper flowers tired, the dingy paper gloves upon which had once been written the name and age of the deceased, faded into illegibility. This evidence of a grief, not yet dimmed enough to see clear to removing such an eyesore, touched upon a tender place deep within Jeannette's heart, a tender place that still made her wince on occasion. Here was kinship with the man who was to be her master, before even they were met. Here, in the wilds of Kent, of all places, for the first time since crossing the Channel, was a connection with home—the thin thread of grief. Weary, but hopeful, she put down her heavy valise, turned her face into the breeze, which smelled richly of sun-drenched growing things, lifted the ring in the brass door knocker's leonine mouth, and banged it smartly against solid English oak.

The hollow pounding echoed the rhythm of her troubled heart as she looked down at dusty shoes and remembered herself. Jeannette Saincoeur should not be banging on the front door at all! She was not a visitor here, to be welcomed by the butler. She was a servant, whose proper mode of entry was through the rear entrance.

The door swung open. It was dark and cool inside, with the closed-in smell of candle wax and unaired spaces.

A severe-looking gent with a stiff collar and even stiffer enunciation, peered down the length of his rather remarkable nose. "May I help you, miss?"

His tone was as cool as his unruffled appearance. Jeannette felt hot and blowsy by comparison. She was fluent in English, but every word flew right out of her head.

"Excusez-moi, monsieur! J'arrive . . ."

The butler held up his hand. "Pray speak the King's English if you wish to be understood."

Jeannette took a deep breath. With a slight inflection she said, "Pardon. My name is Jeannette Saincoeur. I am the new French cook. I believe I have come to the wrong door. Can you tell me the direction of the servants' entrance?"

Her mistake offended him. He raised his eyebrows as though it pained him, and pointed. "If you will be so good, Miss Saincoeur."

Hefting her valise, in one sweating, gloved hand, Jeannette bobbed her head. Her neck felt stiff. *"Merci, monsieur."*

Before either of them could move, an authoritative, female voice froze them in their tracks. "She says she's the French cook, does she? But, that cannot be!" The door flew wide and a starchy, middle-aged female in black bombazine and a spotless white apron and mobcap stood glaring at her, skirt kicking aggressively in the breeze. "I did not hire a female!"

Jeannette looked to the butler for some explanation of such an outburst. His coolly austere expression had grown even more remote.

The woman pulled a bit of paper from her apron and brandished it like a weapon. The breeze tugged rudely at the paper, as though to tear it from her hand. "I did not hire a female! I asked especially not to be sent a female! Who are you?"

Jeannette blinked in the face of such vehemence. "You are Mrs. Gary, the housekeeper?" She drew forth her own documentation, the letter from the hiring service in London, encouraging her to travel far into the wilds of Kent, here to this lovely Elizabethan home called Idylnook, and the widower who lived here, Lord Julian Endicott. The wind snapped her letter to life.

"They have requested that I come," she said.

"Well, I'm sorry for it. You have but to go back again. I'd no intention of hiring a French female for the kitchen. It was my understanding you were a man."

Jeannette felt as if the mischievous wind meant to whip her very position from her grasp. Disappointment bruised her patience. "But I have no money to return to London," she protested, slipping in her distress, into her native tongue. "I have here, a directive to come, and a great many miles have I traveled in order to oblige." The wind whipped the letter about like a standard.

"What does she say, Simms?" Mrs. Gary implored of the butler. "I cannot understand a word. Do make her go away. The dratted wind is blowing all manner of dust in the door. Half the candles in the house have gone out, I'm sure, and she'll be upsetting the master with all the Frenchified noise she's making."

Freed from the constraint of good manners by the knowledge that her native tongue was not understood, Jeannette unleashed a barrage of angry French, battering the two who blocked the door, with the same nagging intensity as the wind. "This is an abominable affront! Have you no honor? It is scandalous to turn a penniless female away without so much as a chance to show you what she can do."

"An atrocity," a cool, masculine voice, also speaking

French, silenced Jeannette from somewhere deep in the shadows of the entryway.

"Master Endicott . . ." the housekeeper began.

"Invite the young lady inside," the gentle voice wearily interrupted in English. "I do not care to have the crowd of you hashing it out on the front step."

Jeannette picked up what seemed to be the growing weight of her valise. The housekeeper scowled. "The young miss has airs, coming to the front . . ."

"Enough, Mrs. Gary." The emotionless voice seemed to grow less animated as Mrs. Gary's grew more shrill. "Simms, relieve the young lady of her burden."

Jeannette stepped into the darkness of the entryway, blinking against the sudden change in light as Simms took the bag from her hand and closed the door on the wind. It was cool here, cool and still, and she was met by the image of what seemed not so much man as wraith.

A figure as gentle and weary as the voice that had addressed them, was supported by the wall beside a door that led off the entryway. There was a sepulchral quality to the man's motionless stance, for the walls and ceiling were draped in black cloth, and the young man clad in the matte, unrelieved black of deep mourning, became a part of the shrouded darkness, like some grim, hollow-cheeked angel, carved from the wall.

The candlelight from the room behind him illuminated an unusually pale face framed by wings of equally pale hair. The face, the hair, thus seemed the only animated parts of him as he stood so quietly before her. This fine, fair, floating hair, which fell sleekly to his shoulders, rather like the feathers on a dove's back, lent his weary face an airy, almost youthful look, a tenderness of years that was not reflected in the shadowed, solemn gray eyes that regarded her.

"I am Julian Endicott," he said. "And you are?"

Jeannette dipped a low curtsy. "Jeannette . . ." Bouillé, she almost said, out of long lost habit, but caught herself. "Jeannette Saincoeur, Monsieur Endicott."

"Saincoeur," he mused with a flicker of interest. "Sound heart? An unusual name. Can you tempt my appetite, I wonder, Miss Sound Heart? I have not an easy palate to please."

Julian gave her one week—the feisty, dusty, little squab of a French female with the great, dark eyes that flashed with anger when told she must be going—seven days in which to convince him that his appetite had not gone to the grave along with his wife, Elinor. She had seemed pleased. The angry fire in her eyes had died down. She thanked him prettily, in the French he was used to hearing in the drawing room and not the scullery, and dipped a graceful curtsy despite the encumbrance of her dusty, white, drab cloak. The vague notion Julian had been harboring, that this young woman was one of the numerous French aristocrats fleeing France with nothing but their lives, seemed more likely than ever.

"But, Master Julian, what about Danny?" Mrs. Gary had hissed. "It was on his account I was set on hiring a man for the cook's position."

Julian shrugged. His head was hurting. This morning's adventure involved too much noise, and light, and decision making for his taste. "We shall see if she can cook first, and then worry about Danial." He waved Mrs. Gary away, convinced this morning's charity would amount to naught. She would be gone in seven days, the dark-eyed little bird whose feathers had gotten so ruffled. Without a squawk, she would fly away when she found she could not convince him to eat. Her going would not pain him, could not pain him. He was too numb with anguish to care what became of anyone, male or female, now that Elinor had slipped away. He was dead to all feeling but the great chasm of hurt into which her passing had plunged him.

Detaching himself from the wall, he withdrew to his study, closed the door, shoved the trouble of Danny and female cooks to the back of his mind, and fell to brooding over the letter from Margaret.

His elder sister informed him she was on her way to visit. She had word that he was still moping over Elinor, still traipsing about in full mourning, with the house still shrouded to the eaves and lit by no more than candles. She had heard that he refused to eat even so much as would keep a sparrow alive. She meant to put an end to it, she said. It was time to put the past behind him. More than a year was gone by, and in all that time his face had not been seen among polite society. Enough was enough. People had begun to talk. It was time to cast off his blacks.

She suggested they go together to Tunbridge Wells Spa, so that he might drink the waters. It was clear he suffered from the melancholy. The minerals of the spring were touted for their restorative qualities, despite the foulness of their smell.

The prospect of both his sister and foul waters, Lord Endicott found rather daunting. There was, in fact, something about Margaret's letter that made Julian want to laugh and cry at the same time. He chose to laugh. A bitter, flat sound, it chased the birds away from the draped windowsill, where they had been fluttering amongst the ivy, searching for bugs. The birds reminded him of the French woman. His laugh sounded again. A ridiculous thing, for any cook to upset herself over, cooking for him. He would not eat, no matter how delicious her recipes. Food was nothing to him, now. It tasted of nothing. He had no hunger in him.

Sorrow deadened one's appetite. It deadened all of the senses. Those who suffered not the loss of their most beloved, had no understanding of such matters. Sorrow could not be turned on and off like the mechanics of a clock. It sat beside one all the time, only briefly forgotten until unexpectedly a sound, sight, smell, or feeling roused it from slumber, and it reached out with malicious indifference, to squeeze one's heart again.

The new cook would cook for him, and his sister Margaret, would come and try to coax him away to Tunbridge Wells. He knew there was no stopping either woman's efforts. But it was all for naught. The only woman whose efforts he had cared about was dead and buried, and he held himself responsible. He wondered if he would ever reach a point of caring again.

Jeannette had no idea that, as far as the master was concerned, her fate was already decided upon. Quite contrarily, she got the feeling, as she was led through quiet, candlelit rooms whose tasteful opulence had been temporarily disguised by the dark draperies of mourning, that she had, at long last, come home. This place called Idylnook was decidedly elegant, but without too much formality for comfort. It possessed, beneath the pall of black baize, a harmonious blending of old and new—a light, airy, feminine quality that had little to do with the sad, brooding young man who had allowed her to stay here. Jeannette felt almost as if the hand that had created such an atmosphere had meant to personify her own worlds; old and new, dead and living.

There was a strong possibility that her feeling of belonging had less to do with atmosphere, and more to do with attitude. She was determined to fit in. But Jeannette had always been drawn to the idea of Fate. She decided Fate was at work, in bringing her both to this place, and to the attention of her new employer, so that she had not been sent away again to dank, dirty London. She had wanted a place in the country to settle, a comfortable nest to feather. Given opportunity to prove herself well suited for the niche that had been made available to her, she was not one to waste opportunity. She passed happily from the dark quiet of the dining and drawing rooms to the bright, noisy, odor-rich heat of the kitchens. Anticipation buoyed her progress. If this lovely house was to be her home, then she must make herself comfortable—especially here, in the throbbing heart of it.

Mrs. Gary paused in her tour, just within the doorway to the kitchen and turned to watch Jeannette as she introduced the staff she would work most closely with. "This is Polly the pastry cook, and our roasting chef . . ." there was a faint hint of censure in her tone, "Danial Fulsom."

Jeannette had the briefest impression of a round, flour-dusted woman and a handsome, florid fellow, who must be the Danny Mrs. Gary had worried over, before her attention was riveted by the roasting range that took up most of the wall behind them. Her mouth dropped open in a little Oh of admiration.

"*Merveilleux*! A Robinson!" She crossed the room to examine the wonder of something so new in such an old kitchen.

Danial Fulsom was quick to take credit for the machine that met with her approval.

"Lady Endicott had the range put in not long before she died," he said with chest-puffing pride. "Saw the one at Brighton Pavilion, she did, and was most impressed. Said she must have one for me." He winked at Jeannette, as if to intimate 'twas charm won him the honor of this oven.

Jeannette's gaze ran appreciatively along the shiny copper canopy above the range. Lady Endicott had been a very forward-thinking woman. Reverently, the pulley wheels that turned the roasting spits were tested, and with a grand flourish of his potholder, Danial opened the cast-iron door to the oven.

Jeannette was suitably awed. The range was a modern marvel. There were removable cast-iron shelves inside. One side of the fire was the oven while the other was made to wind up with a cheek so that the size of the flame might be reduced. The work of cooking would be much simplified with such a contrivance. Jeannette wished for a moment that Yvette might have lived to see such a thing. Yvette had been impressed by all things modern. Sadly, Yvette would never again leave France, and Jeannette, her *petit moineau,* was fortunate to be here in England, with the opportunity to work with such a range if she could but concoct something to tempt the dulled palate of a gentleman so lost in mourning he no longer cared to eat.

"You must be very proud." She faced Danial Fulsom at last.

The young man's eyes glowed as much as his cheeks as they roved over her, head to foot. "It's a rare piece of machinery," he agreed. "Does a roast to a perfect turn."

"We shall see what it does with a Sauce Hollandaise," she said.

He flashed a toothsome grin. "I have always been partial to things with a bit of sauce."

Jeannette was unmoved. She knew his type all too well. He meant to twist her words, to make them suggestive and crude. Gaston, her father's coachman, had been possessed of an equally charming smile and disarming style. He had been grinning as he led the screaming rabble into her father's town house in Paris. He had grinned as Jeannette's mother, father, and brothers; Antoine and Jean, were dragged away to the gaol, for no more crime than their breeding. A smile such as Danial possessed would never win Jeannette.

"You will show me more?" she inquired of the watchful Mrs. Gary.

The housekeeper nodded, and with a quelling glare at Danial, led the way past the marble pastry slabs where Polly was rolling out dough, through the well-stocked larder to the scullery, downstairs to the dark, musty chill of root and coal cellars. Simms, the butler, was persuaded to lead her on a tour of his double-keyed stronghold, the wine cellar. Then, Mr. Sandford, the head gardener, and Thad, his foreman, proudly took Jeannette and Mrs. Gary about the gardens, impressive in their very size and scope. They began in the neatly walled knot garden, where herbs were grown both as kitchen fare, and as decorative borders. They progressed to the more practical vegetable garden, with its snaking crinkle-crankle where the most tender fruit trees and bee boles sheltered from the wind, on to the three glass houses where the odor of flourishing exotics; flowers, melons, citrus, tomatoes, and cucumber, almost overpowered one. Jeannette was even offered a chilly peek into the heavily thatched icehouse, cleverly built into the ground, so that it might keep cuts of meat fresh long after slaughter.

Last but not least, she was led through a gated hedge into the orchards that flanked the gardens.

Here, swaying gaily in the wind, rank upon rank of fruit trees, most of them apple, lifted gnarled arms to the sky. Yellow, russet, red, and green, some of them bore French names that reminded Jeannette of home.

"Kent . . ." Mr. Sandford explained, "is known for its apples, cherries, pears, and plums. So bountiful is the crop here, in harvest, that great quantities of fruit are shipped into London."

Between the apple trees, currant bushes flourished. They, too, produced marketable crop.

Mr. Sandford waved a work-worn hand at a neat row of cottages that sided a narrow lane that ran along the edge of the orchard. "Those houses are occupied by Lord Endicott's tenants. They take care that the trees thrive, keep the weeds here to a minimum, and pick the fruit when it comes ripe."

Jeannette was impressed by the tidy, cared-for appearance of all that she had observed outside the house as well as with the lush abundance of foodstuffs she would have to work with. She had been told this part of England was known as the Garden, so fertile was the soil, so varied the produce. Seeing was believing. She was more determined than ever to make this lovely place her home. There was much to make one happy here, much to thank God, or providence, or the Fates for. In revolution-torn France, she knew, hunger had been a reality for a great many of her countrymen. Jeannette felt blessed to be welcome in this place of plenty. She closed her eyes a moment to soak in the warmth, and the green odor of growing things, and the buzz of happy bees. This place was not called Idylnook without good reason.

"I am, I think, stepped into an idyll, a paradise," she murmured.

Mrs. Gary met her pronouncement with a blank look, and

then a frown. One rarely appreciated the riches one had, until they were gone, Jeannette thought, but really, she did not think she had said anything that would merit a frown. The frown became a scowl.

"What is she doing here?" Mrs. Gary asked indignantly, her hands moving to her hips.

The 'she', referred to, Jeannette realized, turning around, was a simply dressed young woman, heavy with child, who looked to be several years her junior. Mrs. Gary swept past Jeannette.

Mr. Sandford stared without censure at the intruder, his face as clean and open, and weather softened as the soil in his garden. "One must watch where one's seed is cast here in Kent. Most anything will grow," he said evenly.

Jeannette nodded, her eyes following the progress of the pregnant girl, who was, it would seem, being cast out of the orchard. And none too happy about it either. She wept as she went.

Jeannette ventured to ask the gardener something that had been bothering her, for he wore no evidence of mourning, while everyone inside the house was clad in nothing but black. "I know you may find it impertinent of me to ask, but how long has it been since the funeral."

"Funeral?" He cocked his head at her, as though confused.

"Yes," she pressed. "Lady Endicott's funeral."

His brow cleared, and his pale, robin's-egg-blue eyes regarded her wisely. "My lady has been put to rest more than thirteen months ago, now."

Her mouth dropped open. "*Vraiment*! More than a year, and the house is still wrapped in shrouds? Is this the custom here in England? We do not publicly display our sorrow for so long in France."

Mr. Sandford cleared his throat, awkward with the situation. "'Tis the custom here at Idylnook," he said. "We all miss her ladyship, miss, but none more than the master."

Jeannette regarded the back of the house. Twelve weeks

of shrouding was more common than twelve months! She wondered if Lord Endicott had been somewhat unbalanced by the loss of his young wife.

Mr. Sandford seemed anxious to change the subject. "Now, Joss, my garden boy, will come to the kitchen every morning, miss, to inform you what is in season. He'll fetch up what you desire, given a list."

Jeannette looked about her, cataloging what there was to be offered. "*Bon.*" It was a shame the house draped its windows, so that those within saw none of the glory of this garden's lush evidence of life, light, growth, and color. Idylnook seemed distinctly out of character as a sad, lifeless, shuttered place surrounded by the lushest growth of flowers and vegetables she had ever had the privilege to witness. Just looking at the house brought an unexpected heaviness to her heart. She could not remain here if things did not change. She was a creature of light and joy, not dark melancholy. She must make a change here, or leave the place.

Invigorated by the challenge, she gave the gardener her brightest smile. "When Joss comes in the morning, will you have him bring along a young cucumber, and some of the flowering borage I noticed in the knot garden?"

Mr. Sandford smiled back at her, and Jeannette realized that this was the first truly genuine smile she had witnessed on any face in this, her new home. Perhaps, because he spent his days out of doors, amid growing things and sunshine, Mr. Sandford held himself remote from the sadness of the house.

" 'Twill be my pleasure to see it is done, miss," he said with genuine goodwill.

Returning to the house, Jeannette was introduced to the upstairs staff. The master's valet, Alphonse, a haughty, old-school Parisian, made a point of informing her that he, Simms, and Mrs. Gary, took their meals separately from the rest of the staff. Jeannette found such a hierarchy among the servants rather amusing. Class distinctions were severely frowned upon by this man's kinsmen across the waters of the Channel. She could not help but wonder how this Parisian would react, were he to know his supper was to be prepared by a member of the now largely extinct French nobility. Would he cry, "Off with her head?" or grovel to her in subservience and insist she, too, eat upstairs? These were confusing times for French men and women.

Dismissing such fanciful thoughts, Jeannette was relieved to be informed that she should meet the remainder of the household, the footmen, usher, chambermaids, housemaids, laundry maid, and scullery lass after the master's dinner was served, when the staff came to the kitchen in two shifts to eat of whatever the master did not fancy.

"Of late . . ." she was informed, with dour menace, by Mrs. Gary, ". . . the master does not fancy much."

She was shown the dark dining hall, and then the only bright room in the house, other than the kitchen. It was the solarium, where the master took breakfast and nuncheon, and which possessed too many windows to be fully darkened. The parlors where tea or coffee was occasionally served, however, were barely discernible for the gloom, and the ballroom seemed a vast, chill, lifeless place. The rest of the house was largely off limits to her, except, of course, the servants' quarters, in the attic, where she was to share a room with Polly the pastry maker. These cramped quarters were thankfully, not draped, and seemed quite cheery, decorated as they were in a hodgepodge of color and castoffs.

The servant's usher was Polly's niece, a simple, sweet-faced lass of no more than twelve, named Bet. She had seen to it that Jeannette's bed was dressed in fresh linen, her water pitcher filled, and her things unpacked. She had taken the liberty of borrowing a suit of the dour, black livery for Jeannette. It was laid out on the bed, awaiting her pleasure.

"There will be more made up to fit," the girl assured Jeannette, "if you are asked to stay on." Bet pursed her lips. "I've hung about, miss, because there were a number of items I know not what to do with." She held up what looked to be a very fine quality child's dress of quite old-fashioned cut, in a rich striped brocade, and then reached out for the low-cut, blue flowered French muslin dress that lay like an armful of blossoms next to the black livery. "This did not look at all like something a cook would wear—so bright, and pretty . . ."

Jeannette realized it must seem rather brazen to the girl, who had grown accustomed to seeing nothing but blacks and grays about the house. An eye-popping vermillion sash went with the blue sprigged dress, and a tight-fitting, scarlet, short jacket upon whose wide lapels was pinned a jaunty red, white, and blue cockade. She had meant to throw the cockade away as soon as she set foot on British soil. Her hand flew to the scarlet ribbon choker she wore about her neck in remembrance of those who had lost their heads in her homeland.

"Is this the fashion now, in France?"

Jeannette regarded the dress with fresh insight. These things must seem outlandish and strange to the young English lass. "Yes," she said bitterly. "That is the fashion."

Bet seemed to sense she had touched upon a nerve. "And what am I to do with this, miss?" She lifted a heavy green flannel bag from the bottom of the wardrobe. It contained Jeannette's most highly prized possessions: a silver-backed mirror, brush, comb, perfume flask, and salts bottle set. All proudly bore her family crest, a griffin—part lion, part eagle—wings stretched wide, talons extended. A fearsome-looking creature, the griffin was handsomely wrought by a master-craftsman in the heavy, gleaming silver. Jeannette felt they would look horribly out of place displayed atop the only surface that would hold them, a rough chest of drawers that was meant to hold her nightclothes and underthings.

"Wherever did you get such fine stuff, miss, if you don't mind my asking." Bet had pulled open the stringed bag, and was regarding herself cautiously in the hand mirror. "They're lovely." She tweaked a curl into place, and wiped a smudge from her cheek. "As nice as anything Lady Endicott ever had, although all such stuff be packed away now, for the very sight of them brings the master pain and suffering, don't you know."

Jeannette did know. She turned her back on the dresses and the silver. These bits of her past served little more purpose than to remind her of her own pain. The child's dress, especially, never failed to raise gooseflesh, while the cockaded muslin was a calculated mockery of her true feelings. Jeannette had worn it out of necessity in the days before she left Paris, that she might safely appear a champion of the very Revolution she did in fact despise for its heartless destruction of her family.

"Perhaps it would be just as well if you were to pack away the dresses and the silver pieces," she said softly, and bit down on her lip in order to stop even a single tear from overflowing. "They come from another life, and just as the master is pained by memories of his past, so, too, am I."

Bet nodded owlishly. "Best, too, that Danny does not see you in such finery. He'll make a grass widow of you, else."

"Grass widow?" Jeannette had never heard the term, and the last thing she wanted to be associated with was more death. "Whatever do you mean?"

Bet blinked at her as if she could not believe such ignorance. "You know," she insisted, with a suggestive curving gesture over her stomach.

Jeannette's brow wrinkled. "But, I do not know. I would not ask if I did."

"Never tell me no one has told you about Penny?"

"Who is Penny?"

Bet blushed, and leaned forward to speak in a hushed whisper, darting glances all the while over her shoulder, as if there would be dire consequences should someone else hear. "Coo! She was our dairymaid. Helped her father delivering the milk and cheeses and butter, you know. Danny . . . you have met Danny?"

Jeannette nodded. "The roasting chef?"

Bet grinned, revealing a gap where she was missing a tooth. "He's a handsome one, is he not?"

Jeannette shrugged.

"Well, handsome is as handsome does. Danny took Penny for a roll in the hay, but when she comes up with child, he wouldn't do the right thing and marry 'er. His head is as swollen as her belly, you see. Our Dan thinks he's too good for a mere dairymaid. Left her a grass widow, don't you know, to raise the infant on her own." The girl shook her head sadly. "Her dad has given us poor service ever since."

Grass widow. The term made good sense to her now. Jeannette touched Bet's work-reddened hand. "It is good of you to warn me about Danny, and to see to the settling of my things. Now, I must be off to make Monsieur Endicott something tempting for his dinner, else I shall have to pack my bags again and go away."

Chapter Two

~

D inner that evening was regarded as a complete failure by everyone in the kitchen except Jeannette. "Hardly touched a thing," Williams, the long-legged footman, said gloomily as the platters and bowls were returned to the kitchen for the staff feeding. "No more than a drop of the soup, a bite of bread, and a mouthful of the minted peas."

"None of the meat?" Danny groaned.

"He has spooned out a bite of pie here," Polly said hopefully, but Williams as quickly squashed her in saying, "Aye, but no more than a lick of it passed his lips."

Jeannette followed the footman back into the dining room as he continued to clear, but rather than help, as the others had begun to do, she first studied the remains on the sideboard, and scrutinized the pitiful mound of pastry on the bone china plate at the table. Then she drew a tsking from Williams by sitting in the master's chair, so recently abandoned it warmed her backside.

"Jeannette, you mustn't!" Polly gasped.

Jeannette ignored her. She did not occupy Julian Endicott's chair without good reason. She meant to understand the man, and in order to do so, she must see the world as he did.

It was no wonder Endicott touched so little of his food! At the far end of the long dining table, in the shadows of a room lit by no more than a handful of flickering candles, the portrait of a young woman stared back at her.

"Is that Madam Endicott?" she asked.

Williams was drawing back the draperies, so that the brilliance of the setting sun might further illuminate the ill-lit and shrouded room. "What? Oh, yes, Lady Elinor. Quite a good likeness."

Elinor Endicott had been everything that Jeannette was not. A fair, slender slip of a woman, with pansy blue eyes and a cloud of airy golden curls, she had a gay, carefree look about her, as if she were blissfully happy, both in herself, and in her life.

"She was beautiful!" Jeannette breathed.

Williams paused in picking up the platter of roast beef. "Aye, she was that. Always will be, don't you know. The master says 'tis our only consolation for those who die young. They remain ever frolicsome in our memories. Age has no opportunity to tarnish their shine."

"Hmmm." Jeannette found the observation rather extraordinary. She would not have thought the man who left his house draped in crêpe, and lit only by candlelight, capable of removing himself enough from the pain of his loss to make such an objective remark. Turning to the sideboard, she sighed with pleasure over the beauty of the sky as the sun set over the flower garden, and as quickly frowned in noticing the empty windowsills. She examined the table again. No flowers there, either! Vraiment, but this was a dreary place in many ways. She longed to go from room to room, throwing back curtains, opening windows to let in fresh air, and tearing down shrouds.

Jeannette picked up the tureen of minted peas, and took them with her to the kitchen.

Polly was carving up the leftover pie for the staff feeding.

"Polly, does not the gardener decorate the rooms here?"

"Used to." She licked a sticky finger. "The master asked him to stop, after his lady was laid to rest. Said the sight and smell of flowers sickened him. Too funereal. Mr. Sandford was quite put out. Not so the master could see, mind you, but he does like to pretty up the place. He's got quite a deft hand when it comes to the arranging of florals."

Jeannette smiled, and when the foreman came to the house to fetch the dinner buckets for the gardening staff, who ate in their own quarters, she asked him if he would be so good as to require Mr. Sandford to come and speak to her when dinner was finished. She asked the same of Mrs. Gary, by way of Williams, who carried food up to the little parlor where she and the butler and Alphonse, the valet, took their meals separate from the rest of the staff. Word came down again that Mrs. Gary would oblige.

"And very curious to know what it was all about, she was," Williams winked, clearly curious himself, but not bold enough to ask.

"When they come looking for me," Jeannette said in a very conspiratorial whisper, "have them come to the dining room."

The generals in the little army of servants that saw to the running of Lord Endicott's domain, found the new French cook comfortably disposed at the head of the formal dining table, elbows parked on gleaming mahogany, chin sunk in the palm of her hand.

"What is the meaning of this?" Mrs. Gary cried as she and Mr. Sandford came in together. "Remove yourself from the master's chair at once."

Jeannette jumped up. "*Oui!* For you must, yourself, sit here."

"I will not!"

"Yes, yes. Come!" Jeannette indicated imperiously. "You must sit, to understand."

"The woman's gone mad," Mrs. Gary said with conviction to Mr. Sandford.

The head gardener's pale, sun-wisened eyes settled on the portrait at the far end of the table. "Perhaps not," he said. With great care not to scratch polished wood, he changed the chair at the head of the table for another. "Humor her a bit, and we'll see soon enough."

Mrs. Gary sat herself gingerly in the provided chair. Mr. Sandford stood, hat in hand, behind her.

"*Bon!*" Jeannette paced the room with nervous energy. "You are now Lord Endicott. What do you see?"

"This is ridiculous! Whatever do you mean?"

Jeannette looked desperately to Mr. Sandford. "Have I not said the English correctly?"

"Look!" Mr. Sandford leaned in over Mrs. Gary's shoulder to point a gnarled finger.

"Yes, I know, I know, it is the portrait of . . ." The housekeeper paused, realization dawning. "Oh my! Dear Lady Endicott staring down at him throughout every meal! No wonder the poor man does not eat."

Jeannette smiled at the two of them, her eyes brimming with sudden, unexpected tears. "Oui! You see." She reversed the direction of her pacing.

"Indeed I do. But, what is to be done?" For the first time since Jeannette had encountered Mrs. Gary, the woman looked nonplused.

"It has occurred to me that we might rearrange the room," Jeannette suggested, her hands gesturing energetically. Oh, but she would like to make changes here. "It would be wonderful to take down the shrouding. Perhaps open the windows?"

Mrs. Gary shook her head. "That would never do, any of it, without the master asking for it specifically."

Jeannette bit her lip. "*Quel dommage!*"

"Any more ideas?"

Jeannette strode to the window, where a large vase, that should have held flowers, stood empty. "I do have another, but it involves bringing flowers into the room, and more candles."

Mr. Sandford frowned. "Won't fadge . . ." he began.

Jeannette raised her hand. "Wait! I know Monsieur Endicott has complained of the sweet smell, so it did occur to me that if great care was taken not to duplicate the flowers used in any funereal arrangements, and if stalks of fresh herbs were mixed into the bouquets, the smell might not be too objectionable."

Sandford sucked in his cheeks and looked to Mrs. Gary. "It might do."

She nodded her agreement. "If it will break the master's fast, I am willing to give anything a try. He's wasting away, poor soul."

"I'll risk bringing in herbs, but not flowers," Mr. Sandford said. "I'll not go against his wishes, you understand?"

Jeannette beamed at him. "But of course."

Jeannette began to understand Julian Endicott's aversion to flowers a little better when she saw him ride away from the house on the following morning, just as Joss came to the door, bearing the garden's fresh offerings of fruit and vegetables. Along the gravel drive behind the boy, crunched the master's favorite gray horse, a bundle of fresh-cut flowers, their stems wrapped in damp burlap, strapped across his well-groomed withers.

There was a broken look about the way Lord Endicott sat the animal, as though the weight of sadness rounded his shoulders, and took all the starch from his backbone.

"Wherever does monsieur go with so many flowers?" Jeannette wondered aloud. Joss turned to look.

"To see his missus," the lad explained.

Jeannette looked at him blankly. Did Lord Endicott have a mistress? "Where?"

"Graveyard," the boy clarified. "'E goes every Wednesday morning at this same time. Takes fresh cuttings again on Sundays before services. 'Tis the only reason the master so much as looks at the hothouse blooms Mr. Sandford coaxes along. It's a wonder the old gent bothers. Fair breaks Mr. Sandford's heart, it does, to see his prize-winning blooms go ignored. He has got such a knack for growing the persnickety varieties. Takes ribbons at the county showings, does our Mr. Sandford. 'Tis a right shame his lordship holds the things in such disdain, don't you know."

"Oui," Jeannette said thoughtfully. She did know. "Everyone likes to be recognized for their creative genius," she said thoughtfully as she watched Lord Endicott's horse turn the corner of the house. Where did this man's own personal creative strengths lie? She had no real idea of what Julian Endicott did with himself when he was not secreted away in the country, mourning the untimely passing of the woman with whom he had hoped to create a family and future.

"What does the master do?"

Mrs. Gary was the one Jeannette decided to ask, no more than three-quarters of an hour later.

"Why, he's a member of the House, love, an independent Tory, whatever that means, and heavily involved in foreign affairs. He was right in the thick of the decision-making surrounding the attempt to settle things in France not so long ago. You will be interested to hear, I am sure, that he was in the midst of some sort of plan to oust Napoleon when his lady died."

Jeannette was interested, very interested. She only peripherally caught the gist of what Mrs. Gary said next—something to do with Lord Endicott serving as an M.P. for his home county, in Devon, where he had yet another estate.

"And, has he any hobbies?"

"Hobbies, love?" Mrs. Gary looked askance, as though quite at a loss to understand why she should want to know such a thing.

"Yes, I cannot help but think that some occupation of his mind, and time and interest, might lift Monsieur Endicott's spirits somewhat. I know from personal experience, that at the most difficult time of my life, I was very pleased to lose myself in cooking and sewing, embroidery and reading.

These pastimes served well in diverting me from sad and brooding thoughts."

"Hmm," Mrs. Gary mused. "I have never given the matter much consideration. Lord Endicott is not given to hunting, or fishing or cockfights if that is what you mean, and while he does play cards on the odd occasion, I do not think he likes them to excess. Chess! He does play chess quite well, and backgammon, though I have not seen him touch the boards these many months. He occupies himself with reading mostly, and the occasional ride, or a long walk on the downs when he is not working at something. Other than that . . . he is rather fond of travel, but do you know, I think he enjoyed conversation more than anything else. He and Lady Endicott did sit up some nights just chatting away in the most animated fashion. I have thought, on more than one evening since then, how still the house sits. I hesitate to say this, for I am sure you will think me a most fanciful creature, but I have had the strangest impression some nights, when a draught stirs that wretched black cloth above our heads, that Idylnook itself tries to talk, for it is tired of waiting. It longs for voices again."

Jeannette did not find such thoughts in the least outlandish. She found the dark and draped house too eery in the evenings for her own liking.

The housekeeper laughed. "The old house longs for animated conversation as much as I long to tear down these yards and yards of dreadful black cloth. The master's sister will fly into a temper when she finds it still hanging, mark my words." She scowled at the ceiling. "She will find some way to blame it all on me, just you wait and see."

Jeannette regarded the ceiling speculatively. "It is awful stuff and grown quite dusty with the passage of time."

"Oh! We are shabby with dirt. The upstairs maids are forever complaining that it is impossible to keep the stuff from raining down on everything. 'Tisn't healthy! I have told the master as much, at least a half-dozen times."

Jeannette's eyes lit with sudden thought. "When is wash day, Mrs. Gary?"

"What? For household linens, do you mean?" The older woman shrugged. "Next month sometime, I think. You must ask our washerwoman . . ."

"No, no," Jeannette objected. "I think you must declare a washday soon, perhaps before the week is out."

She stared at the dusty shrouding, and when Mrs. Gary turned to her, with a look of understanding dawning in her eyes, she arched her dark brows.

"Do you mean we should take it all down?"

"Oui. But of course. You are a woman who insists on keeping a clean house, non?"

The idea was enlarging itself in Mrs. Gary's mind. "That's my job," she declared stoutly. "The shutters, too, are filthy. We must throw them all open and have a scrubbing."

"But, of course." Jeannette winked at her.

Mrs. Gary sighed. "Too bad we shall have to hang it all back up again."

"Perhaps." Jeannette weighed the idea. "Perhaps not. It is possible, that once down, Monsieur Endicott will decide the hangings should stay down."

"At least until his sister is come and gone." The house-keeper nodded emphatically, quite caught up in the spirit of their plot. "Quite right. We are long overdue a washday, Miss Saincoeur."

The whisper of a sound caught Mrs. Gary's attention. "Hisst, there's the master, come back again already from visiting Lady Elinor's grave. He will be moodier than usual, I warn you."

Small wonder Lord Endicott disliked flowers, Jeannette thought. The only time he had anything to do with them, it had something to do with his tragic loss. He could not fail to be saddened by them.

"*Peste!*" She jumped up, alarmed. "*Peste*! The flowers!"

"What?"

Jeannette did not pause to explain, merely raced out of the

drawing room in which she had cornered the housekeeper, toward the kitchen. She hoped she was not too late.

Before she had begun her conversation with Mrs. Gary, Simms, the butler, had most reluctantly agreed to another of her schemes to cheer Julian Endicott out of his melancholy moodiness. But, in agreeing, he had made it clear that Jeannette must take full responsibility for the outcome of her putting a prettily edged cucumber fan on the lip of the master's claret cup, and a sprinkling of borage flowers on the surface of the liquid itself.

The cup, a wedding gift to Lord Endicott from his late wife, was exquisite, even without the enhancements. Heavy, chased silver, its lip and base were decorated with an elaborate border pattern of fan-shaped chevrons, through which a flowered vine wound. It sat, every morning, upon its matching silver tray, in the butler's pantry, awaiting the master's summons, accompanied by a cut-glass claret jug, with matching silver mount, handle, and lid. Jeannette had cut her cucumber fan to echo the lovely chevron pattern, but Simms had not been impressed with her handiwork.

"He will not be pleased, young lady, mark my words. The master does not care particularly for flowers—any flowers. I do not care if you do insist they are no more than herbs."

He had tried to warn her. Now it was too late. The claret cup was gone, the butler's pantry vacant. Jeannette peeped out of the swinging door. The door to the library clicked shut before her eyes. *Peste*! Why had she not arrived but a moment sooner?

Simms exited the library almost as speedily as he had entered. As predicted, the master was not pleased. She could read as much in the severe elevation of the butler's eyebrows and the pinched narrowness of his mouth.

"Lord Endicott wishes to see you," he intoned, nostrils flaring.

"Oui, monsieur," she said, sighing.

"He was not pleased," he saw fit to warn her.

With sinking heart, and a sense of approbation, Jeannette

approached Endicott's private domain. This was the room the soft-spoken gentleman she had encountered yesterday had disappeared into. Simms was the only servant she had since seen cross its threshold. She had been informed this one room was completely off limits to the staff unless otherwise directed. Taking a deep breath, she rapped on the paneled door.

"Come."

She went in swiftly, her smile forced. Was she to be cast off over a flower in the claret cup?

The library was dark, like every other room in the house, but in a way it was also vastly different. This was very clearly a man's room, untouched by the pale, feminine taste that influenced the decoration throughout the rest of the house. There was instead a mellow, well-worn comfort to the place, a rich wood and leather repose so insinuating that Jeannette was moved by the thought that were her circumstances different, she would have liked to come to this room to kick off her shoes, take down one of the moroccan-bound books that filled walnut step cases almost wall to wall, and curl up in one of the deep, leather chairs. Circumstances being what they were, she restrained herself to dipping a graceful curtsy.

"Monsieur?"

A dark silhouette against the single bar of light that dared leak through the dark draperies over the window, he turned. His face swam in the golden light, like a dust mote, his hair lit up like a halo. Sad, gray eyes studied her with baffled interest beneath pale, glowing pigeon wings of glossy hair. "There is a flower floating in my claret cup, Miss . . ."

"Jeannette Saincoeur, my lord."

"Yes. How could I forget—Miss Sound Heart. Simms informs me you are responsible."

"*Oui*. For the cucumber as well."

Pale eyebrows rose into the windblown forelock of pale, backlit hair. His eyelashes, she saw, were pale gold. "Very pretty, but I do not think . . ."

"It is not just for beauty's sake, sir."

"No?"

"No, monsieur. Borage is imbued with the power to light en men's hearts and drive away sadness."

Quietly he regarded her, as though seeing her for the first time, his compelling gray eyes like deep wells of sorrow. "All of that in such a little flower?"

She smiled. "So they say, monsieur."

He stared down into his exquisitely embellished cup, his lashes a pale golden fan against the bruised blue of sleep-deprived skin. "You deem my heart too heavy then, Miss Sound Heart?"

"Oui, monsieur. Much too heavy. You do not agree?"

He was a moment in answering, but at last his hollow gaze rose to regard her with as much interest as he had bent on the cup.

"My heart, Miss Saincoeur, is not sound, like yours. It is sunk so low 'twill take more than flowers to lift it."

Jeannette read the pain in his eyes. It reached out to prod the ache in her own heart. Maintaining eye contact, she said softly, "Oui, monsieur, I know. But it is a small step in the right direction, non? And, your wife, did she love you, would want you to sip happiness and not sorrow, from the cup she gave you, yes?"

He looked away from her, into the darkness of the room, his jaw working. With shaking hands he raised the claret to his lips, that he might sip it. "Yes!" His tormented answer echoed tragically in the cup.

She took that as dismissal, and turned for the door.

The gentle voice stopped her. "The cucumber, Jeannette, does it possess medicinal qualities as well?"

She pivoted, smiling ruefully.

His lips lifted ever so faintly. He had a tight rein on his emotions again.

"The cucumber is to please the eye, monsieur. Beauty is, I believe, strong medicine for the soul. It reminds those who pine for the dead that there are reasons, small though they may be, both to remain in this world and to admire it, while we are given the precious breath with which to do so."

The gray eyes locked onto hers, as if to probe the very depths of her scarred soul. Jeannette understood the intensity of his searching gaze, and returned the look without blinking. This man stood in the shadowland between the living and the dead. She had herself once stood in that lonely place.

Something he saw in her eyes made him frown. "You are a most curious cook, with a most curious name, Miss Sound Heart. I will drink your flowered herbs for one reason. I should like to taste joy again. Do you know, I have quite forgot its flavor?"

Head bent into that single shaft of light leaking through the dark draperies, he turned to look out of the window, sipping the claret.

Julian saw an uncertain view of the garden through the ripples that marred the clarity of the windowpane. He could no longer claim indifference where Jeannette Saincoeur was concerned. His conversation with her, over the little blue flowers in his claret cup, was too unusual to relegate to a state of forgetfulness. Like the mild cucumber taste of the borage flowers that bobbed in his drink, her observations left a mildly pleasant aftertaste lingering in his mind.

She understood him. He sensed it. She understood the place he occupied, as no one else seemed to, since Elinor's death. He could see it in her great, brown eyes, hear it in the soft, melodious rhythm of her voice. He found himself faintly irritated by her awareness, and mildly threatened by such acuity in a stranger. This unprepossessing female upset his daily pattern, both in thought and deed. She intrigued him, and he was not really in a mood for intrigue. He had become too comfortable, wallowing in morose inactivity, for intrigue.

He was slightly peeved in noticing changes in his dining arrangements from the instant he was met at the door that evening, by Simms. There was a careful expectancy in the staid butler that immediately put him on his guard. Were there more blue flowers to deal with? Awareness heightened, he could not but anticipate this meal with piqued curiosity, though the nuncheon, brought to him in the solarium, had been nothing out of the ordinary. Miss Sound Heart was an original. No telling what she meant to serve up to him tonight.

The dining room, when he stepped past Simms, met him with a sense of expectancy. The lighting was changed, more candelabra having been added. Altered, too, was the very odor of the place. Sprays of flowers and greenery were arranged in the vases along the windowsills.

He had forbidden flowers.

"Who has placed flowers in here?" he demanded of Simms.

The butler bowed. "They are not really flowers at all, milord."

"Are they not?" Julian asked, his voice dangerously soft. "They look remarkably flowerlike to me, Simms."

"Herbs, sir." Simms sounded calm, but he was nervous, Julian could see, by the beat of his pulse in the blue vein that throbbed above his temple. "Thyme, Rosemary, Rue, Lavender. To freshen the air. Miss Saincoeur, my lord, asked Mr. Sandford if he would make an arrangement of them. She complained of the room's mustiness, my lord. Shall I have them removed?"

Julian leaned forward to sniff. It was true, these flowers, small and pungent, like the borage in his claret cup, had not the sickly sweet odor that he associated with his wife's demise. He had not expressly forbidden herbs being placed in the room. A smile touched his mouth, and was as swiftly gone.

"The room was musty, was it?" Julian looked about him, as though seeing the space around him for the first time. How did this place look and smell to a stranger? To the curious Miss Sound Heart? Did it reek of sadness, of sorrow, of death? "Well, we cannot have that, now, can we?"

Simms nodded agreeably, as he drew Julian's chair invitingly from the table. "Quite right, my lord."

The arrangement of the table, too, was changed. A great glossy tower of apples: all perfectly formed, and in a variety of color, stood as centerpiece, where flowers might once have been decoration. Miss Saincoeur, it would seem, had been informed of his command, and sought to honor it, in her own peculiar way. His napkin was the only exception to his ban on flowers. It had been folded into an attractive white rosette. He shook it out and placed it in on his lap.

"Simms?"

"My lord?"

"Has the lighting in this room been rearranged?"

"Yes, my lord, Miss Saincoeur . . ."

". . . feared I might not be able to see to eat?" he broke in sarcastically.

"Oh no, milord! Not at all. She pronounced this a delightful room, sir, once the gloom was dispelled."

"Gloomy and musty, are we? It would appear Miss Saincoeur is accustomed to far finer accommodations than we have to offer."

He did not expect an answer, but Simms would seem to have possession of a bit of gossip too good to be kept secret.

"I daresay you may be right, my lord. I am informed our new cook carries with her a crested, silver dresser set. She may very well have once been a member of the French nobility."

Julian had no retort ready for this divulgence. He had already suspected as much. "You may serve," he instructed.

The food William brought to him in steaming courses, he had expected to be different, and indeed the meal wore an entirely fresh face. The platters were artfully arranged. A harmony of color and texture and form transformed even the most ordinary of dishes into something that required his attention. Fans of fresh herbs freshened the trays along with piquant sauces that had been dribbled into the plates in attractive lace patterns. Roses, birds, and curlicue shapes cleverly cut from radishes or carrots, enlivened many of the platters. Even the bread had been braided differently, and dusted with patterns of sesame seed. Presented in such a fashion, his food took on a foreign look, an exotic allure.

"What is that?" he asked of Simms.

"Layered crepe with smoked salmon, my lord."

"And that, and that?"

"Ratatouille in aspic, my lord, followed by veal scallops in a hazelnut sauce, and wild mushroom tarts."

Tempted by the selection— what Julian could not ignore, he began to taste. And as he considered the variety of flavor as it was here presented to him; creamy, herbed, tart, smoky, buttery, nutted and sweet, he thought of what Jeannette Saincoeur had said about the small things that made one glad to be alive.

A rich bouquet of flavors beckoned. There were dishes he sampled, that once tested, he must eat. He could not have stopped himself if he had tried. He did not try. For the first time in over a year, his mouth watered. For the first time since the funeral, he had an appetite. He took pleasure in the meal.

There was a niggling guilt in this fleshly fulfillment, that had him lifting his head to gaze at the far end of the table, where Elinor might have sat. But every time he looked in that direction, his eyesight was assaulted by the overwhelming vision of the enormous silver epergne usually reserved for banquets of state, that had been so thickly piled with apples of every variety, shape, and color, each of them glossy and perfect, and so overwhelmingly artful in their arrangement, that he was distracted. The source of his uneasiness eluded him.

It was not until the desserts were brought in, the hero of which was a fantastic floating island à l'orange, a melt-in-the-mouth meringue concoction coated in caramelized sugar, and floating in a sweet, custard sauce, whose beauty

he felt compelled to share with someone, that he realized the
most dramatic change in the room had less to do with what
he saw, than in what he did not see. He did not, for the first
time in months, have the beloved specter of Elinor staring at
him from the far end of the table. The change of lighting,
coupled with the breathtaking epergne mountain of fruit,
blocked what might have been his ordinary view of her
painting.

Considering the implications of this change, he sipped
hot, fragrant coffee, toyed with a serving of the floating
island, and felt there was something poetic in his consuming it. He was himself, become an island of sorts. Jeannette
Saincoeur was a clever woman! He had not realized until
this instant, that he had spent the last year eating dinner,
not alone, as he had supposed, but with a ghost for company.

He could not help marveling over the hands that had
brought him such a beautiful gift, a small thing, really; a
meal he found appetizing—a meal he had consumed with
the appetite of a man who had never tasted food before. "My
compliments to our new cook, Simms," he said, patting napkin to lips.

"Yes, my lord," Simms said with his customary stoicism.

"Simms . . ." Julian pushed away from the table, took up
one of the branches of candles, and displaced the darkness
that gathered around the portrait of Elinor.

"Milord?"

The food in Julian's stomach seemed suddenly very
heavy, as he stared up at the cold, lifeless rendering of what
had once warmed him. Jeannette Saincoeur's tower of fruit
had not completely deceived him, and yet her canny
arrangement made him realize he could not continue to sit
table with the dead. "It is time we removed Lady Elinor's
portrait to the family gallery," he said softly.

Simms's jaw waggled for no more than an instant. "Yes,
milord."

"Will you see that it is replaced with . . ." Julian paused.

What would be appropriate? His gaze fell once more upon the apple centerpiece that was Jeannette Saincoeur's handiwork. Yes, of course—art imitating life. "Bring the still-life from the library, Simms."

Chapter Three

~

Jeannette was summoned to that same library only moments later, as she arranged for the feeding of the servants. Polly and Dan took over her responsibilities, that she might go at once, flushed and heated from her efforts in the kitchen, to see why Lord Endicott required her presence. She put on a fresh apron and smoothed her hair as she went. What did the gentle, mourning soul have to say to her? Did he mean to tell her she might stay on as cook? She hoped so. He had eaten well.

He was seated in a wing chair by the cheerless fireplace when she entered, nursing a glass of brandy in the bowl of his hand. The room seemed cool and quiet, far removed from the noise and bustle of the kitchen. A clock ticked with steady precision from the mantel.

"Jeannette Saincoeur, monsieur." She dipped a curtsy. "You wished to see me?"

The sad, gray eyes swung away from their study of the brandy. "I remember your name, Jeannette. You need not identify yourself to me every time you enter my presence. And yes, I wished to see you."

He paused, the brandy swirling in his hand, and she was struck by the notion that he had in fact wanted nothing more than to look at her, for his gaze took her in, in a most searching manner, head to foot.

She waited, stomach growling with hunger. She had not yet eaten.

There came a knock on the door.

"Come!" Lord Endicott called, pulling his gaze from her. Simms entered, the footmen behind him.

"We have come for the painting, my lord."

Julian Endicott waved them inside. Jeannette found herself fascinated by this small, fluid movement of his hand. There was a gentle grace about this man, an ease and naturalness of presence that reminded her of the movement of swans on water. Jeannette jerked her attention away from the swimming hand. He must not catch her staring.

With a great deal of careful maneuvering, the large still-life above the desk was taken down, the footmen never lifting their voices above a murmur in their instructions to one another.

Julian Endicott's lips curled up ever so slightly as the door closed behind the last man out as the painting was carried away. His attention returned to her. "Your tower of fruit was most effective, Miss Saincoeur, but I am relieving you of the burden of building a wall between me and my sorrow, by changing out the painting in the dining room."

Jeannette could not tell if he meant to amuse or reprimand her with his remark. Hoping for the best, she said softly, "How wise of you, monsieur."

He allowed the upward tilt of his lips to increase. His sad, gray gaze traveled over her face, as if he found something unexpected there. "How is it, Miss Sound Heart, that a stranger in my house can see what is wrong with my appetite more clearly than I see myself?"

Jeannette could not stop staring into the sad, troubled face. "Your eyes are dimmed by sorrow, monsieur. It hangs like a cloud in front of your vision."

"And my servants, most of whom have known me all of my life. Are the windows of their vision shuttered, too?"

Jeannette nodded. "They are blinded, sir, by their very closeness to you—by their love for you."

He looked into the swirling brandy, as if he might find answers there. "And you, Jeannette? Do you see me clearly because we are distant?" He presented the thought as if it puzzled him. His searching gaze took her in again, head to foot. "Because you have no love for me?"

Gooseflesh raised the hair on Jeannette's arms. This talk of love sounded strangely improper on the tongue of this very proper Englishman. She felt a flame begin to burn in her throat, in her cheeks and temples. The room seemed suddenly too warm. She nodded, with a feeling of self-consciousness, and her words fell thickly from her throat. "I do not know you well enough to love you, monsieur. My objectivity has a clarity that comes with distance."

Round and round the brandy swirled. "Hmm. Do you think someday you will love your master too much to remain objective in serving his needs? Will affection, like a fine mist, hamper your ability to see?"

Tick-tock, the clock marked each passing moment as Jeannette collected her thoughts enough to answer such a question. Tick-tock. This conversation was disturbing. Her hands felt awkward, her back too stiff. Tick-tock.

"Shall I guard my heart against all affection for you, monsieur? I had hoped to make this my home."

Julian took a swallow of the brandy, and leaned forward in his chair, as though the better to impress on her the importance of his words. "I would advise you to guard your heart against loving anyone, Jeannette. It hurts, far too much, losing a loved one. You must not invest yourself lightly in any such a connection."

She smiled inside. A wistful smile, it bespoke experience rather than humor. His pain spoke with a bleak force equal to her own not so many years ago. The intensity of that pain would fade with time. She no longer guarded her heart so closely. She knew there was a pain in loneliness that outstripped even that of loss. Very carefully, she suggested, "Was it not an Englishman who said, 'it is better to have loved and lost, than never to have loved at all'?"

Julian studied his little French bird with faint surprise. She was not so tame a creature as he would have supposed, to dare to remind him of his loss. Odd. In all the time since Elinor's passing, none of his servants dared broach the subject of her death to him. In the past two days, this audacious stranger seemed to speak of nothing else.

"You read Shakespeare?" he asked, and then wished he had not. It was a stupid question. Of course she read Shakespeare. The woman was obviously well educated. "If you appreciate literature, Miss Saincoeur, perhaps, as my little way of thanking you for the return of my appetite this evening, you will feel free to accept the loan of some of my reading materials? There are a number of French volumes. Will you select something?"

"You are very kind." She smiled, a light kindling in her eyes. He decided she was very pretty when she allowed such a curve to grace her lips.

Mellowed by the excellent brandy he swallowed, the delectables that had satisfied his hunger, and the pleasure of his own generosity in allowing a servant free run of his library, Julian watched Jeannette Saincoeur with lazy fascination as she began to circle the room, hands clasped in the small of her back. There was something foreign—decidedly French—in the way she walked and tilted her head to examine the spines of the books he had to offer.

Through the veil of his lashes, Julian decided Jeannette was not the squab of a woman he had first imagined. She was small, yes, but lithe, in the way of the French. Very neat she looked in the black livery all his servants wore.

Black did not especially suit her coloring or complexion. There was too much dark about her already, in the glossy curl of her hair, and the sparkling depths of her eyes. The translucence of her skin seemed too pale against the void of black. Black swallowed her up, making her seem unworthy of note, when he could not think of anyone he had met of late, more worthy. Rose would suit her better, to bring out the fragile roses in her cheeks.

He blinked. Rose-colored livery? There was something rather Baroque about the idea, that brought to mind the ser-

vants in his grandfather's house. They had worn puce until
the old man's death, no matter that such a color was decidedly passé. Elinor had found the old man's livery vastly
amusing, but had always waited until they left his presence
to let her amused gurgle to voice itself. Elinor. She was the
reason his servants still wore black, though she would have
laughed at such excess as much as she had found puce amusing. "How very dour, Julian," she would have pouted. "To
look at black, and think of me. I will not have it, for you
know how much I hate the absence of color."

Julian raised the brandy to his lips again. Why did such
thoughts plague him? Why did fragmentary conversations
with a dead woman sound with such substance in his ears?
Why could he not stop the hurting and forget?

Jeannette Saincoeur reached for a book in the same
moment that the sip of brandy slid over his lips. As the warm
fire of liquor cascaded over his tongue and into his sated
stomach, Julian found his attention fixed on the sweet curve
of breast exposed to him in her movement. God, how he
missed the soft comfort of Elinor's breast!

His attractive little cook turned toward the nearby branch
of candles, that she might examine her find. The candlelight
radiated with a gentle, saffron light upon her features. Face,
figure, and hair, she seemed gilded by the light. For an
instant, sweet and golden in his gaze, like the ripe fruit that
had filled his eye through so much of dinner, she stirred a
hunger in him. It disturbed him, that this woman, who so
deftly roused his appetite, should as easily rouse another
appetite within him. That even a flicker of this more fleshly
hunger crossed his mind, seemed a betrayal of sorts, a
cheapening of his loss of wife and companion.

Julian had not realized how starved he was for a young
woman's company, a young woman's voice. He longed for
the intimacy of a woman's touch as he gazed at Jeannette
Saincoeur. Loneliness, sorrow, and suffering, none of these
had killed off completely his appetite for warmth and com-

forting, for the driving rhythm of life. Need and desire came growling into his awareness with startling force.

Ashamed and angered by the strength of his baser needs, he wondered if the desire he was feeling somehow voiced itself in his eyes, for when Jeannette Saincoeur approached him, with the work she had chosen to peruse, she met his gaze for a moment, as though something in his regard surprised her, and then swiftly looked away.

The book she had chosen surprised him. It was a current collection of essays, including *Reflections on the French Revolution*, by Edmund Burke.

"Heavy reading," he observed, more fascinated than ever by this surprising young woman. He had expected her to choose a gothic romance, or a book of poetry.

She shrugged. There was something very French in the gesture, something that would seem to establish a casual camaraderie between them.

"I have heard a great deal said about these words," she said. "I should like to judge them for myself."

"A very sensible endeavor," he said, impressed by her orderly thinking. She was an admirable creature—attractive, and creative and vibrantly alive on a variety of levels. He wondered again as to her background, and was left wondering, for she briskly excused herself, and as briskly abandoned the room. He found himself alone again with his brandy and his books, a cheerless fireplace and cheerless thoughts.

Chapter Four

~

There was a noisy celebration in the kitchen that evening, as the remains on the elegant platters and bowls were devoured with high acclaim by the staff. The master had eaten, for the first time since his lady's passing, really eaten! And no wonder. The table had looked a picture, and the food . . . my, wasn't everything delicious? There was no doubt in anyone's mind, that the lengths gone to, in preparing room and food to Jeannette's specifications, had proven worthwhile.

"You've been asked to stay on now, haven't you, Miss Saincoeur?" Williams, his cheeks bulging with salmon crepe, winked at Jeannette when she returned to the kitchen.

Jeannette shook her head. It was strange that with so much revealed, nothing had been said to relieve her mind on that score. "Monsieur Endicott has not yet said," she responded. "I do hope you are correct. I've no place else to go."

Three days passed, and each one brought no definitive word as to Jeannette's continued status as French chef for Lord Endicott, no matter that she drove herself nearly witless with the planning of her menus and the arrangement of his food. Julian continued to sample whatever Jeannette put before him, and the whole household seemed to breathe a collective sigh of relief. The master would not be wasting away of a broken heart, after all. Jeannette, however, could not share in the general easing of tension. She still had no idea if she were to remain. She had no plan of where to go should she be turned away, nor any money with which to instigate such a plan, unless, after all, her treasured silver set was to be sold. So much padded her fall into penury, no more. Unfulfilled expectation and the worry of waiting took its toll on her.

She managed to hide her uneasiness, putting on a cheerful facade in order that she might go about her daily business. It was only in the limited privacy of her room, after Polly began to snore, that she allowed her concerns to surface. There, or in the fountained knot garden. Her haven, she began to consider it—the place she might go to get away from the heat and hustle of the kitchen, the closeness and gossip of the servants' quarters. After the sun went down, after Polly blew out the candle and her breathing grew deep and ragged, Jeannette went then, to listen to croaking frogs and plashing fountain, to gaze at the stars, as she had done when she was a child, in order that she might in some way relax before crawling into bed. Like an open pair of arms the night embraced her.

In the peaceful, herb-scented knot garden, Jeannette soaked up the balmy stillness like a bath. It loosened the tension in her neck, the tight spot between her shoulders and in the small of her back. She had need of such a place as this. There were few places that someone of her order might find solitude in a house as well-manned as Lord Endicott's. The areas that were open to her were always abustle. Kitchen, washroom, scullery, and servants' quarters, even her own room was a hive of activity. Polly was not only a talented pastry chef, she was also considered the most knowledgeable gossip among the members of the staff. The chambermaids seemed to take great pleasure in keeping her informed. The latest on-dit was that Lord Endicott's sister, Lady Margaret Crawford, meant to visit. She was convinced her brother must waste away to nothing were she not there to watch out for him. There was talk she meant to bundle him off to Tunbridge Wells for the water cure. This information was delivered with a great deal of eye-rolling, and the complaint that they should be dreadfully crowded when madam descended on them, with her expected entourage, for she always brought a retinue of her London staff.

"You must expect some interference in your menu-making," Polly warned Jeannette. "Lady Crawford, bless her soul, is notorious for sticking her nose into everyone's business when it comes to the running of her brother's household, and she is sure to bring her own kitchen staff. She puts Mrs. Gary in a devil of a temper whenever she arrives."

Jeannette should have been happy to be included in such confidences. She should be thankful for the coming of Lady Crawford, too, for the expected invasion of company suddenly thrust her into the plural 'us' that the servants considered themselves against the 'them' of the Crawford staff. She should be very happy. She kept telling herself as much as she escaped into the cool stillness of the night by way of the servants' creaky back stair. She was getting on well with the staff, and had coaxed the master out of his extended fasting, just as she had set out to do. She should be pleased. But, she was not content. Her goal was met, her energies spent. For a week she had concentrated on lifting someone else's spirits from the pit of despair into which she herself was now sunk. No one was there to cheer her out of the mopes. No one was left who cared.

For nine years, Jeannette's focus had been on survival, and on the dangers of remaining in France. Like a fractious child, throwing tantrums as it grew, her homeland had become an unpredictable, and sometimes senselessly violent place. She had stayed as long as Yvette was alive. When Yvette had passed away in her sleep, Jeannette had at last discovered what was kept in the box that Yvette stashed away under her mattress. Inside it was a stack of letters addressed in her own handwriting, and beneath them, a set of heavy silver serving knives and spoons, each of them bearing the familiar Bouillé griffin. Jeannette had sat on the floor, the box between her knees, and cried. Not because this was all that was left of the riches she had once taken for granted, nor because there was enough silver to consider the option of leaving France behind her—she had cried because Yvette, her dearest friend, had betrayed her. The letters were those Jeannette had written to relatives in Austria. Yvette had been entrusted to post them. These letters, never sent, had of course, never been answered. Abandoned as she had felt by her relations, it was far more of a crushing blow to discover them completely ignorant of her very survival.

The correspondence had been forwarded, of course, eight years late, and with little hope of reaching those they were meant for, but rather than herself follow their uncertain trek, Jeannette had liquidated the silver serving pieces, and set off for England, across the newly opened Channel, intent on securing a decent and paying position for herself. There were jobs to be found in England, she was sure of it, just as sure as she was that Austria was already teeming with refugees. She would not be so welcome in that country, were there no relatives left to be found.

In an upside-down Paris she had learned to cook, with Yvette at her side, the two of them hired on to serve in one of the many new restaurants that sprang up in the city, to feed the hungry rabble that flocked to see a Revolution occur, at the hands of executioners who lopped off people's heads as readily as Jeannette learned to lop off a chicken's. She had been thankful then, as she was thankful now, for the years she had spent as an indulged if wayward child, who would rather play with the pots and pans under the family cook's feet, than with china dolls in the nursery upstairs. Yvette had adored her, had allowed her free run of her domain, first in playing make-believe cookery, and later in actually showing her the real thing as patiently as if she had been her own daughter.

Jeannette's parents, wealthy, influential, and preoccupied with their own lives, had blithely given her into the care of her nanny, who was too occupied with chasing after her mischievous brothers to mind if Jeannette content herself with playing in the kitchen and gardens. As long as she did not soil her clothes too horribly, she was left to her own devices.

Yvette had become surrogate nanny, surrogate mother. In the end, when the house was sacked and the wealthy and influential Bouillé family carted away in a tumbril, it was Yvette who saved Jeannette from certain death. Yvette hid her away in the pantry, and then provided her with safe passage to Paris.

Yvette had picked her up, on the bloody day when Jeannette's mother and father bravely bent their heads to the guillotine while Jeannette fainted away in the crowd. Jeannette could not bring herself to go and witness the execution of her brother Jean. The old woman had gone in her stead, and come back to praise Jean's defiant acceptance of the inevitable. Of Antoine, Jeannette's youngest sibling, she heard nothing, but there were rumors he had been held in a gaol that was swept by a purulent fever from which few survived.

Dry-eyed, Jeannette had borne the shocks, too stunned to believe that all she knew and loved was shattered beyond repair, too intent on living up to the example her parents set in meeting death, to break down and exhibit the emotion she hid within. Yvette had coolly suggested she change her name—recommending after some consideration, Saincoeur. A strangely theatrical name, Jeannette had decided it fit her nicely, for did she not act a part, in pretending to be happy and brave? Citizen Saincoeur she had become.

Receiving word that some of her relatives might have gone to Austria, Jeannette had written hope-filled letters which Yvette had supposedly seen to the posting of. The box beneath the bed proved her deceit.

Hurt and betrayed, Jeannette turned her back on France without a backward glance, making her way to London, where a registry office listed her as a French cook, seeking employment.

Here she was, at Idylnook, employed after a fashion, with promise of a comfortable future that might keep her alive.

She should be happy and content with her lot, but Jeannette found herself overwhelmed with the enormity of her losses. Strange that it was only now, when she stood securely in the midst of this promise of plenty, that sorrow breached her defenses.

Pacing restlessly around the neat, box-hedged squares and triangles of the knot garden, Jeannette decided the chuckle of the fountain was far too carefree. She plucked a handful of tarragon, stripping the leaves from their stem one by one. The herb smelled of home, of the garden on the east side of the estate, now destroyed, never to be her home again. The evocative smell triggered tears. Impatiently, she dashed them aside, and threw away the tarragon. Sadness could not so easily be tossed aside. An overpowering wave of grief and anger and profound loss rose from the tightness of Jeannette's chest into her throat. Why now? So many years had passed with scarce a tear. Why did she suffer now, when she should be happier than at any time in her recent past? She paced the silence of the garden, and breathed in the perfumed air of freedom and safety and promise, and was consumed by the realization that she, and only she, survived. She was alone, dreadfully alone, and here, in a household drawn together by the grief of losing a single loved one, no one knew or cared about the torment she suffered in having lost everyone and everything she had ever cared about.

The life she had known did not fall into neatly boxed squares and triangles, like this garden did. It was as walled off and separate from her now as this walled-off garden was separate from the grounds. What a contradiction life seemed. She had become one of the very class that had shattered her past and reshaped her future. There was something unnatural in such an abrupt change of circumstance, something as bent and twisted as the espaliered fruit trees that made patterns against the walls on this tiny, secluded corner of the world that she wandered.

A moan escaped her lips. A tiny sound, it tore open the

dam of her feelings. She had not known herself capable of such a pitiful noise. Tears flooded her cheeks. Another moan wrenched itself from her aching throat, then another and another, little hiccups of unleashed anguish. She could not contain them, though she clamped her lips shut in an effort to hold back sound. Blinded by her tears, and startled by the pain that spoke so eloquently in each of the uncontrolled sounds that wrenched from her throat, she sank down on the lip of the fountain side, bent her face into her hands and let the sobs loose. It was time to unleash the pain. No one would know. No one would hear. She was safe here, and very much alone.

Julian had been having trouble sleeping since Elinor's death. The bed she had so often warmed, seemed too large without her, too cold. He clutched a feather bolster to his chest, an approximation of companionship, but not a very comforting one. The room, dark and empty, echoed with the ticking of the clock on the mantel. Julian stared without seeing, at the bed hangings above his head, and listened without hearing, to the frogs croaking rhythmically outside his partially opened window. Exhaustion would claim him sometime before dawn. It usually did.

When the first moaning sound reached his ears, he thought that a cat had caught some unsuspecting rodent in the herb garden, but the second cry jerked him upright in the bed. This was no animal sound. A woman was weeping! He froze for a moment, listening. He had heard a great many women weeping in connection with Elinor's death, but nothing so perfectly mirrored the anguish deep within his own constricted heart as this animal moaning. Tears stung his eyes just in hearing such a sound. With the feeling that he intruded in witnessing such as outpouring of despair, he flung himself out of the tangle of bed curtains, with the thought that he must shut the window. And yet, as he padded across the room, he was filled with curiosity and a concern as to whom, among his household suffered so.

He stood at the window and stared down into the shadows of the garden. The heartrending sound rose like the wailing specter of his own unhappiness, raising gooseflesh all along his arms. The garden looked empty.

The unrelenting cries touched him somewhere deep inside. A tear rolled down his cheek. Hot and salty, another burned in the corner of his left eye, but he refused to let it fall, refused to abandon himself to the immense stony wall of sorrow that he had so carefully constructed. This one tear was the first he had allowed to fall since Elinor's death. Jaw clenched, he blinked the moisture from his lashes, licked the bitter salt from the corner of his mouth, and swabbed at his eyes and nose with the back of his nightshirt sleeve.

The sobbing in the garden spent itself eventually, reducing itself to a soft, mournful sniffling. Unable to resist now his curiosity as to who had so nearly unleashed a torrent within him, Julian pushed wide his window and stuck out his head. Unfortunately, as the window reached its zenith, the rotating sash let out its own cry of anguish.

The sniffling sounds beneath him ceased. The pale moon of a face lifted to regard his.

"Mon dieu!"

It was Jeannette, the new French cook. He could not mistake her voice. The black shape of her gathered itself swiftly from the edge of the fountain and fled into the night.

Disappointed with his own intrusion on her private expression of grief, Julian closed up the window and took himself back to bed. He should have known it would be Jeannette. He had seen the pain in her eyes, had witnessed her uncannily empathic compassion for his own loss. What catastrophe wrung such sounds from her? What specter from her past did she face, there in the garden, with only the moon for company? He lay pondering the matter until sleep claimed him.

Chapter Five

⁓

Jeannette was not surprised she had been summoned to the library with an order to bring tea for two, though all of the rest of the servants were pop-eyed with curiosity as to who was to share tea with the master. The fair, floating wings of hair, the pale, angular face that had gazed down on her the night before, had been unmistakable. Unfamiliar as of yet, with the second story of this house, she had poured out her grief, all unknowing, beneath Lord Endicott's open bedroom window, most likely disturbing his sleep. She was mortified. Of course, he would expect some sort of explanation—at the very least, an abject apology. She steeled herself for what was to come, and rapped twice on the door panel.

"Come!"

Licking her lips, she took a deep breath, tried to still the uneasy clattering of the china on her tray, and went in.

He rose from his desk as she crossed the room. The china chattered in earnest now, but he pretended not to notice, and drew a little drum table between the two overstuffed chairs that flanked the tallest of the bookshelves.

"Shall I take that?" He relieved her of the tray, and when she made a move to turn toward the door, said softly, "Do you take your tea white, or with lemon, Miss Saincoeur?"

"Lemon," she said shakily, highly conscious of the faint odor of Lord Endicott's cologne and the ticking of the mantel clock, of the smell of leather and steaming tea and freshly squeezed lemon.

He waved her to a chair. "Please, do sit down."

Uneasily she perched on the creaking softness of a leather chair that threatened to enfold her in its depths.

"Of course," he said. "The French prefer their coffee, is it not so?"

She shook her head. "Tea is fine."

He handed her a steaming, aromatic cup with the same kind of friendly nonchalance she had used to expect from her brothers so very long ago. The cup and saucer began to clatter as soon as she lay hand on it. The space between them seemed too narrow. He was not her brother, he was her employer. This was not going to be easy. She closed her eyes and concentrated on steadying her grip.

"I must apologize," he surprised her by saying in his gentle way. "I know you are uneasy, Jeannette." He was regarding her, with deep, wounded gray eyes, that appeared to understand everything there was to know about her. "I wish to apologize for intruding on your sorrow last night. It was most unmannerly in me. I wish, too, to let you know that while I have not been myself of late, I am usually considered an observant and caring person. I do not like to see others suffer, most especially those whose livelihood and care I am responsible for."

Jeannette began to blink very quickly against the threat of tears. "But are you responsible for my livelihood, monsieur? Does this mean you wish me to stay?"

He straightened, his spoon dripping in midair, staring at her as if completely surprised she should ask. "Have I not said as much? I do beg your pardon. Of course I desire you to stay."

Relief washed through Jeannette.

"Monsieur!" Impetuously, she abandoned her cup, fell to her knees and grasped his hand, that she might kiss his knuckles.

"Beware, my dear," he admonished, lifting her chin with the knuckle she had just pressed lips to. "I would not have the keenness of these eyes grow dim." He looked at her, as if for the first time—a deep, searching look. "They are remarkably fine eyes. Hazel, and all this time I thought them brown."

She pulled away, afraid he saw too much. What did he look for, in her eyes? Something he had seen in his wife's regard? She returned to the uneasy comfort of the leather chair, to the steaming luxury of a fresh cup of strong tea. Tears sparkled in her lashes, tears welled in her eyes. She was to have a home after all.

"I'd no idea the position meant so much to you." His sad, gray eyes wandered over her face, his sad, soft voice soothed. "Nor that I had been so lax in informing you of your status among us. Perhaps I had best tell you, your thoughtfulness in the face of my own suffering has not gone unnoticed. I am quite selfishly happy you have come to Idylnook. I might have wasted away, otherwise." The ghost of a smile touched his lips, but then his expression grew serious. "I would not have you unhappy, Miss Sound Heart. I encourage you to make yourself free with the knot garden whenever the spirit moves you, and can only hope, when you are become more comfortable among us, that you will perhaps feel free to share your loss." He hesitated. "I know that you are of gentle birth . . ."

Jeannette could not hide her surprise.

The ghost of a smile returned. "Your speech, bearing, and manner give you away, and I have been informed by two of the nosier members of my staff that you bring with you a few items that do not normally fall into the possession of a household cook."

She smiled sadly and regarded the swirling, brown leaves in the lower reaches of her cup. "It is true. I did once live a very different existence, but the past is dead to me. I cannot go back, nor would I burden others with the sorrow of it. I am very desolate to have disturbed you last night with my outburst."

Thrusting aside his cup, he leaned forward in his chair to grasp her, cup and hand combined, between his palms. The warm pressure of his flesh rivaled the hard warmth of the half-empty cup.

"I do understand, Jeannette."

Her gaze flew from the engulfing urgency of his touch, to the equally engulfing urgency of his eyes as they sought hers. There were depths in the soft, charcoal gray that opened to her, reaching out with understanding and empathy. She shuddered under the impact of such a look. There was something so loving and open in his eyes, that her head swayed for a moment with the inclination to take succor in his arms, to rest her cheek against his chest, to let his back bear for a moment the weight of her sorrow.

As if he read her thoughts, his clasp upon her hand tightened. He took the cup from her grasp, and lifted her hand to rest for a moment against the cashmere softness of his cheek. His eyelashes fanned out as though he savored the sensation, and when the gray eyes met hers again, their dark centers swelled with a warmth and interest that was both awesome and frightening to her, for such a look threatened to upset her new stability.

She swayed toward him, as toward an abyss. She had but to fall into those eyes to . . . to what? She jerked herself back, looking away from the great height from which she had been ready to fling herself, and slid her hand from his clasp.

"You give me a decent and honorable future, sir. For that, I thank you, with all of my heart."

She dared to look into his eyes again. They had closed off the depths into which she might have fallen. "Think nothing of it," he said softly, his voice as cool—as closed off—as his eyes.

Chapter Six

⁓

Julian could not deny, that he had, for one wildly deliri-
ous instant, imagined embracing Jeannette Saincoeur. It
had only been a momentary lapse in good judgment, a
moment that had not, thank God, been acted upon.

It was strangely provocative to have an intelligent and
comely young woman in the house, a woman who was not
Elinor, who drew him like a magnet, who pulled his eyes
away from whatever he did whenever she passed. Jeannette
affected all of his senses in a similar manner. His very sense
of touch itched to have its way with her.

Revitalized, that was what Julian felt when he was with
her. Every brush with her person, every glancing moment in
which he encountered her, his blood ran a little faster. He
could not have explained it had he been asked, but Jeannette
Saincoeur brought an invigorating energy into every room,
every space she occupied. The weight of his sorrow seemed
to lighten in the presence of such an energy.

Julian looked forward to the moment of each morning
when she came to ask if he had any special request or
requirement for the day's meals. He stretched that moment
as much as he dared, as she stood, neat and trim, exuding a
lively vitality of purpose, notepaper in hand, pencil poised.
He always pretended he had not given the matter of food a
moment's thought, when quite the opposite was true.
Anticipating these moments, he prepared for them like a
scholar, that all his attention might be focused on her: how
she looked, sounded, and smelled.

He became completely conversant with the energetic approach of her footsteps, the pleasant, singsong lilt of her voice, the enticing rustle of her skirts moving, always moving. She brought into the room with her, the smell of fresh bread baking, and roasting meats, and morning coffee. And beneath these mouthwatering odors, there was the smell of lavender in her clothes, and the faintest whiff of rosewater in her hair.

He could not help but wonder if she tasted of coffee. His own mouth was daily sweetened with claret and borage and cucumber, and with every sip, he thought of her. He studied the tilt of her head, the angle of her hand as she wrote down his requests, the way the morning light gilded the curve of her cheek, the swell of her breast and the tips of her dark eyelashes. She had, he realized, an almost comically retroussé nose that looked anything but English, a decidedly French shrug, and a way of speaking with her hands as much as her mouth when their conversation became particularly animated.

He became intimately familiar with every shade of color in her dark, shining hair, and could trace in his mind's eye the perfectly symmetrical pattern of its growth from her temples. There was a beauty mark on the left side of her neck, just above the line of black bombazine he had begun to find distasteful for the injustice it did her pale complexion.

The black dress did not fit her in more ways than color. It had not been cut to fit her shoulders, and the sleeves were too long. More than once he had watched her shove them back out of her way as she wrote out her daily lists. The cuffs had a worn look.

"Have they not seen to fitting you into fresh livery, Miss Saincoeur?"

She seemed surprised he should ask. "But, of course, monsieur. The seamstress came for my measurements only yesterday."

"We must see to it that the order is canceled."

Her eyebrows rose. "Monsieur?"

"Yes. I have decided it is time all of the servants had fresh livery, in some color other than black."

Her eyes widened in surprise and her hands came together in a sort of applause, as she exclaimed with undisguised pleasure, "How delightful!"

He was pleased to bring her pleasure. An animated creature, her expression was particularly charming when she was pleased. He made an effort to keep her involved in discussion a moment longer than was his custom, that he might enjoy the play of emotion on features fast becoming dear to him.

"Do you have a preference as to color? I had thought blue or brown or navy might be both practical and attractive."

"For the livery, monsieur?" Her brow knit as she gave the matter due consideration. "I think any one of them could be very elegant, in a sturdy, color-fast fabric of the right shade." She frowned. "Except perhaps the brown. There is very little brown in the draperies and upholstery throughout the house, and you will want the livery to complement the setting through which they must daily pass."

He would never have thought of matching livery to the interior of the house. That was something that would have occurred to Elinor. His late wife had had exquisite taste. Her knack for putting colors, and fabrics, and styles of furniture together, had always impressed him.

She shrugged. Strange, how the slight lifting of a woman's shoulders could so completely distract him from any melancholy that would have normally accompanied such a thought.

"I think perhaps the wine color in the dining room would be nice, or the blue from the ballroom. It is not really navy, but dark enough to be serviceable, non?"

He chose a wine color, that perfectly matched the dining room, when the draper came with samples of cloth. It would, he was quite sure, bring out the roses in Miss Saincoeur's cheeks. And he told Mrs. Gary, when she dared approach him about wash day, and the disgusting amount of dust in the draperies, that she had best make haste, for they were sure to raise clouds of dust in the exercise, and he wanted the fait accompli, the house made spotless, before his sister's arrival and while the staff still went about in their old livery.

The days passed in a flurry, and the house was turned upside down in freeing itself from the black pall of mourning. Julian took to sitting in the little walled knot garden, not only to escape the dust, and the clatter of buckets, but also to avoid watching as everything in the house was freed from its darkness. A twinge of guilt beset him whenever he witnessed the bleak festoons yanked down, dust flying. His feelings were wrapped up in the passage of time, and in the progress of his own life, while Elinor and the babe remained fixed in the past. It was somehow offensive to so visibly display his lightened sense of grief. Should he not, in some highly remarkable mode, pine forever? The black pall was swiftly dispatched despite his feelings of indiscretion, and the staff set to with cheerful goodwill in scrubbing, polishing, and dusting till the house shone.

In the knot garden, Julian came to terms with the transition both he and the house must pass through. There were even blessed moments when he allowed himself to forget completely his pain and sorrow and mourning, as he relaxed completely in the undemanding presence of the woman he knew as Jeannette Saincoeur.

She went to the knot garden to pick herbs.

He encountered her there the first time, quite by accident. Thereafter, he went with the intention of intercepting her. Laden with a book, he arranged himself in a sunny, central spot, where he might observe her gathering of rosemary or thyme, or whatever else struck her fancy, under the pretext of illuminating his mind. At first, she had hesitated to intrude, but when he made it clear to her she was welcome, she soon became quite comfortable with him, and on occasion, went so far as to hum as she went about the business of selecting the greenstuff she required.

They did not speak during these interludes, other than to exchange casual greetings, or comments on the weather, or the progress of the cleaning, but it was enough for him, during that time, merely to be close to her.

Thus, Jeannette began to fit, quite integrally, into the mechanics of the household at Idylnook. Like a cog in a sophisticated wheel, she helped to make each day run smoothly. Certainly the kitchen functioned more fully than it had in a long time, and everyone seemed pleased with her performance. Even Mrs. Gary, who had feared her coming so much in contact with Danial Fulsome, had reason to be pleased, for Danny seemed too overawed by Jeannette to cause her any trouble.

Jeannette was pleased and touched to find herself already on such intimate terms with the formidable housekeeper. When Mrs. Gary asked her if she would not do her the honor of taking tea with her one morning, privately, in her room, where they might have a cozy chat, she readily accepted the invitation.

The tea, of course, was a secondhand steeping of the master's own special blend of leaves, a particularly strong blend of Black Bohea, that was not quite so potent as it had been the first time Jeannette had tasted it, in the library. But tea was a rare and costly commodity, and each leaf was washed through hot water as long as it tinged water brown in households such as Idylnook. This batch would likely find its way into the gardener's teapot by the end of the week, and fortified with cream it would not make an altogether tasteless brew. Jeannette thought her cupful tasted quite pleasant with lemon, and could not but be reminded of the moment she had shared her first, more potent brew, with Lord Endicott himself.

It was his lordship, whom Mrs. Gary wished to discuss with her, though she went about it in a roundabout fashion, in a kind attempt to approach the topic with some subtlety. When she at last came to the point, it was to remark very carefully, "As I am myself quite taken with you, Jeannette, it comes as no real surprise that the master is equally taken with you, dear girl, but I hope you will not be offended if I offer a well-meant warning in expressing to you some concern that this affection not be misinterpreted, or taken advantage of. One has only to look at poor Penny Fairing, after all, to see the folly in overestimating a man's honorable commitment to his affectionate nature. Silly girl, she must be unbelievably foolish to trust Danny, of all fellows, to do what is right by her."

"Foolish, or very much in love," Jeannette said softly, with a wise little nod. Mrs. Gary told her nothing she had not already considered, so she strove to shift somewhat the direction of the conversation. "One's heart can so easily lead one astray, if one relies on its direction, without consulting one's intellect as well."

"'Tis true, and very relieved I am to hear you say so, for we have become so comfortable with you here now, and so nice a table do we set, that I should hate to see any folly upset us, don't you know?"

Jeannette quietly sipped her tea. She was set firmly in her place by Mrs. Gary's words, firmly brought down to earth again. She could not help but wonder if there was any possibility she might find herself foolish in love, as foolish as poor Penny Fairing. Having never fallen slave to that emotion, she had no way of knowing. The warm feelings, the tender concern she had for Julian Endicott, could surely not be classed as love, could they? She shook herself mentally. What rubbish! Of course it was not love. She changed the subject, quite consciously, to prove her disinterest in its focus.

"Your mention of poor Penny Fairing reminds me, Mrs. Gary, of something I have been meaning to discuss with you."

"And that is?"

"The excess food we find ourselves daily throwing onto the compost pit, madam. Would it be too much to ask, that we might see it delivered to Monsieur Endicott's tenants perhaps, or some indigent family, before it spoils. It breaks my heart to see so much waste. We suffered great shortages of foodstuffs in France during the worst days of the Terror. A great many displaced citizens could not even afford what was available."

Mrs. Gary looked thoughtful. "Do you know we always did used to deliver our excess breads and meat to the poor and infirm. I do not know how we got out of the habit. Perhaps because it was Lady Endicott herself who used to make the deliveries, and no one has thought to fill her shoes, we have been lackadaisical. I think reviving the practice a very good idea. We shall put it into effect immediately."

With a robust sense of purpose, Mrs. Gary got up from the tea table she had so carefully laid out for her guest, and began to clear away the crockery.

"And do you think we might make poor Penny Fairing one of the recipients of Lord Endicott's largess?" Jeannette dared ask.

Mrs. Gary paused in what she was doing. "I do not see why not!" she stated. "Will you make the deliveries, my dear?"

"*Oui, oui! Enchanté!*"

"Excellent!" The older lady's eyes twinkled with mischievous goodwill. "I believe you will require assistance in carrying everything, and I cannot think of anyone better suited to such a calling than Danial Fulsom."

Jeannette laughed. "He will hold us both in great disgust over such an order," she forewarned. "I have heard he refuses to so much as step into the lane, for fear he shall see poor Penny."

"And do you mind so much being held in disgust by such as he?" Mrs. Gary asked with a wise look.

"Not in the least," admitted Jeannette.

Chapter Seven

~

There came a morning when Julian realized he had become most inappropriately fixated on Miss Jeannette Saincoeur. Guilt weighed down his spirits as all evidence of his grief seemed to disappear before his eyes. The house, no longer draped in black, yet reminded him of Elinor. Her hand was wrought too plainly in the color and furnishing of every room but his study. Elinor seemed closer to him now than before her touch had been disguised by the all-encompassing pall of black. There were times, as Lord Endicott passed through the drawing rooms, that he expected to find his pale, frail loved one sitting with her embroidery frame, chortling over some awful mistake she had made in her stitchery. There were haunting moments when his memories spoke so vividly that he almost thought he heard the echo of the flute his dear one had taken such joy in playing ringing through the halls of the old house. It was always Vivaldi he heard, the light, quick, cheerful riffs from the Four Seasons concertos. She was "Spring" of course, she would always be spring to him; pale and golden, and fragile as a flower.

The thought came to him, unbidden, that he wondered what season Jeannette Saincoeur was, and yet even as he wondered he felt as though he betrayed the memory of his wife with his very curiosity. His thoughts might continue to wander, but his person did not. He abruptly withdrew from all excessive contact with his new French cook. He stopped lingering over his daily orders for dinner, stopped his visits to the herb garden and stopped straying thoughts before they wandered far, for while life went on around him, he found some part in him that could not. He buried himself in paperwork. There was a great deal of it to attend to, and when his pen was not scratching, he was haunting the long, narrow, portrait gallery at the top of the great flight of stairs. There, spring was captured forever in the face of his beloved.

Jeannette noticed Julian Endicott's sudden withdrawal, his curt dismissals. After so many days of warm companionship, she was pained by the abrupt snub, and wondered not only what had become of the master of Idylnook, but what it was she might have done or said to alienate him. His absence did, she had to admit to herself, trouble her with pangs of regret. Could it be, she wondered, that her feelings were more engaged than she had realized? An answer was not long in coming. Jeannette saw Lord Endicott when she stepped inside with her basket on the following morning. That is, she saw his legs, for they were all that was visible from her vantage point at the base of the stairs. Strange, the thought ran through her mind, how drawn one could be, to no more than a set of limbs.

In fact, overcome with curiosity, she crept halfway up the stairs to see what kept Julian Endicott standing there so still. He was, she found, staring at the painting that had been removed from the dining room. Jeannette could tell, by the set of both head and shoulders, that Julian Endicott had loved his wife and loved her still. A pang of emotion troubled her. She recognized the feeling. It was jealousy, there was no mistaking it. She would have liked very much to be held so high in this gentleman's esteem.

So lost in contemplation was Lord Endicott, she did not think he heard her approach. Without a sound, she turned about, to go down the stairs again. Her presence she felt could be nothing but intrusive.

"Don't go."

His voice, no more than a murmur, startled her.

Jeannette froze in her tracks, embarrassed to be caught with her nose where it did not belong. She wished she might sink into the floor and disappear. This personal moment was not hers to share.

"Please, don't go."

She was his servant. She did as she was bid.

"Come up," he beckoned, when she turned uncertainly to face him. "It is your doing that she hangs here. You must tell me if you approve."

She topped the stairs and went to stand behind him. The striking young woman in the painting looked out over her shoulder. She seemed as pleased with her lot as ever. Small wonder, really. She was adored, even in death. Jeannette did not feel herself qualified to pass judgment on one so beloved, not even in the placing of her portrait.

She lobbed the question back into his court. "Do you think mademoiselle would approve? I think her opinion carries far more weight than mine in this instance."

He sighed. "Yes. I think she would approve. She was, on the whole, easily pleased."

He looked at her, really looked at her, for the first time in days. There was a pulled look to his features, a brooding sadness about his eyes, but there was, too, a sense of resolution in his posture that she had not noticed before today.

"She would, I am convinced, have liked you, Miss Saincoeur," he said firmly.

"Monsieur!" Jeannette wanted to sink with her own unworthiness of such a compliment. "I take that as praise of the highest order."

"I miss her," he said softly, gently, as though he might bruise the memory were his words spoken any louder. "And it pleases me that you will speak of her with me, though you never knew her. Most everyone I know avoids the mention of her name, or any reminder to me of her, and yet there is not a day that passes when I have not thought of my dear Elinor."

He smiled at her. It was a bleak, faltering smile, that

masked great pain, a smile so emotionally charged, so tremulous, that it seemed to hang his lips on the uncertain brink of an emotional outpouring. Jeannette was awed that any man would share such a smile with her. He turned away, and took a deep breath, and when he met her eyes again, the smile was gone, and with it his emotions.

He frowned, and regarded the portrait of Lady Endicott.

"With all that thinking, strange as it may sound, there are moments when no matter how hard I concentrate, I cannot bring her face, whole and complete, to mind. I cannot fix it firmly in my memory. And so, I come and look at her, to refresh my recollection." He set his mouth and turned his back on the portrait, so that he might face Jeannette. "Is there a face that grows dim in your mind's eye, Miss Sound Heart? You, of all the people under my roof, would seem to perfectly understand my suffering. I read such empathy in your expression, I cannot help but believe you, too, have suffered a great loss. Can you tell me? Or is your grief too private to share?"

Jeannette sighed. No one had asked her such a question since she had left France, and there was a crying need within her to be asked. Sudden, blinding tears dimmed her view of the kind and gentle man who stood ready to fill that need, even as he stood before the reminder of his own loss.

This tie of sorrow, of mourning, of death, was what had bound the two of them together from the first day she had come to this place called Idylnook. Right or wrong, improper or no, Jeannette opened her heart to him.

"The faces I have begun to forget . . ." her voice wavered, "are those of my family." The word family broke into two pieces as it left her lips, and though she twisted her face, and bit down on her lip, she could not stop the tear that slipped down one cheek.

"Are they all gone?" His voice was so shocked, so sympathetic and sincere, that a little sob tore at her throat in a choking sound. She whirled, unable to confront a stranger with such raw, pent-up grief.

He was beside her before she could find her way to the danger of the stairs. His hand touched upon her shoulder, turning her into his, so that she might press her wet face into the sturdy prop of his chest. She clung to him, in need of such a prop, in need of warmth and kindness. He held her securely, without any awkwardness, pressing her to him, as if he would give to her his strength, his compassion, his unspoken understanding. His arms encircled her with a warmth more intimate than that shared by some lovers, for this warmth was from his heart and soul. It was the warmth of human kindness, of understanding and empathy for the helplessness one feels in the implacable face of death.

His hand pat a comforting tattoo in the small of her back, while his voice crooned a soothing litany. "There, there. I know. I know." His cheek, he pressed to her temple, his lips slid close to her ear, and in the soft, cajoling tone a father will use to comfort a child, he said, "Do you know, I am told that crying lets a little of the hurt out? You will feel much better in a moment, despite a red nose and puffy eyes, and then I shall pour you a little claret, and float a blue borage flower on its surface, for I have it on excellent authority that the blossom will gladden your heart."

She laughed in the midst of her crying, and he lifted her chin, and handed her his handkerchief. She took it, still laughing and he, too, let loose a chuckle, and giving her shoulders a comforting squeeze, he kissed her on the forehead.

It was as she stood thus, teary-eyed, in the arms of the man whose wife looked down on them from the wall, while he pressed lips to her forehead, that Julian Endicott's sister, Margaret—just arrived—entered the hallway, flanked by a retinue of footmen, carrying her bags.

"Julian!" she exclaimed, inhaling sharply, clearly misinterpreting the situation.

"Margaret."

As Julian Endicott released his comforting hold on Jeannette, laughter welled up from his chest, deep, belly-rocking laughter. Jeannette had never seen the man really smile, much less heard him laugh with such abandon. It was totally unexpected. His laughter chased all thought of tears from her mind. Feeling abandoned, and decidedly de trop, she edged away from him.

His hand flew out to stop her, and turning all his attention to her once again, he smiled rather sheepishly. "You know I am not laughing at you, Miss Sound Heart, do you not?" He said the words softly, in French, so that they sang like music in Jeannette's ears. "I do not make light of your pain." His expression was very serious. "I could not. The timing of my sister's entry was just so . . . so . . ."

Jeannette dimpled. It was rather funny. "Your handkerchief, monsieur."

She returned it to him, carefully schooling her tear-stained features into an appropriately servile mask when Margaret Crawford, demanded of her brother, "Who is this woman?"

"Margaret." His voice was under control, though his eyes still sparkled with mirth. "I am so pleased you have come. I am happy to introduce to you, Jeannette Saincoeur, our new French cook. Miss Saincoeur, this is my sister, Lady Margaret Crawford. She will be staying with us . . . how long, Margaret? Your letter did not say."

Margaret's mouth dropped open. "Until I decide to leave," she said stoutly.

Jeannette executed a flawless curtsy. "Madame must inform us if she has any special needs from the kitchen."

Margaret Crawford regarded her haughtily down the length of her nose. "To be sure," she snapped. "If I have any special needs my own cook will see to them. He is preparing a nuncheon for my entire party even as we speak."

Jeannette bobbed another curtsy, and made her way down the stairs to see about this invasion into her domain, but as she went she could not fail to hear Lady Crawford's irate hiss of, "Special needs, indeed. Is that what all that was about, Julian? I was never more shocked than to find you kissing that female. How could you?"

And then, very faintly came the soft, calm voice that had begun to sound very dear to Jeannette. "How can you barge into someone's home uninvited and unannounced, and feel it is your place to judge something you know nothing about, Margaret, my love?"

Jeannette stifled a laugh. She had a feeling that she had not heard the last from Margaret Crawford. She and madame had gotten off on the worst possible foot.

Chapter Eight

W ith such an introduction to start things off, Jeannette was not surprised to find that both Lady Margaret's dresser, and her personal maid, should regard her with narrow-eyed suspicion. The two women were assigned to share the little attic room with her and Polly. The narrow, slant-ceilinged space seemed fair to bursting with two extra occupants, and the bags that accompanied them. Sleeping arrangements were cramped and uncomfortable. Head to toe the women arranged themselves in the two small beds. Jeannette could think of only one time when she had felt more encompassed, and that was the day Yvette had locked her in the dark, spicy confines of the pantry, while her family was dragged away in the tumbril to the gaol. To be so pressed for space left her feeling breathless, and in danger.

Danger came from an expected quarter. Jeannette was summoned to the library, and while such a summons was not unusual, the person who awaited her there, was. It was Lady Margaret who sat, fingers steepled, behind the mahogany expanse of Lord Endicott's cluttered desk. She looked out of place there, despite a strong resemblance to her brother in bone structure and coloring. She was too pale and perfect, like a marble statue blocking the sun from the window. She looked enormously stiff and proper and unbending to have sat herself in the midst of so much yielding leather. The pale, floating hair that so enlivened her brother's face, graced her head as well, but there was no life left in it. It had been crimped into submission in the front, and tightly bound behind. Sausage curls, like the ears of a spaniel, hung down around her chin.

Margaret Crawford fingered a familiar green flannel bag that was prominently displayed on the desk before her. Jeannette recognized it immediately. It was the bag that held her silver! However did it come to be here?

Lady Crawford chose not to get right to the point when Jeannette stood before her, taking instead a rather circuitous route, by way of a strange compliment.

"I feel it incumbent upon me to let you know, before we begin, how very happy I am that my brother is eating again. I understand we have you to thank, for rekindling his appetite. We can only hope that hunger is the only appetite you intend to arouse in poor Jules."

Jeannette frowned and watched the woman warily. Where did this odd, one-sided conversation lead, with such an opening?

A fat, golden bumblebee flew in the open window at that moment, hovering in the air beside Lady Crawford's right ear, and though she must have heard the hum of its wings, she in no way acknowledged its presence, either by the slightest movement, or by any change of expression, until it settled on the corner of the desk. It was with an economy of movement that Lady Crawford then dispatched the poor creature by whacking it briskly with one of the books from the desk.

Lady Crawford turned to close the window, so that no more bees might interrupt her. "Out of my gratitude . . ." she said flatly, as she coolly returned to their conversation, "and unwilling to appear churlish, I would also have you know that my brother is currently in a very vulnerable position, a position I will not allow anyone to take advantage of. He must, as a titled gentleman eventually, and I would hope sooner rather than later, remarry. He must, you see, and do forgive my bluntness, beget a legitimate heir, else our family line shall die out and the inheritance and a great many properties will fall into the hands of some distant cousins."

Jeannette knew all she needed to know about family lines perishing. All too many had been obliterated in France. Her own died with her, for all the males of the family had been eradicated by the bloody Terror. She knew, too, what this woman was hoping to get at, in her roundabout fashion. She was warning Jeannette off, afraid that her brother might take too great an interest in a servant upon whose brow he saw fit to rain sympathetic kisses. This woman was afraid that her brother's name, and her own, might be besmirched by an inappropriate dalliance with the kitchen help. It angered Jeannette for a moment, that she should have to stand here and take such tripe from a woman whose blood ran no bluer than her own. But Jeannette had learned in the past nine years that it was far better to hold one's tongue than to speak out against an injustice. Life was not fair. It never had been, as far as she could tell, nor would it ever become so. She had no response for the presumption of this stranger.

Margaret's tone grew severe. "Your position here, Mistress Saincoeur, is in grave danger of dismissal."

"Dismissal?" Jeannette had been staring at her flannel bag, wondering, astonished, how it was that this woman justified her own behavior in taking someone else's belongings. She felt violated to watch as the bag was unrolled without so much as a by-your-leave. One by one, the only items she still possessed to remind her of her family were held up to the light and carefully scrutinized.

"My brother will never allow a young woman to remain in his employ, no matter how she may tempt his appetites, if he finds her to be a thief."

"I am not a thief," Jeannette said clearly, with low-voiced outrage. "Whoever brought you my things without permission is the thief."

"We shall see about that," Margaret said with condescending righteousness.

"See about what?" It was the cool, quiet, beloved voice of Julian Endicott that floated gently to them from the doorway.

For a moment Margaret seemed flustered. She could not brush aside her brother as easily as she had a bee.

"These silver pieces, Julian. There are five of them. A mirror, brush, comb, scent flask, and salts bottle. There is a tortoiseshell comb here, too, encrusted with what appear to be diamonds, unless they are paste. I am sure they must be stolen items. They were all in this woman's possession. Only look, the silver pieces are marked with a crest."

Julian gave the silver a cursory glance as he crossed the room to stand behind Jeannette. "Yes. Who has taken these from Miss Saincoeur?" His manner, as always, was languid.

"Wallings has. She . . ."

"Wallings? *Mon dieu*, what cheek! The woman shares my bed." Jeannette was so shocked she did not think to speak in English.

Lord Endicott moved into her line of sight, eyebrows raised. "Your bed?" he asked.

"What," Margaret huffed. "Does she proposition you right in front of me?"

Julian laughed. "No, Margaret," he explained patiently. "She tells me this ungrateful Wallings woman has been sharing her bed."

"But of course she has."

"Why?"

"Because I put her there."

"And did you know her to be a thief?"

"A thief? I would not hire a thief to dress me."

"It would appear she has changed her habits. Perhaps you had best dismiss her."

"Dismiss Wallings? What nonsense!"

"But did you not just tell me she had stolen these items from Miss Saincoeur?" He took up the silver-backed mirror, to pass his swimming hands across the finely worked griffin.

Margaret waved her hands at him. "Wallings did not steal

anything! It is this French cook of yours who has stolen the things. Can't you see that?"

Margaret had begun to sound shrill. Her brother, who now gazed into the mirrored surface of the object in his hand, was looking not at himself, but at Jeannette's reflection. Their eyes met for an instant in the glazed surface.

"I see nothing of the kind," he said.

Margaret flung open a large, leather-bound book of heraldic patterns, that had been marked with a bit of ribbon. "See, here, it is the crest of the Marquis de Bouillé on these things. The same Bouillé who botched the king and queen's escape from France. He was executed, along with all of his family, if the reports are accurate. These things, therefore, must be the spoils of war, stolen heirlooms."

Julian Endicott drew himself up from the languid stance he had taken against the doorjamb. His was the voice of reason; calm, collected, and level. "Wallings has taken these things from Miss Saincoeur, and yet it is Miss Saincoeur you call a thief. I do not understand, Margaret. But perhaps you will be so good as to return to Miss Saincoeur her things, now that they have been located."

"You cannot seriously believe such stuff belongs to the woman, Jules." Margaret flushed an angry red.

"I have no reason to believe they do not, Margaret."

"You are bedazzled, Jules!"

"You overstep your bounds, Maggie."

A terrible silence fell.

Margaret rose from her position behind the desk, and as she did, she rolled the silver into its flannel bag. With as much dignity as such circumstances allowed, she made her way past Jeannette.

"I leave it to you, to settle this." She thrust the bag at her brother. "But I warn you. This woman means to deceive you."

Jeannette sighed deeply when Julian's sister had sailed out of the room and down the hall. The air about them seemed to hold some residue of her anger. She made a powerful enemy in Margaret Crawford.

Julian gently closed the door in his sister's wake.

He held out the flannel bag. "I believe this is yours?"

Jeannette took it from him, and clasped it to her breast. "Oui, monsieur. It is mine!"

He nodded. "I do apologize for my sister and her servants," he said as he watched her. "They should not meddle in matters that do not pertain to them."

The bag felt heavy in Jeannette's hands. She was jealous of this little piece of her past, but even more jealous of her pride.

"I did not steal . . ."

He raised a languid hand. "I did not believe for a moment that you did." He seemed to require no explanation at all, and because of that trust, Jeannette felt an overpowering compulsion to tell him something about herself, so that he might begin to understand.

"The silver set belonged to my grandmere. She gave it to me on my tenth birthday. So I should not forget who I was, she said. Nor, who I was related to. I have, out of necessity over the past nine years, parted with everything else that was salvaged from my parents' house, even my name. It is far easier to be plain Jeannette Saincoeur, than a relative of the infamous Bouillé, whose untimely mistake during the king's attempt to flee France, may have cost the royal family their lives. I have left it all behind me, but for these few pieces, and two dresses, neither of which fit me anymore. I have, strangely, been most reluctant to part with them."

His gaze passed over her, as if he found her a curious creature. "These dresses . . . I am baffled. Why does a woman with so little to her name, hang onto dresses that do not fit? Surely they would be of more use to you in the hands of a rag merchant, for the pocket change they might bring you."

Jeannette frowned. Her reasons for keeping the dresses sounded farfetched, when one tried to put them into English.

"Oui. It is perhaps an eccentricity in me, I know. The dress- es do not fit, nor ever will they again, and yet that in part is why I hang onto them. I was wearing one of them on the day that I lost my family. I have kept it through the ensuing years, to remind me, of how very young I was when so many terrible things happened." She shrugged away a twinge of pain in her neck. "I keep it to remind myself that I was too young to have changed the course of events. I need to be reminded of that now and again, else I suffer guilt, both for being a Bouillé and for surviving when the rest of my fami- ly did not."

She turned away, eyes burning, and wondered why it was that she felt so free to tell him these things, that she had never before put into words. "The second dress . . ." she went on, "I can fit onto my figure . . ."

His eyes seemed to be studying the figure she mentioned when she looked up again. She flushed, and went on. "But it does not fit my way of thinking. It is the dress I wore on the day I departed France. Red, white, and blue, it sports a cockade with the word Patria emblazoned in the middle, but I felt no patriotism in wearing it—only a sense of self- preservation. Women, you see, have been required to wear a cockade in public, to prove their allegiance these days in France, on pain of arrest and fining. But the dress and the cockade were to me no more than a sort of costume, that I might pass unnoticed from the prison my country had become to me. I keep them—useless threads—to remind me what I have left behind, that I might never be homesick, and that I might never forget."

Julian Endicott remained silent throughout her diatribe. His eyes, soft and gray, and so very kind in the manner that they settled on her, spoke to her as eloquently as did his mouth. "You said once, Miss Saincoeur, that you wished this to be your new home. I hope that you have begun to regard Idylnook as such, for in that respect, you need never be homesick again."

With the heartfelt conviction that this strange interview

had ended on a much more promising note than it was
begun, Jeannette tucked the flannel encased roll of silver
under her arm, and with a smile and a curtsy, she went back
to the place she had made for herself, in the kitchen of an
English manor house.

As little Miss Sound Heart slipped out of the door to his
study, pieces of the past clasped to her breast, Julian thought
about what she had said with regard to feelings of guilt in
having survived when no one else did. He identified with
those feelings. Such mindless, and pointless guilt had
plagued him for months. It had become fixed in his mind
that had he not gotten Elinor with child, the course of events
that had since governed his life would never have come to
pass.

How was it that he, the perpetrator of death, survived,
while his loved ones did not? And yet, such thoughts were
as foolish as Jeannette Saincoeur's guilt in surviving, when
all about her had perished. There was some comfort, he
decided, in realizing that there were others who suffered the
same, mad feelings of inadequacy and impotence in the grim
face of death. Julian considered Jeannette Saincoeur's loss
with reference to his own. Each of them had lost a family,
and the future promised in those missing lives. They had
both of them suffered the loss of potential, and that was a
heavy loss indeed.

And yet, as great and all-encompassing as his own private
tragedy had been, Julian could not help realizing it might
have been much worse. His grief was assuaged, if only a little bit, with such a thought. He had lost a great deal, but not
everything of meaning in his life. His work remained, and
his siblings; Margaret, bless her interfering soul, and Letty,
who, with the assistance of her husband Peter, had produced
his nieces, Emma and Jane. He still possessed the lush,
green, peace of Idylnook, as well as a comfortable town
house in London, his family estate in Devon, and a hunting
box in Surrey—all of them home to him whenever he should

require them, here in England, a country that he loved and trusted with every fiber of his being.

Jeannette could lay claim to none of these. Her identity, her home, even her country, was lost to her. Yet, she survived. No, she thrived! She went on about her daily life, taking full advantage of the gifts God had given her. She did not whine, or beg for special compensation, she merely went on living, testing her talents and creativity to the limits of her ability. She was, in every way, a most admirable creature!

What strange patterns life fell into. Julian pondered the embossed cover of the book of heraldry that Margaret had been examining. The ribbon marker still identified the page she had turned to. He could not resist the temptation of peeking in at the Marquis de Bouillé's griffined crest and shield.

Margaret was right. The pattern was identical to the one so elegantly wrought on the back of Jeannette's mirror.

Julian's mouth twisted. It was no surprise that Margaret had trouble believing that his cook might be a Bouillé. He had trouble swallowing the premise himself. History hinged on the name, history gone terribly awry. It was no wonder that Jeannette now called herself by the fabricated pseudonym, Saincoeur. The citizens of France hated the name Bouillé, because Bouillé was a royalist, and because of his connection with the attempt to whisk the ousted king from the country. Aristocrats and royalists despised the name as well, because the Bouillés had come so close to saving the royal family only to fail.

Julian's eyes narrowed. Margaret would never believe any of this, for a moment. He had no idea what he was going to tell her. Perhaps it would be best to say no more than that the matter was settled. Margaret was the one who had to live with doubt and suspicion, with regard to Jeannette, not he.

Chapter Nine

~

"I am convinced your precious French cook is no more than a trollop." Margaret could be vicious in her right- eousness, especially when she had been thwarted. She stood staring out of the nursery window, where she and Julian had come in investigate the rooms, in expectation of the impending party of weekend guests. Every room in the house was to be put to use, in some fashion, even this one. Margaret thought the nursery would be the perfect place to house the excess of ladies' maids that would accompany every female on the guest list. Pallets on the floor would make them comfortable.

Julian did not much care, as long as they might decide, and leave the room with some swiftness. Memories hung like cobwebs between these pale, sky-blue walls and beneath the cherub-adorned ceiling, fragile, fluttering mem- ories of what might have been. The furniture had long ago been removed to the attic: the cradle, the bassinet, wash- stand, and rocking chair, along with the leather horse, and painted blocks, hand-tinted books and silver rattles. The tiny woolens, tiny linens, and tiny eyelet dresses, the tinier knit booties and caps were all carefully packed away—in the attic, and in Lord Endicott's memory—packed so tightly, that it all tumbled loose again whenever he stepped into this room. Something inexplicable hung here, like spirits that might whisper to him did he but listen hard enough. The room pained him.

Devoid of understanding, Margaret was not about to leave

quickly. Her attention was riveted to the window, and what she saw through it. There would be no hurrying her. She was practically plastered to the pane. Her breath fogged the glass when she spoke.

"Look! Just look at her down there with that handsome fellow. I would have you know that I have seen her at this same time the last two days, coaxing that same young man away with her. You must come and look, Jules."

Margaret was forever bringing his attention to some deficiency in the appearance, productivity, skill, or character of Jeannette Saincoeur. Julian chose to find her pettiness amusing rather than annoying. Margaret was as transparent as the glass she peered through.

He did not so much as glance out the window. As much as he liked to look at Jeannette Saincoeur, he was not willing to give Margaret the satisfaction of thinking him concerned. He knew where Jeannette and Danny were off to. They went with his blessing.

Margaret punched him in the arm, as she had used to do when they were children and he utterly frustrated her. "Julian! Please do pay attention. There they go, through the side gate, laden with baskets full of household silver or some such thing. Do look up, or they shall be gone from our line of sight."

Still, he did not bother to gaze out of the window. He had already done his share of spying on the two below. He knew where they went because he had spotted them days earlier, traipsing off together, picnic baskets in their arms, just as they were today, at this same time. He had, he was ashamed to admit, even to himself, jumped to a conclusion very similar to the one his sister offered up. He had been convinced that the two young people, as young people will, went off together for a romantic interlude.

The thought that his pretty cook could turn to another man so soon after he had bared soul to her and she had cried on his shoulder, rankled. That she should turn to Danial, of all men, filled him with the very real fear that Miss

Saincoeur might soon make a grass widow of herself. The master of Idylnook had set off in pursuit of the two—ready to do what had never occurred to him to do at any other time in his life—in spying on his servants.

He had been chastened by what he discovered. No romantic trysts for these two. They seemed more quarrelsome than romantic in their conversation as they walked through the apple orchard and into the lane lined by his tenants' houses.

"They go to deliver food that would otherwise spoil, from the kitchen, to two of my tenants, a cripple, and the dairyman's daughter, who is soon to be delivered of a child," he said aloud, with gentle conviction. He wondered if Margaret had any notion that she pressed him into the role of defender of the very female she was determined to undermine in his opinion, and that this talk of Penny Fairing, and the child she carried, in this room, of all places, only served to harden his heart toward her interfering ways.

Margaret was peeved. "And what of the dairyman, and the young woman's husband? Can they not provide this wayward dairyman's daughter with sufficient sustenance?"

Julian sighed. "The handsome young man you just remarked upon, is father to the child, though he refuses to marry the girl." He moved to the door. Margaret might amuse herself here if she would. He had better ways to pass his time.

"Disgraceful!" Margaret seemed put out, but content to follow. "Whatever would Elinor say to such goings on?"

Julian rubbed at his temples. Did Margaret mean to give him murderous thoughts as well as a headache? "Since the practice of delivering excess food to the needy was first put into effect by my late wife, I should think she would be pleased we still honor the commitment."

That was all it took to silence Margaret. Julian did not mention that he had discovered it was Miss Saincoeur's outcry against wasted plenty that had revived the practice. Margaret was sure to find something offensive, even in charity, were it Jeannette's cause. She had taken his French cook into instant and powerful aversion, from the moment she had entered the house to find him comforting the poor young woman. Had the girl been her own servant she would have tossed her out of the house on her ear. Denied that prerogative, she contented herself with maligning her character given the slightest provocation.

Margaret loved to involve herself in the lives of her siblings. As the eldest, she was convinced she knew what was best for everyone. As heir to the family title, and the only male among a host of sisters, Julian knew he was singled out for more managing than most.

"I am quite sure you will find any number of equally charitable young women amongst the company I have invited for the weekend," she said forcefully. Julian wondered if Margaret realized that she had far better chance of success in turning his attention away from Miss Saincoeur, if she but took it into her head that Julian must marry her.

"I'm sure it will be an exceptional gathering," he agreed with a notable lack of enthusiasm. His remark was an honest one. He had already taken exception to the approaching invasion of both privacy and peace.

Margaret could not leave well enough alone as she followed him out of the nursery and along the corridor. "I know the prospect of meeting these young women may seem a little daunting at first, Jules, but you have, I am quite certain, a complete understanding of your position, and the importance of taking this next big step in putting the past behind you. Elinor would have wanted it, you know. She always wanted what was best for you. I'm sure whoever fixes your affections will be a credit to her memory."

They arrived at the stairway landing, where Elinor's portrait hung, the same place in which he had been discovered planting a kiss on the forehead of one of his servants. Julian cringed beneath the pressure of Margaret's warm, wheedling words. She had no surer way of putting his back up than in assuring him she knew, and the insinuation was, better than he, what Elinor would have wanted for him. In this instance, she deftly wielded his pain and guilt over the loss of Elinor to get another dig in against Jeannette Saincoeur, or Bouillé. Whoever she was, Margaret had judged his interest in her unseemly.

Did his curiosity in a titled young woman's strength of purpose in setting out against all odds to support herself in a world gone mad, dishonor his dead wife's memory? He thought not. Elinor would have admired Jeannette. She would have recognized and valued strength in another. He was sure of it.

Jeannette did not realize she and Danny were being watched from the house, as the two of them pushed through the gate into the orchard, with Danny insisting at every step that he had no intention of setting foot in Penny Fairing's cottage.

"I'll be happy to carry the load for you as far as the end of the lane and no further. No further, mind."

"*Assez!*" she silenced him. "I do not understand you, Monsieur Fulsom. Have you no feeling at all for this young woman whose child will be blood of your blood? I find it puzzling that you can seduce a female, get her with child, and then abandon her and your own progeny to the vagaries of Fate."

Danny glared at her defensively. "What I feel, or don't feel for her, is none of your business."

"It would appear to no longer be your business either, more's the pity!" She could not resist sniping at him. Jeannette had little patience with men who would be the undoing of a maid. But for the grace of God, she might be wearing this poor girl's shoes.

"I do not understand men," she mumbled under her breath, in French.

"What's that you're muttering? I do not understand you."

Jeannette laughed. "*Vraiment!* That is only fair then, for I said, I do not understand men."

"Women!" he groaned.

"Men!" she shot back at him.

* * *

Fifteen-year-old Penny Fairing stood silhouetted against the light from the only window in the cottage, arching her back, her hand pressed into the small of it, as though it pained her. The roundness of her belly was more pronounced in such a stance, and Jeannette, fascinated by the profound, womanly changes going on in this girl's body, could not help but stare. Penny resembled nothing so much as a ripening plum.

Penny turned her head, caught the direction of Jeannette's gaze, and nodded knowingly, unseemly wise for her tender years.

"You're wondering how it is a girl gets herself into such a predicament."

Jeannette frowned. She had been wondering just that, but did not like to pry into such a personal matter. "I was wondering how a young woman can be so free with herself as to allow a young man dominion over her future."

Penny said sagely, "Passion done it. One does not think sensibly when gripped by passion. You, of all people must understand the power of such an emotion."

"Me?" Jeannette was confused.

"You are French. The French are a passionate people. All that fighting going on. Some of it quite senseless. Just like a woman in love, your whole country."

"Oh! Yes, I suppose you are right."

"There are few here in the country who do understand the force of passion. I did not myself comprehend, until the age of nine, when I first met Danny. From the moment I laid eyes on his beautiful face, I was smitten. He is handsome, think you not?" She threw an anxious look at Jeannette, as if she saw some sort of competition in her, for the handsome Danny.

Jeannette could not help but think of wise, young Bet's pragmatic, "Handsome is, as handsome does," but she could not say as much to Penny. The girl needed reassurance in her difficulties.

"Yes, the baby will be comely, I'm sure," she said as she wondered what was to become of this poor, pretty girl and her fatherless babe.

Penny seemed content for the moment not to think too much of the future. Her remarks conjured up only the happiness of the past. "Danny had but to come into my line of sight, and I could think of nothing, and no one else. I used to dream about him at night, and touch myself." She stroked the bulge of her tummy, laughing ruefully. "I was given to flights of fancy, and imagined it were Danny's hand upon me. He took no notice of me for years though, and then only when I began to take on a woman's shape, though I made a point of throwing myself in his way whenever opportunity offered."

"That must have changed."

"Aye. One day he looked at me different, when he run onto me and me dad at chapel. I had a new frock with a pretty tatted collar, and for the Sabbath my hair was dressed high. This look he threw at me . . . it were all warm, and glowy and ever so friendly. It fair took me breath away. The next time we made deliveries at Idylnook, he snatched a kiss, behind me old dad's back. It were me first such kiss from a man. It were as breathless as the look he'd thrown at me the last time we had met. I thought for a minute he meant to steal it quite away; me breath, me soul, or both. Lightheaded I was, for days. Danny made a habit of stealing kisses from then on, and I got right sly about kissing him back."

"And the kisses led to . . ." Jeannette prompted, caught up in the story. She did not want the girl to stop talking. She had herself fallen prey to thoughts of passion, and kissing, with regard to Lord Endicott of late, and it concerned her more than she would have liked to admit.

Penny lowered her eyes, and stroked her taut belly again, with a brave laugh, that made light of her predicament. "My shoes had the queerest way of wanting to come off my feet when Danny was about, and off they eventually came. It never occurred to me to refuse the man when he asked me to lie with him. I were that besotted."

"And do you regret it now?" Jeannette could not help but be awed by this girl's devil-may-care attitude, for it reminded her of the moment in the library, with Julian Endicott, when she had felt the surge of just such a wave of passion as this girl spoke so casually about.

Penny looked very young as she twirled a lock of hair about one finger. "I regret the babe has got no dad, but for myself, I've no regrets. I had a little bit of heaven in Danny's arms. I'd not wish that away. Once I'd lain with him, I could not get enough of having him near me. His touch . . ." she paused, "made a wanton of me, don't you know. It were magic, that touch. It melted away all resistance; all that the church had taught me, all that me mum and dad warned me about, it was all gone in an instant. Me knees turned to butter, me insides to jam, and up come me skirts. 'Tis a funny thing, passion."

Jeannette cleared her throat, and shook herself, in an attempt to clear her head.

"Tell me, Penny, would you object to my asking Lord Endicott if there was any position you might fill in his staff, either here, or elsewhere? It had occurred to me that you would be needing some form of living."

Penny sat down with a sigh. "Would you do that for me? How very kind. I had thought I might find a position as a wet nurse somewhere. And if anyone around here would be likely to understand me predicament, it must be Lord Endicott. 'E's one who understands passion."

Jeannette was intrigued. "What do you mean?"

The girl picked up a bit of knitting that was meant to be some sort of clothing for the child when it was done. "You was not here for his lady's funeral, was you? You could not ask such a question, had you been."

"Will you tell me about it?"

The girl's eyes misted over with the memory, as swift fingers made her needles go clickety-click. "What? The funeral? Well, if one must go, one can only hope to go in such style. It were the grandest thing I have ever seen. Far more pomp than any wedding I have been to. There were flowers everywhere. The air was thick with them. In addition, the whole of Idylnook was shrouded in black baize, and shuttered up as dark as night, with candles the only source of light. Length after length of black stuff they had draped from the ceiling, and around the windows and doors. I could not help but think how many shifts and shirts the ells of cloth might have been made into. Of course, you could not find a soul who was not already clad in black of some sort, almost everyone in Kent seemed to have been invited, and most of them head to toe in black. There were great parties from London who came, as well, and of course all of the villagers, and the household staff traipsing in and out, handing out chamois or lamb gloves to all, and silk hatbands and feathers to them that meant to take part in the funeral procession.

"Poor, lovely Lady Endicott was the only one among us who was not shrouded in black. They had her laid out very pretty, all in finely worked white woolen. The poor little mite swaddled all in white as well, and each of them with lovely white Brussels lace collars and cuffs. And though the lace was in direct contradiction to the law, there was not a soul there to complain, much less report the infraction, so beautiful did the both of them look. The coffin was almost hid by mounds of flowers, all of them white, except for one pretty little blossom. It was in shades of amethyst, to match the mourning rings, which all of the females of the family, and several of Lady Endicott's close friends were given.

"Lord Endicott looked very much like he had not had a wink of sleep for days, yet he sat ever so long beside the coffin, while all of the company came in to see his poor, poor wife and babe. He did not cry. He just sat there, all stiff, like he was carved from wood. His eyes, I shall never forget, were flat and cold like a fish's get when you take it out of water. There was an unnatural stillness about him, even when people spoke to him, a cold, frozen look. Numb, he was, me mum said. Numb with the shock of losing both her and the babe."

"A child had died as well?" Jeannette had heard no whisper of this element of the tragedy. Lord Endicott's loss seemed all the more poignant.

"Oh yes. A terrible thing. The babe was not turned the right way, and tangled up in the cord besides. The midwife told me the details of it, not a sennite ago." Penny swallowed hard, her mouth sour with the thought of such a death.

Jeannette gave her arm a squeeze. "It will not be so with your little one, you know."

Penny squared her shoulders. "Nay!" she said with emphatic good humor. "Best it doesn't, for I'm not one as shall have plumed horses, six mutes, and a dozen pages to grace my passing."

"There you are," Jeannette agreed, her mind stuck on the image of Julian Endicott, mourning not just the loss of his wife all this time, but his first-born child, as well.

For once, Jeannette was glad Danny chose not to wait for her when she made her delivery to Penny Fairing. After such remarks as she had heard fall from the girl's lips, she did not think she could face the man, or any man for that matter, with complete composure. Life and death and passion were heavy subjects that required a quiet moment to ponder alone.

Jeannette was not completely naive. She had seen animals, on more than one occasion in the act of procreation, and had supposed that men and women went about it in much the same way. She had also witnessed the exchange of kisses and squeezing hugs among some of the members of her family's household staff. She had even walked into the stables one day to find her brother, Jean, bare buttocked and very red in the face, fornicating with one of the upstairs maids. He had been furious when he opened his eyes to see her watching. He had shouted at her most awfully. She had been no more than curious, but their actions, their nakedness, had revolted her. She had certainly never involved herself in such a perversion as a result of what she had seen. The maid had been yelping, as though she were in pain. As a result, the thought of lovemaking frightened her. In Paris, she had avoided men who tried to pinch at her, or put an arm about her waist.

Never before had she heard the act of lovemaking described enthusiastically by a female. Her mother had certainly never discussed it with her, and Yvette had called what men and women did together, a nasty business. To hear sex spoken of in glowing terms, and by a young woman whom she would have assumed to rue the day she allowed herself to be carried away by such yearnings, was curious indeed. It demanded consideration.

Jeannette could think of nothing else all the way back to Idylnook, where she cut into the apple orchard, empty baskets swinging in her arms, so that she might approach the house from the rear.

The last person she thought, or even hoped to encounter, was Lord Endicott. But as she ducked under the low-hanging branches of one of the older, more substantial fruit trees, her thoughts too centered on the things men and women did while private with one another to watch where she was going, her straw bonnet was knocked loose. In returning it to its proper position, she paid more attention to what she was doing than where she was going. Awareness reclaimed her when in tilting her head up so that she might tie the hat more securely beneath her chin, she found herself confronted by a shapely pair of male legs, clad in tight, buckskin breeches and black boots, dangling just above her head. Her gaze followed the familiar limbs upward. There, clinging to the trunk of the tree, sat none other than Julian Endicott, an unusually sheepish expression in possession of his features.

"Mon dieu!" she exclaimed.

For a strangely exhilarating moment he smiled at her with the air of a conspirator, and then, his finger rose to his lips.

"Shhh!" he hissed, pointing in the direction of the great house.

Puzzled, Jeannette turned to look. The reason for his concern was clear. His sister, Margaret, approached.

Julian held himself very still, and listened to the wind in the trees, and the voices of the women below him. He was wondering what it was he had seen that was different in the eyes and lips of Jeannette Saincoeur as she stood looking up at him just now. Perhaps it was his changed perspective, and nothing more, that had made her seem unusually alluring. But, no, it was something else, something besides her surprise in finding him there above her, something soft and melting and vulnerable. It was an arousing glance she had leveled at him, akin to the look a woman gives a man when she comes into the circle of his arms. Yes, that had been the look. For the life of him, he could not understand why Miss Sound Heart should have such a look, now. He wondered if she meant to go away and leave him here, up a tree, and wondering.

He could hear the lilting music of her voice. It held some hint of the look he had surprised in her eyes. Soft, sultry, warm, and sensual, like the sunshine that filtered through the leaves of the apple tree, her voice always seemed to hold a seductive hint of promise, just as the look that he could not dismiss from his mind, held promise.

There was nothing at all sultry to be heard in Margaret's voice. "Are you sure you have not seen him?" she insisted. "He entered the gate here no more than a quarter of an hour ago. It is most urgent I locate him. We have a great deal to attend to before his guests arrive."

Julian squeezed his eyes shut. That last remark did it up a bit brown. These people whom he had agreed to allow to overrun his home, came at Margaret's beck and call, not his. They came to see if the rumors were true, that he wasted away to a shadow of himself. They came, too, with the intention of removing him from the peaceful idyll he found in Kent. Some of them meant to drag him back into the frenetic activity of London, and his job, and the political mayhem that involved France. Some came, too, to see if they might interest him in a replacement for his wife; a sister, a niece, a good friend or connection, all of them excellent women, he was sure, who would not be at all averse to catching themselves a member of the House for a husband. He wanted nothing to do with them at the moment. He would meet them all too soon, and be expected to pander to their every wish. For now, he had a far more interesting puzzle to solve in the riddle of Miss Saincoeur's smoldering gaze. He stared at the ground far below, and tried to recreate the image of her face from memory. He was surprised at how clear that memory was. He had not thought her so firmly fixed in his consciousness.

The voices ceased. The creak of the gate made him frown. Was that Margaret going, or the intriguing Miss Saincoeur?

A moment of suspense, and the little French cook appeared beneath him. The bonneted head tilted upward. The smoldering look was no longer there. Had he imagined it?

"She is gone, monsieur. And, before I, too, must go, there is something I would ask you. Is this perhaps, a bad time?" Her eyes were twinkling. She did not mean to seduce him. She was trying her best not to laugh at him.

"Ask away," he encouraged. "Wait, I shall come down." With a sudden desire to examine her expression from closer range, he swung down out of the tree, and landed nimbly right in front of her, on the balls of his feet, just as he always had as a boy.

Her eyes grew large, confronted with his presence so suddenly, and so close. For an instant, the heat of that elusive, smoldering look returned. It was, for the flicker of an eyelid, as if she let down her guard, and allowed a possibility to reveal itself. As swiftly as it came, the look was gone, and in its place was a more guarded young woman than ever before. She seemed reluctant to directly meet his gaze. "I wonder, monsieur," she said, fingering the lip of one of the baskets she carried, "if you might have some sort of employment available, for a young woman who is about to have a child?"

Julian knew immediately who it was she referred to. "So, you wish to champion the cause of Penny Fairing, do you?"

Jeannette's chin went up. "Yes, my lord, I do. No one else seems inclined to do so, not even her family, and surely her crime is no more severe than Danny's . . ." Who remains happily in your employ, her tone meant to imply.

"I had hoped that Danny himself might come to his senses and do the right thing."

"Would you, were you in his shoes?" she challenged, flushing when he looked at her sharply.

"I would not leave a young woman to fend for herself were I to father a child on her, if that is what you ask," he said vehemently, thinking of the damage he had done the last time he had fathered a child, and that to his wife. He felt a sudden burning anger toward Danial Fulsom. The man was a complete cad. "What position do you think Penny Fairing qualified for?"

Jeannette started, as if he surprised her with the question, but she had an answer for him. "She would make an excellent wet nurse at this stage," she suggested. "Or perhaps she might make a start in a kitchen."

He smiled at her indulgently. "I wonder, Miss Sound Heart, do you find an answer for all problems in the kitchen?"

She regarded his question in all seriousness, as if it had never occurred to her, that she seemed to seek succor and safety, in kitchens. "No, she said at last. "Not all of them, my lord." As she looked up at him, he got the feeling that he posed some problem to her that would not find answer in kitchens.

"I shall see what I can do," he agreed, and because he wanted to see if he could stir the embers of that smoky look in her lovely hazel eyes again he leaned very close to her, closer than was either warranted or appropriate, to say, "Thank you, for diverting my sister. I do appreciate it."

She backed away from him a little, and lowered her head, so that the rim of her bonnet hid half her face, but not before he saw a flicker of the look he sought. The heat was still there. It warmed him, just as before. He wondered what roused such fire, and how he might go about keeping the flames of it alive.

Chapter Ten

~

With no idea that a glance might cause so much speculation, and no idea what Julian might have said to his sister, Jeannette was pleased to note an uneasy truce seemed to exist between herself and Lady Crawford. Margaret carefully refrained from any open confrontation with her, contenting herself instead, in making a plethora of unnecessary demands on the kitchen staff as a whole, and thrusting herself quite conspicuously between Jeannette and her brother whenever the two happened to cross paths. Her tactic irritated her brother no end, and made the running of the household more difficult.

Jeannette bore the punishing pace and unceasing demands, with stoic good grace. Complaining, she had long since learned, merely sapped one's strength, and made malcontents of one's fellow laborers. So, she held her tongue, and focused her energies on producing mass quantities of delicious food for the occupants of Idylnook, and planned her part of the menu for the upcoming entertainment that Lady Margaret had talked her brother into hosting.

There was something enjoyable in the ensuing bustle and activity, and because Lady Crawford had seen fit to bring kitchen staff among her entourage, the extra hands made the work, extraordinary that it was, go much faster than she might have anticipated.

So helpful, indeed, was the extended staff, that Jeannette suggested that by rotating their talents, everyone might enjoy one day of leisure a week. Her suggestion was met with hearty approval. Mrs. Gary declared it should be so.

Jeannette took advantage of her own day off, four days later, to see a bit of the English countryside. She begged the use of a horse off the head stable lad and asked him to recommend a pretty bridle path. Packing up a cold collation of bread, cheese, and fresh fruit, she set off on the provided mare, Rosy, a gentle, aging roan that had once been a favorite of Lady Endicott, and was in sore need of good exercise.

She was not disappointed. The day was a promising one, bright, clear, and warm, with just a breath of a breeze heavy with the perfume of clover, honeysuckle, and roses. The bridle path Jeannette had been directed to take was verdant with green things. Small, cob-nut trees stood back from the recommended track, and all along the sunny wayside a riot of wildflowers nodded their colorful heads, while bees and butterflies, and the occasional dragonfly, flitted between them. Rambling blackberry vines, pink with blossom, reached out for the roan's fetlocks, while house martins fluttered in the low spots, gathering mud for their nests. Blackbirds and cuckoos called from the hedges. Beyond the cob-nut trees stretched the distinctive, staked fields of hop vines, and low growing beds of strawberries, or orchards, where sheep grazed between twisted trees, weighed down with ripening apples, pears, or plums. Through the foliage of these trees one might glimpse the lovely, well-kept, black-and-white timbered houses, their second story overhanging the first, built by the yeoman farmers who had first cultivated this land. Everything was interesting, and foreign, to Jeannette, especially the odd, conically roofed oast houses, where she had been told, hops were dried for the making of ale. She reveled in the differences, and reveled in her freedom, which she had not tasted in what seemed the longest while. It seemed odd, and rather wonderful to be free to do whatever struck her fancy.

She rode a winding, hilly course, gently rising until the

farms fell away behind her, and the chalky white outcroppings of the downs cut into the fertile soil, until she came to a large, jutting rock that offered a lovely view of the surrounding countryside from its highest surface, and a shaded, but dry area for the spreading of her picnic.

Unsaddling and hobbling the roan, she let her loose to crop grass, and with a contented sigh, spread out the carriage blankets that the head lad had offered up for just such purpose. Taking care that her foodstuffs were placed in the shade, she raised her rather worn parasol, and climbed up onto the rock, that she might see what there was to be seen. The view was very satisfying, and from her elevation, she spied a thin clump of elm and beech that seemed worth exploring. She set off toward them, with the thought that nothing so keened the appetite as a bit of exercise.

The trees, once reached, could not hold her attention, for beneath their arms, in the filtered shade, was something far more interesting. A display of delicate, amethyst-colored blossoms met her eye. Perhaps three-score tender spikes of pale, speckled, purple blooms on tall, sturdy stalks. Orchids! Lovely, cultured-looking flowers, growing wild, in fact thriving, in this lonely place. They were almost too exquisite to be real. The sight stopped Jeannette in her tracks.

Awed, she stood looking at them with a speechless, singing sort of joy, pleased beyond measure that she should happen so casually on something rare and breathtakingly beautiful. She wished for an instant she were not alone, for something so spectacular was meant to be shared. But she was alone, a circumstance not at all unusual. These days, Jeannette felt a very solitary person. She did not really fit comfortably in any of the worlds she straddled; aristocrat or commoner, French citizen or British.

It was really just simple things that got her up out of her cramped bed every morning with a spring in her step; her joy in cooking, the growing feeling of family that possessed her whenever she entered the hall of Idylnook, and the increasing closeness she felt to the man who held her life in his hands. She added to those reasons the beauty and plenty of the countryside in which she had chosen to make her home. The orchids could not help but remind her of that blessing, with their very beauty. She was filled with delight just in looking at them. Stooping to examine the wonderfully dainty faces of the flowers until her back began to ache, it was her stomach's rumbling complaint of emptiness that moved her to return to her picnic. With a feeling the day had been blessed, she turned her back on the amazing orchids, and returned to her cache of food with good appetite.

As she soothed hunger, and watched the roan munch with equal contentment on the grass, his foraging nose raising clouds of agitated butterflies, she decided the day could not be more perfect. The sky above her head was an eye-watering cerulean, unblemished by so much as a trace of cloud, and the field on the downhill side of her perch, sweet with honeysuckle, vetch, milkwort, purple thistle, showy foxglove and cheerful ox-eye daisies, danced with butterflies; white, and brown, and some, more dashing, their wings tipped in orange. Bees hummed in the clover, lulling her with their busy nectar gathering. The warm somnolence of the afternoon and the sated fullness of her entire being, teased her eyelids with drowsy promises of even greater satisfaction in the Elysian fields of sleep.

Jeannette had not slept a whole night through since Lady Crawford's company had moved into her room. There simply was not enough room in her bed to be genuinely comfortable, and the number of snorers within hearing range had increased threefold.

Perhaps it would not hurt to lie back and catch a few sun-drenched winks. Jeannette carefully removed her hat, gloves, and with a quick look around to see nobody observed, her high-laced shoes. Wiggling her toes in blissful freedom, she unbuttoned the stifling confines of the high, stiff neck of the new burgundy-colored livery that had been fitted so perfectly to her only days before. The color suited her very well, much better than black ever could. She felt pretty in the new dress, despite the fact that every other female on the staff had one exactly like it. Fingering the pleasing texture of the new cloth, she sank back on her borrowed blankets, and closed her eyes.

Julian Endicott, hot and dusty, was returning from an errand into Maidstone, by way of a bridle path that promised more shade than the dust-choked road, when he spotted old Rosy, roaming loose on the downs. Wondering how it was the nag had come so far, he gigged his mount, and went after her, that he might catch her up and drive her home.

As he passed the stone outcropping that looked out over the surrounding orchards and hop fields, a flutter caught his eye. His attention was drawn to what appeared to be a woman, who lay as if dead, in the shadow of the rock. He recognized the new burgundy coloring of his servants' livery. He had chosen the fabric himself. Riding closer, he recognized the woman as Jeannette Saincoeur, and wondered if it was possible Rosy had thrown her onto the chalky outcropping, for she lay rather indecorously disposed, her wine dark skirts billowing about motionless legs, arms outflung. The thought that she might be seriously injured shot bleak terror through him.

Fearing the worst, he slipped down from his horse, and fell to his knees beside the young woman whose energetic company and vivacious conversation he had been missing these past few days of his sister's visit.

The pale, oval face was far too still, the usually articulate hands, motionless. To see Miss Saincoeur lying thus, alarmed him. He leaned in over her chest, prepared to press his ear to it, as he had seen the family physician do over the inert form of his wife when she had ceased her futile struggle to deliver the cross-turned babe he had cursed her with. The similarity of the moment sweated his brow.

But his ear had no opportunity for gentle contact. His very hovering seemed to rouse Miss Saincoeur. Head and shoulders, she rose with alacrity, an exclamation of fear rushing from her sweat-dewed lips.

"Mon dieu!"

They collided with bruising force, her yielding breast and completely unyielding chest bone against the bridge of his nose, and brow.

"Christ!"

"Ow!"

"Ow, is right," he agreed, nursing his abused nose. "I do beg your pardon. I did not mean either to startle or to injure you, Miss Saincoeur. It appeared to me some harm had come to you, so still did you lie there."

Jeannette pressed a palm to her breast, and Julian could not tell whether she meant to assuage the pain there with its pressure or calm her breathing, which came at a greatly accelerated pace. Either way, he felt the proper heel. Why in the world had he leapt to the conclusion she was dead?

"I was asleep," she said, rather unnecessarily, for of course she had been sleeping. She began to laugh, and Julian realized he had never heard a sound that pleased him more. "You gave me a nasty shock. I thought some stranger was leaning over me. I am very relieved such was not the case. It was rather foolish of me to leave myself open to such a possibility." She lay back against the blankets, and exhaled heavily, as if her relief took all strength from her.

Julian, who had sat back upon his heels, blinking involuntary tears that the stinging pain so close to his eyes produced, began to chuckle. "I thought you were dead. I thought docile old Rosy there had tossed you on your head."

"She is still here, then?" Jeannette opened her dark-lashed eyes to stare with amused concern at the sky. "From the position of the sun, I would say I have been asleep for hours."

Julian laughed outright, and when, unbalanced by the laughter, he sat down rather abruptly on the stone, he laughed even harder.

Jeannette, more awake now, propped herself on her elbows, smiling.

Regaining control of his spasm of mirth, Julian licked his lips and faced her, prepared to explain himself. But there was something strangely intimate in their mutual proneness on the rock, something undeniably alluring in her sleepy stance as his gaze roved over stockinged feet, rumpled skirts, and unbuttoned neckline to the drowsy vulnerability of hazel eyes, framed as they were, by dusky curls come loose from their pins. Her appearance stopped all explanation. He felt as if they shared the intimacy of a man and a woman fresh from a tumble.

"Would you care to ride with me, back to the house?" he asked, his voice husky.

Something of what he was feeling must have gotten through to her, for she sat up self-consciously, tucking her shockingly shoeless feet beneath the edge of her hastily straightened skirt, and began to tuck stray wisps of hair, rather unsuccessfully into their pins.

"Yes, if you do not mind the company," she said, no longer able to meet his eyes.

Really, this was most embarrassing, Jeannette thought. She was not at all used to having a gentleman regard her, no matter how kindly, as she tidied her hopelessly recalcitrant hair! There was an illicit flavor to such a pastime, an illicit flavor, too, in the looks he turned upon her. She had seen such a look only once before, in his library. Now, as it had then, it left her shaken.

"There's nothing for it," he murmured, regarding her efforts with his head cocked judgmentally to one side. He reached out to pluck a blade of grass from above her right ear. "You shall have to take it down, comb it out, and pin it up again, else someone mistakenly assume I have been rolling in the hay with you, when we return together."

She gasped, shocked he should say such a thing. "No one would dare to believe such an absurdity!"

He smiled ruefully, "No?"

The image of just such an occurrence could not help but pass through her mind. "But, of course not!"

"You are, perhaps, forgetting my sister. . . ." His hand darted out to capture a twig from somewhere beyond her line of sight. A hairpin came with it. "She has already proved herself ready to believe you capable of any number of despicable acts."

Jeannette had forgotten, blissfully forgotten. She tended to forget many things when alone in the company of this gentle man. She patted her disordered head. The tortoiseshell comb at the back fell out in her hand, so loose had it come. "Vraiment! I must look a sight." She began plucking free pins.

She did look a sight, Julian thought as he began to gather up her picnic things—a sight for world-weary eyes. She looked to him like nothing so much as a budding, young wood nymph. Her cheeks were flushed rosy, the pale column of her neck rose up out of the half-buttoned neckline of her dress with provocative grace, leaves and twigs and grass clung wildly to her hair and the breeze teased and flirted with her freed locks. She was a wood nymph with a mulish expression. The tangles she picked at with the tortoiseshell comb, were more numerous than she had expected, and the breeze hindered her efforts.

Her hair! What a glorious riot of tumbled dark hair! It was magnificent. He had never imagined the careful knot could reveal such waves of wonder. Julian's gaze tangled in the rich, coffee-colored locks. What would it feel like to run one's fingers through such hair, to feel its soft, glossy weight against one's bare skin? He could not look away, could not stand idly by as she tore at it with the comb.

"Gently, Miss Saincoeur, gently!" He slid the instrument of torture from her hand. "You need not tear at it so. We are not in so great a hurry that you should abuse your crowning glory. If you will be so good as to turn around, I would be more than happy to assist."

She frowned at him and snatched the comb back. "I can manage quite well, *merci*."

The breeze lifted her hair, and wafted a lock into her mouth even as she spoke, but with a quick swipe of her hand to rectify the situation, she went back to ripping at the snarls, Julian winced.

"Hand it over," he insisted. "It will all fall out at the rate you are going, and I do not care to find the cook's hair in my soup."

Begrudgingly, biting her lip so as not to smile at his witticism, she handed over the comb.

Jeannette was not prepared for the mind-numbing sensation of this man's hands in her hair. Blinking in complete consternation, for there was a hypnotic lulling quality to each gently stroking caress to her head, she did her best to steady her ragged breathing.

He was incredibly gentle—breath-stoppingly so. Her eyes grew heavy with the erotic pleasure such a simple act engendered. Jeannette felt his every contact, no matter how subtle, with every strand. Gooseflesh rifled her scalp, and shiver upon delightful shiver insinuated its way down her spine. The comb, like teasing fingertips, ran across her crown, her temples, and around the tender tips of her ears. The weight of his hand followed the comb, smoothing the tangle-free strands. And then, an eye-popping change, his hands grazed the nape of her neck in gathering up the bulk of her hair, so that fingers and comb might trail their way up the incredibly sensitive area of her neck. As the weight of her hair lifted, the breeze whispered against heated skin with such sweet delicacy, Jeannette closed her eyes, and swallowed hard. The moan that threatened to slip her lips was quashed.

"Hold this, please," Julian said, surprisingly businesslike, and having split away one manageable hank to detangle, he thrust the remainder of her mane over her shoulder and into waiting hands. Carefully, almost reverently, he worked his way through the length of her hair. She was touched by his gentle consideration in not pulling too hard. Her eyes closed with expectant pleasure each time the firm pressure of his hands weighed against her head, that she might not feel his tug with the tangles.

There was something perfectly in keeping with the heady bliss of her afternoon in the heated sensations he spawned, something as steady and rhythmic as her breathing, as drowsy and comfortable as her sleep had been, and yet as breathtakingly awe inspiring as the orchids she had discovered.

When he touched her, she became the sun-blessed, fertile soil and he the fervent growth of something green, joined to her, rooted in her. Together, they seemed natural and beautiful and verdant, a synergistic blending of two parts that created a greater whole. Time stopped. Jeannette was not sure whether he had been stroking her head but an instant, or for all eternity. She felt a definite sense of loss, of profound parting, when he handed her back the comb, saying, "There, that's much better. Now, you should be able to make it neat again."

"Thank you," she breathed unevenly. With arms gone weak and hands that trembled, she took the comb, and leaning forward, threw the weight of hair over her head. It crackled with the retained energy of his touch. Twisting the smooth, tangle-free waves into a neat chignon, she pinned it in place. The comb was tucked in last, both as decoration and as extra security against loose strands. Her cheeks felt very hot, and her scalp tingled with the memory of his touch. She had no idea of how beautifully pink-cheeked and alive she looked, nor how much restraint it took in the man before her not to reach out to take her in his arms, that he might trace the open neckline of her dress and rain hot kisses on the beauty mark he saw there, the only blemish on the pale perfection of her creamy neck.

Julian turned his back on Jeannette as she finished the work of her coiffure. He could not face her, could not risk

revealing the powerful feelings that had been unleashed
within him in running his hands through the living silk of
her hair. Hunger ached deep within him, a hunger for flesh
upon flesh, for the sweet taste of a woman's lips, for the
closeness of loving and being loved. And with every
moment that he remained in the company of Jeannette
Saincoeur, that hunger grew.

Julian knew within his heart of hearts that his desire for
female companionship was natural, even healthy, but even
as he admitted as much to himself, he could not help feeling
guilty of the capability of such wanton need, when Elinor
was little more than a year taken from him. It was as if, in
his being drawn to any other woman so soon, he showed
some form of disrespect.

He glanced over his shoulder, to see how Miss Saincoeur
progressed with her shoes. She was tying off the top of one
set of hooks and laces. Her other wool stockinged digit was
yet to be hidden, and though the rather bulky stocking was
not as enticing as silk might have been, it was a thing of natural beauty, part and parcel with tumbled skirts, a glimpse of
petticoat and rumpled carriage blankets spread on sun-
warmed stone. Julian wished that he might have spent the
afternoon picnicking in this spot, with the owner of that ill-
clad leg. He wished he might have disposed himself non-
chalantly on a blanket in the sunshine, and been lulled to
blissful sleep in Jeannette Saincoeur's tender arms. Julian
shook himself, took a deep, head-clearing breath, and turned
away from the enticing sight of one shapely, shoeless foot in
its evocatively rumpled stocking.

"I shall just catch up old Rosy," he said, his throat unusually thick. "And throw your saddle onto her back."

"Oui," she agreed, reaching for her missing shoe. "But
there is something *incroyable*, I would show you before we
ride back. Something so *fantastique*, it will steal your breath
away." The fluid Frenchness of her accent worked to mud-
dle his thinking again. There was something that spoke
always of the sensual, the sexual, in such an accent. The

eddying force of that fluid vocal tone resounded again and again in his ears as he saw to the horse, and wondered what it was, besides bared limbs, that Jeannette meant him to see.

"Come, come!"

Temptation beckoned, and before Julian could catch up to her, his beautiful French cook was striding out across the downs, almost dancing in her haste to show him "something *incroyable*."

He set off after her.

Her skirt belled gracefully around her on occasion as she whirled to see that he followed to a thin grouping of trees. She had in fact disappeared among them by the time he reached the first of their number.

She stood in the filtered sunlight, amid a cluster of tall flowers, her face alight with expectation, awaiting his reaction. Are they not wonderful, her expression and the motioning of her hands seemed to say. For an instant, he was inclined to find something wonderful in the sight of his wood nymph, fairly dancing with her delight in the middle of such an unexpected mass of delicate color.

But Julian could not find anything wonderful in the orchids once he recognized them for what they were. Frowning, he turned away from the sight of her, turned away from the pale purple flowers and the memories they conjured, and leaving the stand of elms behind him, stalked back toward the horses, an unexpected wash of tears blurring his vision, his throat so thick he wanted desperately to cough, or choke, or weep.

"Monsieur? Monsieur, you did not even look at them." She came running after him, her wonderful voice plaintive, as though he wounded her with the haste of his exit. "You do not like orchids? You do not find it remarkable that they should grow in such profusion in the wild? I have never before seen such a thing."

He did not answer, could not answer, else he break down. Without a glance for the now breathless Miss Saincoeur, he strode on.

"Wait," she gasped. "I cannot keep up with you." She dropped behind.

He stopped and walked back to her. Her labored breathing only served to heighten his anguish. He wanted to reach for her, to stroke her back, to loosen more of the buttons at the neck of her dress so that she would stop gasping for air. He wanted, quite selfishly, to fall down on the grass with her, that they might think and do only what delighted them. But his arms were bound to his sides.

His voice echoed the hurt in hers as he said very softly, "Kent is the only county in all of England where the 'Lady' orchid grows. My late wife, Elinor . . ." His voice wavered in uttering her name. He cleared his throat and went on, ". . . had a particular fondness for them. We covered her . . ." Again his throat required clearing. ". . . casket . . . with them, at . . ." His voice failed him entirely. He had to purse his lips to stop a great wailing sound from erupting from deep inside.

The puffing of Jeannette's breath hitched up for a telling moment. She exhaled heavily, and while he could not reach for her, she had no trouble reaching out to him. Her hands flew to his shoulder, then his hand, quick fleeting contacts that moved him far more than she would ever know.

"I did not know, monsieur. I am very sorry. I did not mean to cause you grief. They were just . . ."—she shrugged, and her hand darted out to make contact with his back—". . . so very beautiful."

Emotion spoke plainly in her words; shock, distress, and understandable regret. But it was the hint of breathless awe at the end, in the beauty of the flowers she had so desperately wanted to share with him, and the gentle touch, upon his back, that shattered his control.

Shaken, he sucked air into his lungs like a drowning man. A tear welled into the corner of his left eye, and no matter how furiously he blinked, he could not stop its fall.

She understood his sensibilities too well. "I have a shoulder here, for the wetting, should you be so inclined." The warm pressure of her hand upon his back, made a soothing circle. "It does you no good to hold onto such sorrow. Open your heart, monsieur, and release your pain. You will feel so much better afterward."

It was the phrase "release your pain" and, again, the warmth of her touch upon his shoulder, that did him in. His chin fell down upon his chest, so great was the weight of the sorrow she recognized. A shuddering sigh slid involuntarily from the tightness of his throat, and then another. As though the sighs uncorked his feelings, a second tear burned a trail down his cheek. He could not stop it, though his shoulders shook with the strain of trying.

"It's all right, *mon ami.* You have reason to weep, and there is no one here to notice that your eyes are wet, but moi." The warm pressure of the hand at his back gently turned him into the circle of her arms.

With a raw, choking sound, he sank to his knees before her in the grass and buried his face in the comfort of her abdomen, his arms about her waist. He did as she suggested, and released all hold on his tears.

Her arms cradled his head as deep, gut-wrenching sobs tore from his wretched throat, and as he wept, the music of her French, and the equally soothing music of her hands moved in comforting circles through his hair, and along his back and neck. "That's right. *Tout à fait.*" She said it again and again. "Let go the awful hurt inside. Be free of it, monsieur. Do you know, I have been told that each tear liberates a small amount of the pain within us. You will feel much better in a moment, and then we will return to Idylnook and Simms will fix you a cup of claret with a blue borage flower to float upon its surface."

His face was wet, and tears still seeped from his eyes, but he felt a sudden overwhelming happiness. It bubbled up, within him like champagne, and under its dizzying spell, he felt an almost drunken urge to kiss her. He rose from his knees, and responded to the urge, unthinking, eyes closed to the consequences, a man seeking greater comfort in the comfortable arms of a woman who knew how to make him laugh, even as he wept. She smelled of sun-touched skin, and sun-baked fabric, and the promise of even greater warmth. He knew he could keep the fizzing happiness alive within him, did he but kiss her, so he nuzzled her neck, his tears wetting her flesh as hotly as his lips, which he caressed against the satin of her cheek, and then, with gentle urgency, sought out the liquid embrace of her lips.

Jeannette was shocked by that first kiss. She froze, unwilling to brutally refuse the needy embrace of this grief-stricken man, and yet unable to respond to it either. She had not meant the comfort of her arms to be misconstrued as something sexual. She had not reckoned with the possibility of a kiss, despite the fact that she had imagined kissing this man from the first day they had met.

She meant to refuse his second kiss, but found to her dismay that her lips met his with curious willingness. For a lingering instant, there was within her the delicious feeling that everything fell into place with this kiss, that here the promising day found culmination. But the feeling did not last. The alarming sensation that such a course courted disaster, so roused her sense of self-preservation, that Jeannette lowered her head when he would have locked his lips on hers a third time, and let her arms fall away from him, and said, "Non! This is not right. I did not mean it to end this way. I will not be able to continue working under your roof if we go on in this manner."

He pulled back without a word, and turned his back on her, head bowed. After a brief moment of silence, he sighed a deep sigh and agreed raggedly. "No, I do beg your pardon. I beg of you to forget my imposing myself upon you in such a fashion. My emotions quite carried me away. Forgive me."

It had been Julian's own suggestion to forget, but he found in practice, that he could in no way do so. He could not forget the honeyed warmth of Jeannette's mouth, could not keep his eyes from straying to the exposed skin of her pale neck, could not forget the moment of response he had felt from her, the sweet, heated promise of their mutual desire.

For the first time since Elinor's death, he actually found himself seriously interested in a woman, interested to the point of obsession, in the gleam of sunlight on the smooth coil of her hair as she went ahead of him to the horses, in the physical pull that tugged at him rather strongly when he held out his laced palms, that she might step in and be thrown up into her sidesaddle. Keen interest made his blood race when she braced a hand against his shoulder and looked into his eyes for a brief, revealing moment that told him she had as much trouble putting what had happened behind them as he had. He wanted to kiss her again as a result of that look, wanted to pull her down off of Rosy, rather than launching her onto the mare's back.

Their eyes met again, as she hooked her leg over the horn, and straightened her skirt. It was not designed after the fashion of a riding habit, and tended to reveal not only a great swath of petticoat, but a hint of ankle as well. Besides the physical, Julian realized that for the first time in over a year, he felt as though he were connected to a woman's mind, as if the two of them spoke a language that had nothing to do with words, and everything to do with the openness of another's thinking. Jeannette Saincoeur's soul cried out to him through her lively, hazel eyes. This woman understood him; physically, emotionally, intellectually—he ventured to say, spiritually, as no one else had ever done, not even his dear Elinor.

She was right, of course. They could not safely continue to respond to the incredible pull between them while she remained under his employ, and certainly not with Margaret in the house. And yet, his imagination refused to accept such a bleak ruling. Throughout their awkward, silent passage back to Idylnook, he conjured up scenario after scenario in which the little flame of passion that had ignited within him today, a flame that filled him with a level of light and care-free happiness that he had begun to forget, was given fuel, and allowed to blaze.

Chapter Eleven

~

Jeannette found it difficult to forget, even for a moment, what had transpired. That this man she admired should mirror her own desire, was wonderful in its own way, but that he should do so, in the midst of weeping for his deceased wife, threw a definite shadow on her pleasure. She had been quite serious about not staying another night at Idylnook should his passionate claim on her continue. She had no intention of becoming lover to a man who must always imagine in her the lost gratification of a dead woman. Jeannette was strongly drawn to Julian Endicott. She could not deny as much to herself. Under different circumstances, perhaps they might have made a match of it, but reality was very clear to her, and decidedly not in their favor. She was his servant, not his equal. Nothing but ruin lay in her falling slave to unattainable desire. She would end up a grass widow, without a doubt, and she had too recently seen the consequences of such a position, in Penny Fairing's questionable future, to yearn for a moment's gratification at such cost.

Given the events of the afternoon, there was something subtly appropriate in Julian Endicott bringing up the very subject of Penny Fairing, and the position he had found for her as wet nurse, as they rode away from their own brush with such a fate.

"Would you care to tell her of the position, or shall I?" he asked, having described the circumstances to her.

She smiled bitterly at the irony of such a discussion.

Allowed she this man to have his way with her, would there come a time when he went about finding a similar position for her, in order to get an embarrassment off his hands? Pushing such distasteful thoughts away, she said, "Penny holds you in highest esteem, my lord. She would be much moved were you to personally deliver the good news."

He reined his horse in abruptly, and reached out to similarly halt the progress of old Rosy. His gray eyes searched hers. "And you, Miss Saincoeur, do you hold me in highest esteem, or have I fallen horribly in your estimation as a result of my reckless behavior today?" His voice, genuinely concerned, was like a caress to her ear.

Jeannette wished she might somehow erase the events of the afternoon. What did he expect? An open profession of her growing affection for him? A confession of her fears that she did in fact fall in love with him, that he might ruin her, and then cast her aside?

Used to protecting herself, to surviving all kinds of peril, she responded cagily, "I fear I begin to lose my objectivity with regard to you, my lord. That disturbs me. You did at one time profess to value that very trait in me above all others, and I would not lower myself in your esteem."

He understood her dilemma. She could see it in the faint twitch of the lips that had so recently sought out her own.

"I begin to realize I have placed far too high a value on objectivity, Miss Saincoeur."

He let go her horse, though he continued to look at her in a most searching manner. "You have in no way lowered yourself in my esteem. In fact, I cannot think of a female I hold in higher regard. You may rest assured that I would do nothing that threatened that regard." His gaze strayed from her eyes, to her chin, and still further down. A playful smile touched his lips, ever so briefly. "You must see to buttoning your dress, Miss Sound Heart"—he always addressed her as such with an amused twitch of the lips—"else I shall most certainly be suspected of quite different intentions."

Her hand flew self-consciously to her throat, and as she

fumbled with her buttons, he kindly bent to stroke the neck of his horse, so that she did not feel in any way that he wished to leer at her in her rectification of such an embarrassment.

When he was sure she was finished, he chirruped to his horse, and said, "I shall, as you suggest, deliver the news myself to Penny Fairing."

The return to Idylnook was to Jeannette a study in contrast to the peaceful ideal of her morning and afternoon. Like a shock of cold water in the face to wake one, the arrival of guests woke her from a dreamlike state, to that of stark reality. She and Julian Endicott rode side by side up the drive, only to find themselves miles apart in the midst of the bustle of activity surrounding the arrival of two traveling coaches and three outriders.

Julian, immediately the center of attention, dismounted, helped her down, and was swept away into the embrace of his guests' many arms. Jeannette felt herself grow invisible in such company, faceless, an entity glanced over and dismissed as inconsequential by all but Margaret Crawford, who flapped a dismissive hand in her direction and encouraged her to, "Run on to the kitchen. You are doubtless needed there."

Jeannette could not look at the young ladies who climbed gracefully down from the coaches, proper chaperonage revolving around them like moons paled by the star-bright elegance of fair young faces, without remembering rather wistfully, when she had shone just as brightly.

Turning her back on the reminder of her past, she led the roan toward the stables, and when one of the guests' footmen offered, with a flashing smile, "Shall I take the mare, miss?" she smiled at him as graciously as any lady, handed over the reins, squared her shoulders and set off for the kitchen, little realizing that two gentlemen followed her passage with admiring looks—the footman, who had been dazzled by her smile, and the lord of the manor, who felt the day lost a measure of light, whenever they parted.

As Jeannette made her way back to the world of the kitchens, where she was needed and recognized as a force to reckon with, she thought this odd dichotomy ironic. She did not change. The perception of the people around her was all that changed. In one sphere, her name, contacts, appearance, and wealth, or lack of it, were what mattered, while in another it was the talent of her hands, the quickness of her eye, and the smoothness of her sauces that impressed.

Perhaps the deepest irony was to be found in her own personal assessment of who she was in this moment compared to who she had once been. She considered herself a far more worthy individual now, in servants' livery, with flour dusted on her cheek rather than rouge, and a spoon in her hand as opposed to an embroidery tambour. She considered her talents worthwhile. As cook, she could be both an erstwhile contributor to art, and the means to man's daily survival. Surely such a contribution offered the world far more than had she lived a life of leisure.

As she made her way around the house, to the servants' entrance, instead of taking the more expedient route through it, due to nothing more than her station, it occurred to Jeannette that perhaps, after all, she had some slim understanding of what it was her countrymen had fought for and against, so avidly.

Julian watched her go. At every opportunity between greeting the guests and helping ladies down from treacherous carriage steps, and in ordering the disposition of baggage and horses, his eyes followed her unerringly. As she went, he was impressed by the grace of her carriage, and the self-possession of her posture. Miss Sound Heart, or Saincoeur, or Bouillé, whoever she was, the woman had substance. Her spirit somehow occupied a little more of the cosmos than any other female he had the pleasure of knowing.

"Julian!" Margaret firmly brought his attention back to the matter at hand—their guests. "I would introduce you to Miss Sophy Burnett, and her sister Adria."

To please his sister, Julian performed his "how-do-you-dos" with gentlemanly style, but as he bent over each soft and carefully gloved hand, he could not help wondering how these gentle innocents would respond to the demands of a harsher life were they thrown to its mercy without the benefit of family or connections, as Miss Saincoeur had been. He rather thought they would have been thoroughly crushed, or thoroughly embittered by the experience. It was remarkable Jeannette was neither. The more he saw of his guests, and listened to their idle chatter about idle pursuits, the more remarkable she seemed to him.

There were thirty-five guests in all, outside of Margaret, and her staff. Fifteen were females, eighteen males, twenty of them servants; valets, footmen, grooms, and ladies' maids. The house bristled with people from stem to stern, cellar to rooftop. Even the stables housed extra male servants, and the gardening staff was doubled up with still more. The kitchen was a hive of activity. All of these extra mouths must be fed. The larder, wine cellar, and gardens were pillaged, the oven never went out and the dishes that had to be washed piled up in great hillocks in the scullery. Two girls from the village were hired on to help level the mountains.

It was exhilarating and exhausting, and Jeannette rarely left the kitchen, or saw anyone but servants, for in addition to the ordinary table that must be set thrice daily for the guests, the servants must be fed, too, in revolving shifts, and there was the culminating ball to prepare for that was to be held as a grand finale to the weekend, on Sunday evening.

Jeannette did not have much time for ruminating, so much was there to be done, but when she did stop to think, now and again, they were melancholy thoughts that plagued her. Why and how had she gotten the idea that Lord Endicott might be truly and honorably interested in her? She had but to look at the gathering of elegantly gowned young women who fluttered about Idylnook like butterflies, to realize how drab and mothlike she was by comparison. She had been foolish enough to indulge herself for a few days, to believe all things possible, to believe she might herself one day fill the position one of these young ladies was destined for, as wife of Julian Endicott. But, now, reason returned.

Had she so completely fallen from her original station in life? Was she destined to marry one such as Danial Fulsom rather than Julian Endicott, merely because of her name, and occupation? It would seem so. This was England, not France. There had been no Revolution here. The class structure was firmly entrenched. For Julian Endicott to marry her, for him to so much as show a decided interest in her, went against all common sense, against all the unspoken rules of society. It would be as ludicrous as if, as a child, she had told her father she meant to marry his valet.

It was odd how life turned and folded in on itself sometimes, so that one might more clearly see its contradictions.

Jeannette had thought, despite his assurances, that there might be some awkwardness between herself and Lord Endicott, as a result of their passionate confrontation on the downs, but there was in the end, no time for awkwardness. Like a calm before the storm, the day on the downs preceded the steady, attention-demanding influx of visitors who descended on Idylnook like a flock of hungry birds. Jeannette had few moments in which she might so much as ruminate on the strangely peaceful and enchanted day she had shared with Julian. There was breakfast to prepare, and trays to be sent up to the rooms of those who were not seen until nuncheon was served, which must be followed by tea and finally dinner. Perhaps most annoying, every painstakingly prepared meal had to meet Margaret Crawford's exacting standard of excellence—standards that toughened, Jeannette was quick to realize, whenever Lady Crawford assumed that a dish had come from Jeannette's hand.

Margaret had not been pleased to see her brother ride into the drive of Idylnook, with the new kitchen help beside him, while important guests were disembarking at the door, and marriageable prospects among them! She had clenched her teeth on any scolding at the time, but managed to make her displeasure known in sending one after another; a perfectly wonderful béarnaise sauce, a seafood soufflé, a dish of braised endives à l'orange, a cucumber and nasturtium salad, and a chocolate gateau back to the kitchen, as unacceptable and untouched, because her ladyship found them too rich, too salty, too tart, or too sweet.

Jeannette took each rejection without complaint, though she was cut to the quick in being so humiliated before the rest of the kitchen staff. Lady Crawford's own chef, however, put her at ease by dipping into each returned dish for a taste, and then winking at her, saying, "There is nothing wrong here. Madam is miffed with you over something, isn't she? She is hoping to anger you into giving notice. She never sends so much back to the kitchen unless she is on a tear of some sort."

The whole of the household soon caught on to this focused pettiness, and rallied around Jeannette with indignation and sympathy. Jeannette was one of their own. Insult to her was insult to them all. The promptness of service to her ladyship fell off considerably.

Madam's temper did not improve, and she did not hesitate to complain to her brother.

"Really, Julian, you must see to your servants, my dear. Never have I seen them so insubordinate during Elinor's lifetime as they are now. And that new cook of yours—why, I have had to send half of her dishes back to the kitchen, so inedible have I found them."

Julian had listened with only half an ear up to that point. But he knew his sister well enough to know that once again she had taken it into her head to put Jeannette Saincoeur in her place. He lifted his hand, and rang for Simms.

The butler responded with his customary alacrity.

"He comes quick enough when you ring," Margaret muttered.

"Milord?" Simms inquired with a studied deafness for Margaret's mumbled insult.

"You will be so good as to inform the kitchen staff, Simms, that I will personally conduct the tasting of any food that is to be presented to my guests for the duration of their stay. I have relied too heavily on my sister's good nature in conducting duties I should myself be responsible for."

Simms bowed. "Very good, sir. I shall inform the staff."

Margaret was frowning as the butler left them.

"Satisfied, Margaret?" Julian murmured, with a contented twitch of the lips that he would not allow to spread into a full-blown smile.

"Hmph!" Margaret was anything but. "I shall not be satisfied, Jules, until you have found yourself a decent helpmate, to take poor, dear Elinor's place. Tell me, what do you think of Miss Forbisher? She is a very promising girl, think you not? The Misses Burnett are very nice girls, as well."

Julian, who had, until that moment, no opinion at all of either the unfortunate Miss Forbisher, or the Burnett sisters, took them into instant dislike. There was no mistaking these young women must be his sister's favorites, among those who had been invited, and he was in no mood to have his future arranged for him.

"I am sure all of the young women you have invited might be described as promising young women," he said, with gentle irony. "And as such, I promise you, I shall give each and every one of them the attention and respect they are due."

Chapter Twelve

~

Jeannette was restless. The kisses she had tasted at Julian Endicott's lips kept floating to the surface of her memory. The more she tried to dismiss Lord Endicott's physical impact on her, the more insistently he impinged upon her consciousness. She found it difficult to conduct herself with her customary focused attention in the hectic and crowded kitchen.

Equally challenging was the prospect of settling herself comfortably in her crowded room that evening, despite the knowledge that the following day was sure to be frantic. Polly had started up a card game, and half a dozen of the female servants, visiting and otherwise, crowded into their room to play for pennies. Jeannette had no interest in cards. It occurred to her that perhaps, had she a book to read, she might relax in some corner, and escape this neck-stretching tension she could not seem to dismiss.

Taking up the volume of essays she had thoroughly devoured, she made her inconspicuous way downstairs, past the drawing room and the smoking closet, where a number of the visitors were likewise playing cards, imbibing in punch, and talking and laughing uproariously.

It bothered Jeannette to hear the sound of feminine laughter ringing through these halls. Perhaps one of the women here tonight would amuse Julian Endicott to the point of a laughter as engaging as that she had provoked in him this afternoon on the downs. He had a handsome smile. It bothered her to think that she would soon see some other female coaxing dimples into his cheeks. She had allowed herself to dream foolish dreams with reference to this troubled man. Her weakness irritated her. It crossed her mind, that should she stay on here, for any length of time as cook, she must one day face the reality of Lord Endicott's remarrying. She must, as his servant, stand aside, and watch him succumb to another's feminine wiles. The prospect of cheerfully serving another young woman in the position she herself secretly dreamed of filling, was daunting. It had crossed her mind, more than once, that she would like to be mistress of Idylnook, and wife to the kind and gentle Lord Endicott.

She slipped, with relief, into the peaceful stillness of the empty library, and shut out the sound of laughter. She must content herself with the flights of fancy to be found in books, not in the extravagance of unrealistic dreams. She would look for something romantic upon Lord Endicott's shelves. A gothic romance, or a book of poetry might satisfy the yearnings one heated kiss provoked within her.

Jeannette was halfway across the room before she realized it was occupied. She inhaled abruptly. A shadow in the chair by the window moved. Without a word spoken, she knew whose shadow it was.

"Did you enjoy the essays, Jeannette?" It was Julian Endicott who asked. The low resonance of his voice sounded an echoing resonance of expectation within her breast. Her knees felt quite strange, as if they were no longer supported by bone. A similar softening afflicted her spine, and her tongue flicked out to wet suddenly dry lips as he leaned up out of his chair. The light caught his face and painted the planes of his cheek and brow with a pallor that matched his hair. There was something fascinating and reminiscent of the first day she had seen this man, in the way his face, and nothing else, swam up out of the darkness. He regarded her, as he usually did, intently, with piercing gray eyes still weighed down by loss.

"The essays?" she repeated, her mind a blank. He referred to the essays she carried in her hand. "Very enlightening, monsieur." She knew she had thought so at the time, though in this moment she could not recall a word of what she had read. Her mind seemed to hold nothing but memory of the sensations she had experienced that afternoon as he unburdened himself before her, and then took her in his arms to kiss her.

"Come closer to the lamp, Miss Saincoeur," Julian directed her. "I would have you equally enlightened."

She drew near, her heart loping, her hand sweaty on the leather binding that contained the collection of essays. Did he mean to kiss her again? He rose so that they stood together in the circle of light the lamp on his desk threw. Gently, he took the book from her hand and leafed through its pages, his elegant fingers turning the paper, swimming in flashes of light and darkness. Jeannette knew what it was like to be caressed by such a hand. She could not deny her desire to be blessed by such a touch again. Such thoughts brought her to the blush.

"In what way has Mr. Burke shed light on your knowledge of the world, Miss Saincoeur? Tell me, I am curious."

Jeannette concentrated on recalling her impressions of Burke's essay, and not her impressions with regard to Lord Endicott's hands. Such a redirection of her thoughts served to steady her. "A great deal that Monsieur Burke wrote seemed sensible to me. Indeed, there were certain passages that struck such a chord . . ."

She could read the intensity of his interest in his gaze.

"And can you point out these passages? I would be interested to see just how it was this Englishman's opinion struck some note of truth for a Frenchwoman who has lived through the very Revolution he seeks to explain."

He handed the book back to her, and she turned immediately to its front section. Burke would see her through this trying moment. The passion of politics fittingly diverted her attention from the passions of her heart.

"Here, monsieur," she said. "He speaks of his reticence to congratulate France on her freedom. These words seemed remarkably astute. She read. " 'Is it because liberty in the abstract may be classed among the blessings of mankind, that I am seriously to felicitate a madman, who has escaped from the protecting restraint and wholesome darkness of his cell, on his restoration to the enjoyment of light and liberty? Am I to congratulate a highwayman and murderer who has broke prison upon the recovery of his natural right?' "

Julian studied her face with some puzzlement. "Do you see your countrymen, then, in the light of madmen and murderers?"

"I do," she said emphatically. "I shall never forget the screaming rabble that gathered around Madame Guillotine, roaring for blood, and more blood. The faces I looked upon were not those of just and sane men and women. The behavior I observed, was too consumed by passion to be admired." It occurred to her that her own passion was back under her control, reined in by the focus of their discussion. Relieved, she plunged on. "Burke goes on to say, 'I must be tolerably sure, before I venture publicly to congratulate men upon a blessing, that they have really received one.' " She lifted her eyes to his, hoping he would understand. "My own feeling is that my nation has been thrust into turmoil that will not resolve itself for many a year. It is probable that great good will come of the evils of this Revolution, but my own life has been so touched, so altered, by the violences of men seeking this abstraction they call freedom, that I cannot judge completely without bias, just what the good is. I do not find myself made more free by their new freedom. My choices, my direction in life, my very future, have been greatly affected, I dare to say, severely narrowed by events that I had no power to stand in the way of. Should men be free? I daresay yes. But must it be at so dear a cost, and can it not be delivered by men of decency and honor without the sacrifice of the lives of so many innocents?"

He sat forward as she spoke, his eyes alight with intellectual stimulation. "I think I understand your complaint." He stood, and leaning in over her shoulder in a pulse-fluttering manner, pointed out a passage that echoed his understanding. "There . . ." he indicated by reaching around her, so that they did both seem to be bound together by their mutual hold on the book, for one warmly, heart-stopping moment. "Where he speaks of the French Revolution as the most astonishing thing that has hitherto happened in the world." He leaned in close to her cheek, his chest brushing her back in a most disconcerting manner, and read aloud. " 'The most wonderful things are brought about, in many instances by means the most absurd and ridiculous . . .' "

He paused, and she felt his chest move as it took a great lungful of air, and then as he expelled that breath, its warmth titillating the flesh of her cheek, and brow, and earlobe, Jeannette lost all train of thought in connection with Revolution and freedom. She concentrated only on the nearness of this man, and the memory of how much closer they had been in the heat of passion on the lonely downs. She was highly tempted to adjust her stance but a fraction, it would take no more than a shifting of her weight from one foot to the other, and she would come more completely in contact with his body. His cheek hovered within a hairbreadth of her own. His arm, with but the slightest shift, would fit snugly about her. She knew he felt the tension of the moment. She heard it in the abatement of his words— and such words! There was an absurdity to this moment that mirrored those words. She knew that did she but move—a ridiculous thing really—as a result of that absurdity, the most wonderful thing would come about. He would take her into his arms completely, she knew he would, and he would kiss her again. She both relished and dreaded this moment, for the power of events lay within her grasp. She could change history with the mere shifting of her feet.

She did not, in the end, give in to the heady lure of passion. She moved away and not toward him, bringing a closure to opportunity by stiffly picking up the reading close to where he had left off. Something in Burke's words seemed appropriate.

" 'In viewing this monstrous tragicomic scene, the most opposite passions necessarily succeed and sometimes mix with each other in the mind: alternate contempt and indignation, alternate laughter and tears, alternate scorn and horror.' "

He took the book from her, his finger marking the passage. The magic of the moment was lost. He turned away from her, and continued reading, " 'It cannot, however, be denied that to some this strange scene appeared in quite another point of view . . .' " He turned, and lifted his eyes to regard her evenly. " 'Into them,' " he went on with subtle emphasis, " '. . . it inspired no other sentiment than those of exultation and rapture.' "

So intent was his gaze as he spoke that she knew what he said had more to do with the two of them, than with any feelings he might have with regard to Revolution. The word rapture fell from his tongue like a ripe plum.

Jeannette flushed. Flustered, she felt the need to flee. A noise in the hallway outside the library—one of the guests heading off to bed—increased her sense of alarm. Did she stay, she would not be able to refuse the pull she felt from this man. She knew it. He knew it. The space between them hummed with the tension their knowledge engendered.

"I must go," she breathed, and turned to the door.

He stopped her with but a word. "Wait."

She turned, her back against the support of the door.

"There is a poem I have read that I thought you might enjoy," was all he said. Going to the shelf, he plucked forth an ornately gilded book, and brought it to her. "The man's a Scot, and writes with rather heavy dialect, but perhaps you will sift some meaning from the best of it." Then he opened the door for her in a most gentlemanly fashion, that she might depart with all dignity intact.

It was not until he had closed it behind her, and she had taken a deep breath to steady her racing heart, that Jeannette so much as looked at the slender volume he insisted she take away with her. It was a collection of poems by a Robert

Burns, and the silky ribbon marker was placed so that the book opened up to two poems on facing pages. One was called "Afton Water", the other, "Ae Fond Kiss". Heart beating in a decidedly uneven manner, Jeannette took herself off to read the verse, wondering what Julian Endicott had seen in this poetry to make him think she must read it as well.

Chapter Thirteen

~

Jeannette's mind was fixated on the passionate nature of that same poetry the next morning when she went to the kitchen door, in anticipation of Joss bringing her the morning's delivery of fresh fruit and vegetables.

"Afton Water" was a love poem, the writings of a man about his beloved, as she sleeps beside a stream. Its imagery could not but suggest strong parallels between a woman who slept along a riverbank and another who slept upon the downs. "Ae Fond Kiss", concerned two lovers' parting kiss, and despite the difficulties of understanding Burns's dialectical style of expression, the poetry was profoundly moving. The kisses she and Julian had shared took on new meaning with the mirror image of Blake's poetry reflected upon them. Unsettled by the power of the evocative verse, she had gone on to read what would appear to be a poem about corn and barley, only to find that it was even more provocative than the former works, for it dealt with the seduction of a young woman named Annie, in the stubble of a cornfield. So rousing and inappropriate would such poetry appear to be, Jeannette put aside the book, with the decided intention of reading nothing more of Monsieur Burns.

And yet, she had been unable to honor such intention. She could not leave the book untouched. She finished the poem, and read it again, along with the others, and decided she quite liked Monsieur Burns's earnest expression of himself, despite the unsettling nature of his subject matter.

Perhaps even more unsettling, it was not Joss who stood

upon the doorstep, with heavy baskets laden with the freshest of the garden's fruits and vegetables. It was instead, the tall, dark-haired footman, who had, the day before, kindly taken the horse Jeannette had been riding, into his care. He looked down at her with an expectant smile, as though he wished for nothing so much as to see her smile in return.

"Good morning to you, marm," he said, ducking his head in under the low door frame. "Your boy gave me leave to deliver these up to you, that I might introduce myself."

Jeannette felt dwarfed by the magnificence of this young man's height, and quite uncomfortably the focus of attention, as everyone in the kitchen slid glances in their direction, for they realized immediately, with such an apparition's appearance, that something interesting was afoot in the form of this footman. With a tight-lipped smile she suggested mildly, "You might introduce yourself without taking vegetables in tow, you know."

He blushed a fiery red, and ducked his head down, turtlefashion, a sight to behold in a gentleman of such admirable stature. "I know that, marm, as well I know that you are bound to be busy, with so many mouths to feed. I would not get underfoot, you see, but was anxious to introduce myself, nonetheless." He settled the baskets on her work board, taking care not to bruise their contents.

"I am Thomas White." He ducked his head again.

"I thank you, Monsieur White, for so kindly taking away my mount yesterday, and for the delivery of these vegetables today. I am Jeannette Saincoeur." She bobbed a curtsy.

He smiled at her again, as though her formal response amused him. "Aye. I've been after askin' who you are."

Jeannette did not know how to respond to such a bald disclosure. It seemed this great, awkward, young fellow was oddly taken with her.

"And well you might," she said lightly. "It is best we know how to address each other if we are to work comfortably together for the next few days."

She turned away to begin unloading the baskets, hoping

he would be content for now, and go on about his own duties.

Such was not the case. He stood watching her, twisting his hat between uneasy hands, clearly set on saying something more, and oblivious to the stares of the curious in the kitchen.

"I was wondering if you might be so good as to take the air with me, marm, sometime this evening, when you've naught else to do."

"Take the air?" she repeated. "Do you mean me to take a walk with you? I do not have much opportunity . . ."

She was interrupted, with a sly wink and a nod, by Danial Fulsom. "A walk is it, he wants? Well, say no more, lad. You are more than welcome to take my place this afternoon, when Miss Saincoeur and I do normally perambulate about the neighborhood, delivering the spare victuals to the poor and needy. You have but to show yourself again, about half-past two, and you shall have your walk. Won't he, lass?"

"But Lord Endicott will be expecting you to escort me, Mr. Fulsom," she protested.

"Lord Endicott's gone to Biddendon with a gaggle of his female guests today. He'll never know the difference." Danny grinned at Jeannette, whose eyes were wide with astonishment at his audacity. But, before she could think of a word to say, the slender giant of a footman was bowing to them both as though he had just been granted royal favor.

"Half-past two, do you say?" He backed toward the door, beaming. "I shall return in good time, Miss Saincoeur, I surely shall. You'll see."

Danny was laughing fit to burst as the door closed on Thomas White's back. "You should see your face, girl," he crowed to Jeannette. "'Tis a sight to behold."

Biddendon, and not Canterbury, it had been decided, must be the chosen destination for the party of visitors most set on embarking on an excursion to view something of merit in the neighborhood. Julian played host to the party, which included the Misses Burnett, Sophy and Adria, Miss Ellen Forbisher, her mama, and a young Frenchman, by the name of Francois, who was a friend to one of the guests who wished to involve Julian in the business of international affairs once again.

The Misses Burnett were quite thrilled to be going to Biddendon. "We have heard there did live there, at one time, two sisters, joined at the hip and shoulder." Sophy laughed, as if she had said something clever.

Her sister, mind working in concert, picked up the thread of thought as if it were her own. "Yes," she agreed. "My sister and I have always been accused of being joined at the hip, so often are we to be seen in each other's company." She, too, was prone to laughter.

What these two should find in Biddendon, to remind them of the two unfortunate Chulkhurst sisters, Mary and Elizabeth, who had indeed been joined quite inseparably at the hip by a cruel vagary of nature and not their own design, was beyond Julian's ken. The twins, being born in the twelfth century, and having long since died, there was not much left of them to witness in the town.

It was even less clear, however, why Miss Forbisher and her mama chose to accompany their party. Neither of them were at all interested in the Chulkhurst twins, indeed Mrs. Forbisher went so far as to remark that she felt such subject matter quite unnatural as a fascination to young women of any breeding. Her daughter sighed and said nothing.

Francois, alone, would seem to thoroughly enjoy every aspect of their jaunt. He was impressed by the countryside through which the carriage was driven, and fascinated by the process by which hops were grown, harvested, and made into ale. He was also interested in horses, and quite complimentary to Julian with regard to his team. He compared much of what he saw to the France that had once been, and then, his voice falling away, as though he discussed the death of a loved one, he compared that to the pale shadow of itself France had become.

Biddendon was reached, and Julian did his best to make their entry into the village interesting, by pointing out to the party the fine examples of half-timbered medieval architecture lining the south side of High Street, and the great, uneven slabs of the local marble that had been put to use in paving the causeway. He explained that such lengths had been exercised in order that the heavily laden pack animals that had once made this place the weavers and cloth-making center of England, might pass through the streets with ease.

This information was met with a giggle from each of the Misses Burnett, the one of whom said, "How droll," while her sister quite bested her, in remarking, "How very diverting your observations are, Lord Endicott."

Quiet Miss Forbisher surprised him, in encouraging him to continue describing the sights, but her mama wanted only to know, "Wherever do these poor folk shop? Surely this cannot be all that is available to them." She was not often to be coaxed outside of London, and thought all of England must have its equivalent to Bond Street.

"Mama," her daughter quelled her. "You do forget. This is not London!"

That particular phrase came into play more than once as they made their way about the village, until Francois du Bounnet put a stop to the refrain by remarking, "No, it is not in the least like London, thank the gods. This place is far more sunny and cheerful and the streets have a neat tidiness about them that I have never witnessed in the city."

"Wherever do you stay in town?" Mrs. Forbisher asked forbiddingly, eyeing him with disfavor through her pince-nez.

"With whomever will have me," the young man said without the least bit of shame.

Julian tried not to laugh and rather than remark furth- on the history of Biddendon's wealth and fame, came up with the happy idea of examining the brasses in the old church, for he had heard they were quite fine.

Luckily, these relics of the sixteenth and seventeenth century happily occupied the attentions of all concerned. The Burnett sisters were quite set on discovering where the remains of the Chulkhurst twins were interred, while Miss Forbisher and her mama were each of them determined to locate themselves a knight to gawk at, for the people depicted here were very plainly dressed, were they not?

Francois seemed quite astounded, in the meantime, at the proclivity of the citizens of Biddendon in the arts of reproduction and remarrying.

"Six sons, and eight daughters!" he murmured in an awed undervoice to Julian. "It is no wonder the poor man gave out, no?"

Miss Forbisher surprised them both by remarking, "Poor man? What about his poor wife?"

Her mother quelled this slight evidence of spirit in her daughter by pointing out, quite unnecessarily, that John Mayne, Esquire, was a sheriff. "Isn't his armor depicted in an interesting manner, my dear? He was most assuredly a gentleman of wealth, to have been able to afford the luxury of both fourteen children and a brass headstone. His wife must surely have held him in highest esteem."

Francois was not so easily subdued. "Here, we have William Boddingham," he called to them. "He was not content with just one wife, he must have two, but . . ." he chortled, "he is nothing when held up to alderman Allarde, for he had no less than three wives; Helen, Joan, and Thomasin."

Lord Endicott, not amused by this chronicling of lost spouses, and life gotten on with, bent his head to divine from the briefly enscripted marble and brass, what kinds of pain these long dead predecessors had endured. He decided, when all of the brasses had been scrutinized, that it would seem his own particular brand of sorrow was not unique. There were four men here, who had lost wives and remarried, and one woman, a Margaret Goldwell, who had been buried in 1499 with the memory of two husbands chronicled above her head. The loss of a child, too, was not his personal cross to bear. There was a particularly moving inscription on the door to the vestry, for a Richard, son of Henry Allarde, who had passed from this mortal coil in 1593, at the tender age of 2 1/4 years. It was the telling annotation of 1/4 that brought stinging tears to Julian's eyes.

He blinked them away. Strange, that a father, who would understand the broken heart within him, should reach down through the years, to touch him deeply with no more than a fraction.

Julian could not help thinking that Jeannette Saincoeur would have been equally touched by such a commemorative, but she was not here, and no one else in the party would understand, without a great deal of explanation, his feeling for a brass that was neither exceptionally ornate nor noteworthy for its age.

Feeling suddenly out of patience with the sight of so many commemoratives, which far outlasted the lives of those they served to make immortal in their very mortality, Julian made his way out of the confines of the church, and drank in a deep gulp of honeysuckle-scented air. My, but the sky was blue and the air sweet! The soft churring of doves and pigeons from the eaves above him seemed a particularly lively music after so much silence. He had missed such subtle stirrings in the quiet confines of the chapel. There was something far too colorless, too cold and final about figures of times gone by, etched in brass, their clothing and headdress long gone out of fashion.

He did not want to be remembered forever on some brass etching as the faithful mourner of a dead woman and nothing more—not if it meant relinquishing his own grasp on life, and a second chance at happiness. A pair of swifts chittered above him, carefree as they wove a winged pattern against the azure sky. He smiled. Jeannette would have liked to watch the birds. Odd, that though he traveled in the company of so many women, it was the one left behind that his thoughts turned to. Jeannette Saincoeur made him a happy man, despite his losses, despite the impropriety of casting her in such a role.

"So, there you are, Lord Endicott!" It was Miss Forbisher who approached, and put herself forward to him, without benefit of her mama's dancing attendance. "We are, I see, of like mind."

Julian lifted an eyebrow. What could it be, he wondered, led this young woman to such a conclusion?

"Enough of this staring at graves, no matter how pretty. They would trap us in the past, and that is a waste of our time among the living. Do you not agree?"

He stared. This young woman surprised him. There was more here than first met the eye.

Her gaze met his unflinching. "I have little patience with wasting time, my lord, and so I would not waste yours. I do not believe in arranged marriages, or in connections based solely on financial accountability. I have no intention of accepting any offer you may feel inclined to direct my way, and so perhaps you will be kind enough not to offer. My heart, you see, is already engaged." Her mouth twisted. "My mother simply will not accept the fact."

He was jolted out of what he realized to be his own self-absorption by her disclosure. "Since you are so forthcoming, Miss Forbisher, I dare ask, is the match in some way inappropriate?"

She looked about them, as if in fear they should be overheard. "But of course. In everyone's eyes but my own." Her face and person stilled, and a beautiful softness touched her mouth. "I have allowed my affections to become attached, you see, to a gentleman of excellent education and intelligence, who is blessed with wealth, not through inheritance, but hard work. What is he missing, you may ask? A name, my mother would hastily inform you. Jonathan Stiles has no connections, other than those he has cultivated in the gemstones business, where he works. But that does not matter to me, you see. I love him, and he loves me. He has asked me to marry him, and marry him I shall."

Julian thought of Jeannette, the young woman he had begun to fancy himself in love with. Unlike the unacceptable Jonathan, she had a name, though it was not one held in the highest esteem. Money was what she lacked, money and suitable occupation, stupid things, really.

"I think I do see," he said: "May I wish you luck with winning your mother over to your Jonathan, Miss Forbisher?"

"I shall marry him," she reiterated, "whether she is won over or not. I am the one who must live with my choices, not my mother, as much as she might like to convince me otherwise."

Julian decided he liked Miss Forbisher very much. "Your Jonathan is a most fortunate fellow, my dear Miss Forbisher. Rest assured I shall not trouble you with any unwanted offers."

She smiled at him. "I am glad you understand, my lord. Shall we tell the others it is time for our tea?"

He nodded, and took her arm in his. "It is most certainly time for our tea, Miss Forbisher."

Chapter Fourteen

~

Jeannette, meanwhile, was making an effort to enjoy the company of the persistent Mr. White. He was helpfully carrying the food tins and baskets, and he waited patiently beside every door at which she stopped, and spoke both to her and to the people to whom they made deliveries quite pleasantly. He spoke of the weather, the state of the fruit trees they passed, and the quality of her cooking. This last could not but please her, but even compliments grow tedious when they appear to lack substance, and before the baskets were all delivered, Jeannette began to wish herself alone with her thoughts. Mr. White lacked stillness. He could not abide any lull in their ceaseless, and largely senseless, conversation. Not a moment must pass with words unspoken, no matter that the words meant little more than nothing. She would almost have preferred to walk the lane alone, as to walk along with someone in whose company she could not be easy.

Jeannette could not help but think of the comfortable manner in which she and Julian Endicott fell into moments of complete and utter silence after conversation about the most intimate and private of their thoughts and feelings. In so thinking, she had to remind herself that this gentleman she cared far too much for, was out today, entertaining marital prospects. He would marry one of them eventually, and share his stillnesses with her, while Jeannette would end up, she was sure, married to one such as Thomas, did she continue in her place as cook. She had no right to think she might do better. And yet, she could not quash the notion that she deserved more.

As the carriage carrying Julian and his party of ladies entered the lane next to the orchards of Idylnook, a tall young man with dark hair and wild eyes came tearing out in front of the horses, waving his arms.

"Stop!" he cried. "Stop, sir, stop!"

Julian reined in the team. The man looked familiar, but he could not place him. Breathless, the fellow came up beside his perch.

"What is it?" Julian asked.

"Penny Fairing. Her water's broken, my lord! The babe is coming, and the midwife's still to be fetched."

Julian nodded, unperturbed by such plain speaking though the ladies under his escort sucked in their combined breath in shock and alarm. "I shall go for her, immediately."

The young man was dancing from one foot to the other in his anxiety. "I dare ask, sir, do any of the ladies here have experience in such matters? The poor girl's overwrought, my lord, and none but Miss Saincoeur to help her, and she is not easy in the role, for this is the first birthing she has been party to."

Julian looked at his company of females. They stared back at him with a mixture of horror and openmouthed awe.

"Oh my, no!" One of the Burnett sisters tittered, while her sister rolled her eyes as if she meant to faint, and said meekly, "We've no experience in such matters, my lord."

"I should think not," Lady Forbisher said tartly.

"But, surely you, madame," Julian suggested softly, with a significant look at Miss Forbisher, who, after all, was born of this woman.

Lady Forbisher threw back her shoulders. "I have, of course, borne one child, my lord. But I was attended by any number of informed friends, an excellent midwife, and an accoucheur of the highest reputation. I've no intention of subjecting myself to such trauma again, I can tell you."

"Well, my good man . . ." Julian jumped down from the carriage with sudden conviction, "It would appear I must assist with this laying in, myself. I have had some little experience, and would not abandon the girl in her hour of need."

"But, my lord," Lady Forbisher protested, appalled. "Surely there must be someone else!"

He tipped his hat to her. "It would appear there is not, for the moment." He thrust the reins in the young man's hands. "Tom, your name is Tom, is it not?"

Tom nodded, a worried look still in possession of his features.

"You must drive the ladies back to Idylnook, my good man, and then, taking a servant who knows the way, you must proceed with all haste in the fetching of the midwife."

"Aye, milord." Tom leapt up onto the driver's bench. "I shall be back as soon as ever may be."

Julian nodded, and without watching the departure of the carriage, or his guests, he sucked in a great lungful of air, reliving in his mind the horror of the last birthing he had attended. He had little heart for the task before him.

Jeannette was feeling rather panicked, and trying hard not to show it. She had little idea what she was about, but had only to see Penny, as she entered the cottage, standing in an awkward, bent over, spread-leg position, a scared look on her face as she stared down at a huge puddle on the floor beneath her feet, to know that the baby was progressing, and no time should be lost in finding the local midwife.

Tom had agreeably flown to do just that, and now she was alone, with Penny, who whimpered with fear, "What do I do, Jeannette? I'm soaked. I'd no idea it would come in such a rush."

"First we get you dry, my dear," she had said, as calmly as she could, but even as she said it, Penny doubled over with a moan, face contracted with pain.

"Oh! It hurts," she wailed.

Jeannette grabbed at her hand, and gave it a squeeze. "The pain will pass."

"I know, I know," Penny gasped. "It's been hurting off and on all morning, but not like this." Another pang doubled her over.

The pain did pass, and Penny was made more comfortable, the knifing pangs returning off and on as they progressed, and it was as she moaned her way through another wave of it, that a knock came upon the door, and Jeannette went to see who it might be, hoping against hope it was the midwife.

Julian Endicott stood waiting on the stoop, hat in hand. He looked rather fine for a cottage, in tight-fitting, gray coat, handsomely tied cravat, and spotless gloves.

"Monsieur Endicott!" Jeannette was taken aback. She could think of no one whose face might bring her greater comfort, and yet, she felt embarrassed that he should intrude on this very private female moment.

"I've come to help," he said simply, and in looking at him, at his sad, gray eyes, and the quiet, reserved way in which he looked back to her, hat in hand, Jeannette knew she had never loved anyone so much as she loved Julian Endicott in this moment. What he offered was dear indeed. She opened the door and welcomed him in.

Jeannette and Julian shared the trying moments that ensued, as they had never shared anything before. Together, their strength on either side of the girl as they made her walk about the cottage, they shored up poor Penny Fairing. In long, meaningful glances, they met over Penny's head, as she bent into the pain of the coming child. Jeannette felt she had been given opportunity to witness the measure of this man's quiet strength as his tragic past was reenacted before their very eyes. His features assumed an almost unbearable seriousness, a quiet sadness that drew deep lines in his forehead, but despite what his personal feelings might have been, he was gentle, calm, and soothing in his manner.

Penny seemed not in the least awkward around him. She leaned quite gratefully into the steady strength of his arm as he walked her about the room.

When Penny said she felt unequal to the feat of walking any longer and that she felt an urge to bear down with the increasingly frequent waves of pain, he directed Jeannette, with quiet assurance, to make the bed ready, for it was time for Penny to lie down in it, upon her side, with her back to the edge of the bed, that they might more easily access the baby, when it came.

It was Lord Endicott who held poor Penny's head while she vomited what little was on her stomach into a bowl Jeannette provided. And he daubed at the girl's sweating brow as the pain reached new proportion, while Jeannette was instructed to check the baby's progress, for it must be crowning now.

The idea that the child's arrival might supersede the mid-wife's, made Jeannette's pulse race with uneasiness. She kept looking to the door, expecting, nay praying, that the midwife might arrive. Julian serenely focused on Penny and the increasing waves of her pain. He was a deep well of calm in the midst of troubled waters.

"It goes well," he kept soothing, when Penny wanted to panic, and screamed with the pain, and begged of him not to let her die, for she could bear no more of this.

Jeannette wanted to cry as well, that he should relive the horrific moments of his wife's passing, in such a possessed fashion. She could not help but notice the anguish that twisted his lips whenever Penny fell to ranting. He looked up at one point, and correctly interpreting her concern, tried valiantly to smile, with no success in the endeavor.

"It progresses nicely," he insisted, as though to calm all their fears, even his own. His coat was off, along with his waist-coat, and cravat. His sleeves had been rolled back, his collar unbuttoned, and yet, sweat sprang profusely from his brow.

His assistance took a toll, she could see.

"Courage," Jeannette whispered, for the benefit of both of her companions.

He looked up from Penny's face in that instant, bending a look upon her that acknowledged her understanding of his position. It was a special look, an intimacy that had nothing to do with passion, and everything to do with a profound, shared understanding. A rare and beautiful thing, it was an unspoken comment from his soul. She would never forget the drama that played itself out in their eyes in that moment.

The midwife arrived at last, in a flurry of self-importance, to push Jeannette out of the way, and insist that she must go to the far side of the bed, in order that she might pull forcefully on Penny's hands, during the final push. Penny was examined. The matronly woman crowed with pleasure at how far they were come, and she encouraged Miss Fairing to, "Bear down now, love, and we shall have that baby out in a trice."

Penny complied with a great deal of wailing. She took short, puffing little breaths, and pressed her feet against the bedstead, and held onto Jeannette as though for dear life. Julian, at the head of the bed, looked lost, almost forlorn, as though his lack of involvement were much harder to bear than being in the thick of it only moments before.

The baby, when it came, came quickly, and the midwife expertly caught it up in a blanket, and made sure its airway was clear, and the cord not wrapped around its neck, and as it began to wail and flail arms and legs, handed the wet parcel off to a startled Julian, while she tied off the cord.

"Hold him high!" she instructed Lord Endicott. "High as you might safely hold the howling mite, that he might rise in the world, milord."

He seemed to know what she meant, and lifted the protesting baby as close to the rafters as could be safely reached.

"Saturday's child has a journey to go," Penny said with satisfaction.

The midwife made a point to inform Penny as to the exact

time of the baby's birth as she and Jeannette awaited the afterbirth and made the exultant new mother comfortable with a warm sponge bath, heated on a fire sprinkled with ash twigs.

"To keep evil spirits away from the newborn," the midwife explained, when Jeannette wondered why ash should be important.

Jeannette looked up at that point, from what she was doing with the sponge. Lord Endicott held the baby without the awkwardness she usually associated with men and babies. As with everything he touched, or said, his hands and voice were gentle as he rocked the child. He walked about the little room, cooing and talking, and reciting unfamiliar children's rhymes, in his quiet, gentle manner, trying fruitlessly to soothe the bitterly unhappy wails.

"It's his mother's breast the little man wants." The midwife relieved him of the child and placed the new life in its mother's welcoming arms. She shooed Jeannette and Julian from the cottage. "Best leave them be, now. I'll see to bathing the babe once its suckled a bit. And you can be sure I shall leave the right hand unwashed."

Jeannette looked at Julian with complete confusion as the door closed behind them. "The right hand must not be washed?"

Julian smiled. "Superstitious nonsense, as was my holding the child as high as I could, and the ash wood on the fire. It is believed among the common folk that the child will gain riches if his right hand is left unwashed."

She laughed, dimples flashing in both cheeks.

Brimming with an ebullience of spirit that had them grinning rather fatuously at each other, Julian and Jeannette paused to wash themselves at the pump in the yard, before setting off for Idylnook.

He pumped the cold water for her, his face alight with inner thoughts, with inner joy, and as he pumped, and she splashed her hands clean, both of them, he watched her, still beaming and speechless from the happy outcome of their afternoon's efforts.

It was his turn for ablutions then, and he splashed about quite merrily, as she, in her turn, watched him, her own lips curved in a most satisfied expression.

"That was wonderful," he said at last, having come up from a face splashing that had him thoroughly drenched, without concern for the condition of his clothes. "It was invigorating!" He cupped his hands under the water, and held them up, dripping over the pump, cradling his imagination. "To hold new life in one's hand." He smiled, and breathed deep, as if to fill his lungs with the power of the image that still fired his imagination. Water seeped from his cupped hands. He stared a moment at damp palms, before flinging what little moisture still clung to him away, with an impatient shake. "I could but wish it had been my own."

His energy level subsided. Picking up his shed clothing, which was piled beside the pump, awaiting clean hands, he seemed to focus on anything but Jeannette. Wordlessly, she helped him into the waistcoat and jacket, and watched as he pulled his crushed neckcloth into a careless knot under his chin.

Their eyes finally came together, in his reflection in the water that pooled beneath the pump, met in a look that spoke volumes, a look of intimate understanding and mutual admiration. There was something so powerful, so compelling in that shared look, that she longed to throw herself into his arms, to beg him to kiss her again, to tell her that he loved her, and loved life as much as she did in this moment.

"I could not help but think that a new family is started today," she said softly, a world of meaning pent up in those simple words.

The depth of his sigh stirred the water.

"I am pleased that the child lived," he blurted, and for an instant the sadness she found so familiar in his features, touched his face. "I do not think I could have borne it, had it been a difficult labor."

Jeannette could not resist reaching out to him. Her hand, not quite dry, caught his before he slipped a glove upon it. "You were superb!" she breathed. "Absolutely superb. I could never have managed without you being there." Tears welled into her eyes, tears of empathy and pity, but most of all, joy. His warm, damp hand came up to cup her cheek, to catch the tears.

"Nonsense." He gave her other hand, still clasped in his, a squeeze and then carried it to his lips for a much more intimate salute. "You underestimate your own strength, Jeannette. We worked quite splendidly together."

"We did, didn't we?" She beamed at him.

A breeze was blowing out of the east when they left the cottage behind them, arm in arm. A playful wind, it plucked at Jeannette's skirts, and did its best to knock Julian's hat askew. It had the apple trees dancing when they entered the orchard. In their rustling boughs and the occasionally thunking timpani of apples jostled loose from their perch, Julian heard some form of music. He let go her arm, and as if he could no longer control the feeling of joy that struggled within him, he began to dance. It was a reel, Jeannette decided. He did but grasp the swaying leaves of each tree he took to partner briefly before moving on to the next leafy hand. Now and again, he paused and bowed to a current bush that got in the way. On one old dame of a fruit-bearer, her arms lifted high enough that he might swing from them, he got caught up in the exuberance of the moment. Both of his feet came off the ground. He spun around the swaying skirts of the bushes, and came stepping lightly back to Jeannette, a sweet, boyish smile upon his face.

Jeannette had never seen Julian Endicott look happier, or more alive. There was something in his voice and eyes, in his manner, that declared them happy equals here in the middle of the orchard. She was impressed by the feeling that something of moment was released within them both, there in the orchard, something primal and vital and alive, that had nigh been extinguished.

He bowed before her, as he had before his more wooden partners, his eyes alive with a light that was not to be denied. He caught her up in the tempo of his strange dance, and whirled her about in his arms, as though he were the wind, and she but a leaf, slipped down from one of the apple trees. His usually solemn gray eyes lit up with inner glee as he led her through their apple-treed ballroom. The sparkle in his eyes told her things as he swung her adroitly under his arm, things that made her blood race faster—things that made her cheeks flush as she nimbly fell into the steps of the figure he meant them to move to. Eyes locked, they moved with perfect understanding together, without a word exchanged.

Jeannette felt the pleasure of the day, and what they had just accomplished with it, singing in her veins. She knew Julian felt the heady rush of this ecstasy as well, and reveled in his willingness to share this newfound lightheartedness with her.

As they brought the dance to a breathless close, she was convinced that he must surely try to kiss her again, as caught up in the passion of the moment as he was. She was disappointed in this. He took her arm in his, and stood staring at her a moment, with such a look shining in his eyes that she knew it must be love he felt for her in that moment, or something very like, but the only thing he touched lips to was the back of her hand. Very correctly, he escorted her toward the gate through which they must pass to reach Idylnook.

Jeannette could not but feel it was a shame such feelings as they had shared together on this day did so rarely fill one's heart and soul and entire being, with glowing happiness. She went out of the orchard on his arm, with a warm feeling of accomplishment and content.

He seemed to share her feelings, for rather than allow her to part from him in the gravel drive—he to go in the front entrance, she to make her way to the rear—he said, with a hint of the bubbling ebullience that made a man dance with trees, "It has been a precedent-setting afternoon, Miss Saincoeur. Would you not agree?"

"Unforgettable."

He winked at her with an earnestness about the set of his mouth that made her heart race. "Then we shall continue to set precedent," he said with a grin, and rather than allow her to pull away from him, that she might make her way around the house to the servants' entrance, he led her up the steps and past Simms's high-nosed, censuring frown.

Chapter Fifteen

~

It was Miss Sophy Burnett who caused a stir at dinner that rivaled the stir at Penny's that afternoon. She came in late, her sister fluttering uneasily in her wake, and her hand fluttering uneasily at her throat. "My rubies! They have been stolen!" she exclaimed, in a voice that reached new heights with every word she uttered.

Everyone at the long dining table looked up.

Margaret leapt with alarm from her chair. "Do you mean the pretty pendant you wore last night? Is it really gone? From your room? Are you sure?"

"Oh yes. This is dreadful." Sophy was in tears.

"We have searched everywhere," her sister said faintly. "The necklace is not to be found."

Francois du Bounnet closely followed the whispered conversation from his chair at the table. "Could the clasp perhaps have broken while you were wearing it?" he suggested hopefully. "It might be anywhere in the house if that is the case."

Miss Burnett primly wiped at her eyes with a lace hankie her sister thrust into her hands. "I do not think so," she said doubtfully. "It was of the finest workmanship, its clasp of quite superior quality."

Her sister nodded. "It was very dear. Papa will be furious to hear it is missing."

Sophy was not comforted by such a prospect. She began to weep in earnest, but just as suddenly stopped, to insist, "No, I have a very clear remembrance of taking it off last night, and placing it on the chest of drawers. A silly place to have left it, I know. Someone had but to glance in the door to see it, and with little more effort, it was taken." Tears slipped down damp cheeks again.

"Oh, who could have done such a treacherous thing?" Adria came to her sister's defense. "Are the servants not to be trusted, Lady Crawford?"

Margaret fired a speaking look at Julian as he removed himself from the head of the table to join them. "Julian, you must summon your French cook and question her on this matter. I told you she was not to be trusted, but you would not listen."

"This cook has been known to steal in the past, and you allow her to remain under your roof?" Adria Burnett was indignant.

"I have no reason to believe Miss Saincoeur is a thief." Julian said mildly.

Margaret did not agree. "I have every reason to believe she is."

"Based on what proof, Margaret? Miss Saincoeur is not allowed on the floor where the Misses Burnetts' chambers are located, and she has been gone all afternoon delivering food to the poor and assisting in the birth of a baby to a young woman in the neighborhood who no one else saw fit to help."

His sister interrupted him. "Really, Julian, I do not see how you can go on defending her so stoutly. She has in her possession all of those silver pieces, each bearing the mark of a once prominent French family. She would have us believe the French nobility is reduced to stirring pots in the kitchen of an English country house! I think it is hardly likely."

"You accuse one of my countrywomen, madame?" Francois rose from his chair. "What is the name then, of this cook of yours? If it is a noble house she descends from, I would know of it."

"Her name is Saincoeur, monsieur."

"Saincoeur?" Francois shook his head. "No, I have never . . ."

Margaret interrupted. "Oh, but it is the Bouillé crest emblazoned on the silver she secrets in her room. Perhaps you knew the family, Monsieur du Bounnet, before the Terror?"

"Bouillé?" Francois repeated in almost breathless disbelief. He laughed bitterly. "Everyone in France recognizes the name Bouillé."

"Yes, dreadful really, how close he came, but for so many blunders," Margaret said. "You might have a monarchy yet, and the king his head, but for the Marquis de Bouillé, who did not wait long enough, and his son, Charles, who held the change of horses in the wrong place, and a duke . . . um . . . what was the other fellow's name, the one who withdrew too soon?"

Francois frowned. "Duc' de Choiseul. He was the one who withdrew his cavalry too soon, and wrongly sent word ahead by way of the royal perruquier, Leonard, that the convoy would not arrive that day."

Margaret arched an eyebrow. "Quixotic, think you not, that the fate of the king's head did rest for an instant in the hands of the royal hairdresser?"

All of the gathered company laughed but Julian, the Burnett sisters, and Francois, who struggled to return a level of seriousness to their discussion. "I had heard that the de Bouillés who are not similarly missing their heads, had fled to Germany and Austria. I should be very surprised if your cook is in actuality a member of the ill-fated family, but bring her in. She has piqued my curiosity and I will do my best to tell you if there is any family resemblance to be seen."

"You knew the family well enough to judge such a resemblance?" Julian asked dryly.

Du Bounnet nodded. "One branch of the family, in any event."

"And what of my necklace? Do you mean to question her with regard to my rubies?" Sophy Burnett wanted to know.

"We will question every servant in the house," Julian promised, "if it will please you, Miss Burnett, but I will not single out Miss Saincoeur as our only suspect without further evidence of her culpability."

"Simms," his sister commanded imperiously. "Fetch Miss Saincoeur from the kitchen, please." She snapped the word kitchen as if it left a foul taste in her mouth.

Simms regarded Julian dubiously, waiting for such an order to be contradicted.

"Perhaps we had best settle this thing once and for all," Julian said softly. "Please, Simms, will you be so good as to inform the staff that a ruby necklace is missing. Any information as to its whereabouts should be brought to me immediately. Then, require Miss Saincoeur to come to me in the library if you will."

"The library?" Margaret squawked.

"Yes, Margaret, the library. I shall interview her there, on this rather sensitive issue, with Monsieur du Bounnet at my side. If you will be so good as to see to our guests, we will not allow this matter to interrupt the serving of dinner any more than it already has."

Word came to the kitchen that a ruby necklace was gone missing, and Jeannette's presence requested immediately by his lordship. She was bade go to the library of all places, which seemed most inconsiderate, for the kitchen staff was right in the midst of serving up a great many of the dishes that were to be carried in to the table for the third course.

Jeannette was hot and harried, and there was a soufflé in the oven that was sure to fall was it not handled with infinite care, but she knew better than to argue, and went swiftly, as she had been bid, to the library, smoothing hair, and removing her apron as she went.

She did not look forward to facing anyone other than Lord Endicott, for none of the guests were familiar to her, and all of them of the class of people she had once thought her brethren, who had a tendency to look down their aquiline noses at her now that she was nothing but a cook. But Julian was not alone when she went in to him. There was a second gentleman in the room.

He was French. She knew as much immediately, though he stood with his back to her as she crossed the room. There was no mistaking his Frenchness. It reached out to her across the space that separated them, like a ghost out of her past in the cut and color of his clothes, hair, and complexion. His very stance whispered of home. His voice, too, for the two men were chatting as she came in, held a familiar fluid, musical rhythm that touched a chord of familiarity within her memory. When he turned, Jeannette froze in midstride, her hand leaping to her throat, for it felt as if the wind were suddenly knocked from her lungs. A strange light-headedness made the man's image jiggle about before her.

"Antoine!" she tried to scream, but all that came out was a terrified whisper. It was a ghost she encountered. Her brother, it could be no other, had turned to face her, and her brother was dead. Jeannette had fainted only once before, on the day of her mother and father's death at the guillotine. And now, with the brother she had assumed dead all these years staring her eye to eye, she slid into a dead faint once again, dropping to the floor like a bird shot down with the swiftest arrow.

She revived, to find herself in Julian Endicott's arms, his face doubled, and swimming before her like twin, tethered balloons. Her head ached where it had connected with the floor and her breath seemed difficult to catch, but the memory of what had cut her down so suddenly was fresh and clear in her mind.

"*Fantôme!*" she managed to croak in French. "I have seen a phantom!"

The phantom was no phantom at all, but a flesh-and-blood fellow who bore strong resemblance to a taller, thinner, graying version of her brother. He stood looking down at her a moment, his eyes hard and shuttered in a manner she could not recall ever having witnessed in Antoine. There was something closed in his attitude toward her, something remote and reserved and distancing, as if he held her at arm's length with his very gaze. This could not be Antoine. And yet, she squinted at him, unconvinced. Antoine would be changed. Nine years had passed.

The phantom intruded on her thoughts, killing hope. "My name is Francois. It is not often I have the privilege of causing young women to swoon. Have we met?" His voice bore little resemblance to what she remembered of her brother.

"*Pardon.*" She sighed, and tried to sit up. Her head whirled. She felt so very tired and saddened by this cruel reminder of what Antoine might have been today, had he survived. She could not get over how much like her brother this young man looked.

Julian Endicott pushed her back into the supine position. "Lie back now, Miss Saincoeur. You are overheated." He pressed a coolly pungent vinegar compress to her forehead. "We've no wish to see you go crashing to the floor again."

"*Certainement non,*" the man who called himself Francois remarked, and all the while he seemed to be watching her, not with the straightforward gaze she met from Julian Endicott, but in a furtive, sideways manner, as if he had no wish to be caught in such observation.

Jeannette felt shaken, weak. The ashes of her past had been stirred to life, when she had thought them long since cold. She could not remain in the same room with this man and the powerfully unpleasant memories his appearance provoked. She wanted to get away from the cause of such memories now, as far away as she could. At least as far as the kitchen. Perhaps if she dove back into the normal, the everyday routine of work, she might forget the feelings that churned in her stomach, the ache that weighed down her heart—and head. She pressed a hand to the knot at the back of her cranium.

"I'm sorry to have caused a fuss. I thought for an instant,

Monsieur du Bounnet, that you were . . . someone I knew. Someone very dear to me. He was killed during the purges, you see, and so it was in essence as if I came face-to-face with a ghost. I am quite all right now, and must get back to my work." She removed the vinegar compress. Julian Endicott's hand caught her wrist. His sad, gray eyes probed hers. He understood. She could see it in his gaze. She read it in the slow release of her hand.

"If you are certain you feel up to it," he allowed. "Perhaps it would be best."

Jeannette gave the man, Francois, a last, piercing look and left them.

Julian watched her go. She was still as white as a sheet. The shock of facing what she thought to be a ghost from her past was still evident in her pallor. He wondered who Antoine had been, friend, family, lover? Jeannette's face had been beautiful, awestruck, in the moment she first laid eyes on Francois. Whoever Antoine was, she had loved him.

He wondered what it would be like to inspire such a look from Jeannette. He wondered, too, what it would be like to run into Elinor, or someone who so resembled her that he might feel compelled to believe her a ghost. The idea made his skin crawl. Elinor was gone. There was no bringing her back. Julian had at last come to terms with that idea. He could not go where Elinor now resided, and there was no wishing her back to this plane of existence. He lived here, now, and with him was a young woman whose well-being he cared deeply for.

He took special note, therefore, the rest of the evening whenever he caught a glimpse of Jeannette, to see that she was, as she said, all right. He did, in fact, instruct both Simms and Williams to keep an eye on her, and peeped, himself, into the kitchen on two occasions to see she fared well.

Margaret waited until after dinner, when Julian and his guests removed themselves from the dining room to the large drawing room for cards and conversation, to find out what Francois du Bounnet thought of their cook.

"Is she the imposter I think she must be?" she inquired. "And did she tell you what it is she has done with Sophy's necklace?"

Francois stood up suddenly from the soft cushion of the chair that he had just sunk into, with a yelp for answer. "Madame! The chair. It bites me!"

And then, as he massaged the bitten spot on upper thigh, he reached down between the cushions, and came up with the missing ruby necklace. "What beautiful teeth," he exclaimed.

Margaret was silenced, the Misses Burnett ecstatic. Sophy, so much so that she planted a kiss on Francois's cheek, to the indignant disbelief of her sister, who had no kindly cheek to salute.

Francois winked at Adria, who was not at all pleased by such casual familiarity." It was not the cook after all," she remarked to Margaret, and then with a trace of jealousy ruined the effect of her clever deduction. "'Twas only poor Sophy's carelessness."

Francois whispered to Julian. "Pardon, but I fear we are about to witness an altercation. Care to join me for a smoke?"

Julian declined.

Francois shrugged and headed purposefully for the peace of the moonlit terrace.

Sophy rounded on her sister, her color high. "I was not careless. I remember putting the rubies on the dresser, I do. I do not know how they have managed to make their way into the cushions of this chair, but 'twas not I dropped them there, I can assure you."

Adria was not at all ready to relent. "We shall see if you can similarly assure Papa," she said spitefully.

Julian turned his back on them. Such bickering wearied him. What did it matter how the necklace was lost, now that it was found? Parting the curtain that looked out over the rose garden, he considered the wisdom of joining Francois after all. He did not smoke, but he realized that du Bounnet had never said whether or not he believed Jeannette to be a de Bouillé, and he could not deny himself curious.

He wondered how Jeannette was feeling, no matter her name. He had known she was not a thief. He should have trusted that feeling, and spared her the pain of an encounter with the past in Francois du Bounnet's features.

It was curious how the roses in the garden lost all color in the moonlight. They were all of them shades of gray, he was interested to note, barring the few that his parting of the curtains threw into adequate light to prove scarlet. Even Francois was gone gray, though the smoke from his pipe plumed whitely in the meager light, like the plume of steaming smoke that had gone up above so many of the dishes that had come from the kitchen tonight. How did a young woman manage, he wondered, to go from delivering a baby to delivering course after course of delectable viands? His little French cook was a remarkable woman, she was. She never ceased to surprise him. That she would faint this evening when throughout the afternoon she had shown no sign of vapors . . .

Even as Julian's thoughts lingered on her, Jeannette appeared before him, her head down, as she stepped away from the shadows that enshrouded the servants' entrance. She set off briskly, into the darkness.

And suddenly, Francois du Bounnet was lunging down from the terrace, and on his way down the gloomy garden path as well, following her.

Julian spared not a glance for his guests. He was out the door, and after them. What did Francois du Bounnet mean to perpetrate against his cook? Whatever his intentions, he meant to find out. The Frenchman had troubled her enough.

He thought Jeannette would lead them to her favorite haunt, the herb garden. She did not, making her way instead, through the torch-lit formal garden outside the dining rooms, around the topiary and the vegetable garden, to the glass houses, that were Mr. Sandford's private domain.

The music and laughter from the main house dimmed, replaced by the lonely warbling of a single nightingale accompanied by a croaking chorus from the toads who stood night guard on the garden. Jeannette walked with purpose. Francois followed with equal purpose, though what that purpose was, he alone knew. There were three glass houses. The central one, the largest, was lit by Chinese lanterns this evening so that guests might wander through to view the lush variety of flowers. But it was not to the central house his little bird flew. One of the flanking glass buildings drew her, and as Julian followed, at a more leisurely pace, he kept his eyes on the dark figure that shadowed her. He would not allow du Bounnet to disturb her again. Guest, or no guest, Jeannette's peace of mind was too important to trifle with.

Francois did not so much as hesitate to follow her into the heavily scented darkness of the melon house. Rather than interrupt immediately what promised to be an interesting tête-à-tête, Julian folded himself into the space between the two glass houses, that he might discover the Frenchman's intentions. There was enough light for him to see there, light that flickered from the gay lanterns in the flower house. It was just enough light to see that Jeannette had thrown herself down upon the gardener's workbench, her apron clapped over her mouth, that she might stifle her sobs. She was weeping, as he had seen her weep only once before.

He would have gone to offer her comfort, had not Francois du Bounnet beaten him to it. Julian stiffened over such an intrusion, his hands clenching into fists. He would call the man out, did he dare to take advantage of Jeannette in such a moment!

There was no need for heroics. The two spoke, the tenor of their voices intense, as if something of moment were discussed and then with a little cry, of joy, it could be nothing less, Jeannette threw herself into the young man's arms, and kissed him with disturbing fervency on each cheek. She made no move to push him away when he reciprocated her kisses and clasped her tight to his chest.

She clung to him. It hurt Julian to see it. There was no mistaking her affection, no mistaking the emotion in her voice, as it rushed to express some truth so urgent that she could not wait for his lilting tongue to still. Their voices met and tangled as completely as their bodies did.

Julian watched the two together, and could come to no other conclusion than that they knew each other, and rather well, at that. The embraces they shared were joyfully exuberant. Lord Endicott, who had begun to think himself trusted, perhaps even beloved by the young woman before him, felt his heart shrink. He had deluded himself. Miss Sound Heart's affections were quite clearly, elsewhere engaged.

Chapter Sixteen

~

Jeannette's heart soared like the song of the nightingale. Antoine, for it was Antoine after all, was alive! She was not alone, as she had so long believed, in this lonely world. Her brother sat beside her, on the rough wood of a gardener's bench, his hand clasped in hers, his dark eyes gleaming in the dim light.

"But, Antoine, why do you pretend to be someone other than yourself?" She could not understand why he had postponed identifying himself to her.

Antoine placed a finger in a hushing gesture against his lips. "You must be careful no one else hears you say such a thing, *mon petite*," he cautioned. "I am here on sensitive business, and it will not do for anyone to know I am not who I say I am."

"Sensitive business? Whatever do you mean?"

He looked at her steadily, his face changed, made unfamiliar to her by the passage of time. In the flickering light she thought Antoine looked first timeless and unchanged, and then old and tired. There was about his expression, a hunted look, a wary tightness to his mouth, a watchful narrowness to his eyes. He shook his head impatiently. "There is too much to explain, and not enough time. The reason I followed you here, other than that I might relieve your mind as to who I was, is to ask you if you would care to return with me, to France!"

She frowned. "To France? But, Antoine, there is no going back. It is all gone, the France we once knew."

"Perhaps not quite all of it, Jenny. There are princes of royal blood who yet might be crowned. There are Royalists, here in England, plotting no less than that, even as we speak. I have today, with your Englishman's compatriots, discussed what may be done in France."

"Mon dieu!" she breathed. "Are there still those who hope to assassinate Bonaparte then?"

"That would seem to make sense, eh, little one. We must hope they succeed this time. In the first attempt, the Fates were against us. It cannot always be so. You miss the old France, do you not?" His words were more statement than question.

"But, of course," she said wistfully. "Life was very good to us then. Little did we know, or appreciate, how good."

"Oui!" A fire gleamed in his eyes. "I mean to have it back again, cherie! I mean to help these Royalists in any way I can."

Jeannette frowned. Such aspirations seemed unrealistic to her. "You really believe you can reclaim what has been so thoroughly cast aside? How? How does one go about stuffing freedom back into the box it springs from?"

His face shut down. His gaze shifted about them, searching the shadows. "It is best, I am thinking, that you do not know." He smiled, and the dark wariness seemed to fall away from his features. For an instant, he was again the mischievous boy she remembered, ready to talk her into some scrape. "Tell me, how do you come to be here? I thought I was the only one of us left alive."

She wished to tell him everything, and in return, to learn everything there was to know of the years, and time, and places that separated them.

"Yvette saved me," she began with a laugh. "Stuffed me into the pantry, between the vinegar jug and the sacks of flour. She had stuffed a great bit of the family silver there as well, in preparation of the potential sacking of the house. She took me and the silver to Paris with her. We worked in one of the restaurants that sprang up there. It was not until

Yvette died, that I discovered what was left of the silver. I found too, Antoine, that she had not sent letters that I had written to Tante Natalie, and cousin, Claude. The letters, I sent on to the family, of course, but by then there was no way of knowing if the addresses were current, so I sold the silver and made my way out of the country? What of yourself? How came you to be here?"

"The story is a long one, cheri. There is much I would tell you, but perhaps it is best if I begin with telling you that I return to France in a few days. I would know if you mean to come with me."

"To France?"

"Oui."

"To what? We have no house, no family, no money. What is there in France to lure me back?"

Antoine looked at her in disbelief. "I cannot believe you've no wish to return. How can this be? But of course you will go back with me. We are family. We must stick together. Reclaim what is rightfully ours. Men of good breeding and education shall reign supreme in France once again. You shall see I am right. This young upstart, Napoleon, will soon be ousted. I'm convinced of it. I may even be fortunate enough to have some part in it."

Jeannette could not comprehend the fire that blazed in her brother's eyes. No such flame burned within her—there was only a leaching coldness in her thoughts as she considered returning to France. She had built herself a new life here in England. Her memories of France were too violent, too terrifying, for her to feel drawn there again. "One cannot turn back the clock, Antoine, no matter how hard one wishes for the past. There is nothing there for me, in France. We cannot raise the dead, cherie, any more than we can stuff liberated thought back into the heads of radicals."

"But neither is there anything here for you, Jenny. What do you do? Cook?" he scoffed. "What is stuffed squab and buttered prawns in the grand scheme of things?"

Her chin came up at that. "I am not really interested in the grand scheme, Antoine. I do not need to move mountains to feel that what I do—what I create, the people's lives that I touch—is important. I am weary of politics, and philosophy, especially when they involve death and destruction. If this is the engine that drives you, then follow its course, but do not, I beg of you, try to drag me along. I fear I will only be crushed beneath its wheels. Each of us must determine the course of our own lives. Mine will be lived out here, in England."

"And do you think this fine English lord you work for will take you to wife? You, a penniless refugee? Think again, sister dear. This country has engaged in no revolution. The nobility and the common man live in completely separate worlds." He grasped her hands fervently. "Here, you have been cast out of the nobility as surely as ever you were cast out of France. It is no wonder. What is it you call yourself? Saincoeur? I have never heard such a name, and just look at your hands. They are rough, and red and swollen. Common! Mother and father would be appalled!"

Jeannette snatched her hands away from his. "Mother and father are dead! Pale, gloved hands will not bring them back. Neither will my starving on the streets out of some misguided loyalty to a name that will not bring me a crust of bread, either here, or in France. I do not mind hard work, Antoine. I have chosen to do it here, where there is no killing, no guillotine, no heads on pikes, no scheming of one party to violently overthrow another. Perhaps, had I been a man, I might answer your blood call, but I am not hungry for revenge. Go, and may God go with you. I do not encourage you to stray from your chosen course. Do not, I beg of you, insist that I stray from mine."

He stood, impatient and put out. "Well, perhaps it is best we say *bonsoir* before any more is said. We might each of us live to regret our words. I am very glad to find you alive again, Jeannette, but I am disturbed by the direction of your thoughts. You would almost seem infected by the fever of this pestilential Revolution. If you change your mind about leaving, let me know."

He embraced her somewhat stiffly before leaving her alone with her thoughts.

"So, she means to conduct an affair with this Frenchman, right under our noses!"

It was Margaret who spoke. She had come up quietly beside Julian as he walked away from the tableau in the dimly lit melon house behind them. The last thing Lord Endicott wanted at any time, was his sister pointing out the obvious to him, but in this instance she would appear to be no more than honest. It hurt him, far more than he would ever admit, to feel as he did now, abandoned. The sensation reminded him too painfully of his suffering following the loss of Elinor. He did not want to believe what he had witnessed with his own eyes tonight, any more than he had wanted to believe that Elinor, so full of life's promise in one moment, might be dead the next. It was too much to absorb, too contrary to the picture his mind had created of a future filled with hope, and love, and companionship.

"She is a hussy, Julian. I knew it from the start." Margaret did not want to stop once she got started. "She means to take advantage wherever she can. You may recall I tried to warn you? You are well shut of such a busy piece. You are most fortunate that she should be so exposed to you, before this folly went any further."

Her words beat against his brain with the steady wearing nature of rain. He was ready to say anything, if only to stop the dithering of her tongue.

"Am I a fortunate man, Margaret?" he wondered.

"But, of course you are, Julian, dear."

"Of course." He nodded, not at all sure himself, and strode quickly away from her, away from the truth he had just uncovered, and away from his fortune, good or bad.

Chapter Seventeen

~

It was late in the evening on the following day that Jeannette took herself to the herb garden, to cool her cheeks and enjoy the first moment of peace she had anticipated all day. Her work had trebled, what with the large retinue of family and friends that had taken over the house, and with the additional demands for tonight's ball. She had been on her feet since dawn. Her arms ached with stirring, kneading, and grinding. Her cheeks were flushed with the heat of the ovens, and the back of her neck was damp with sweat. Her hair had begun to fall down in wispy tendrils, from the neat chignon she had twisted it into so many hours ago.

An yet, as weary as she was, the music as it floated through the garden, stirred her. She swayed to its rhythm as she sat on the lip of the fountain, watching the play of moonlight on water. Her mind fixed on the dance she had enjoyed with Lord Endicott among the windblown apple trees, and then reached farther back. It had not been so long ago, that she would have been on the other side of the music, enjoying the luxury of eating and drinking and dancing, without a thought as to the preparations required from an army of servants. She had, at that time, nothing to think about but looking pretty and enjoying herself. It had not been so long, and yet it felt like an eternity separated her from that reality. Here she sat, hot and exhausted, and still longing to dance and look pretty.

She unpinned the damp weight of her hair, and with the

comb she kept tucked in her apron, she shook it out, and freed it of tangle, and twisted it into fresh neatness, all the while thinking of the day on the downs when Lord Endicott had combed her hair for her. A sweet, nerve-tingling awareness of how close she had come to succumbing to her own passion lingered, like an unusual and indescribable flavor. Dipping her fingers into the flow of the fountain, she patted away the heat in her cheeks and brow, and all the while her body swayed to the strains of the music that came faintly to her on the breeze. The music seemed to echo that memory of passion. So compelling were its strains at last that she stood and swayed along the pathway, in order that she might get as close to the sweet sound as possible within the confines of the walled garden.

Julian fled from the heat of the dance floor, and the press of the crowd and his sister's insistence that he be happy to dance with any female she could push in his direction. He fled through low windows that opened onto the terrace and had been built with a sill low enough to accommodate just such an escape. Afraid he would yet be discovered if he remained in the rose garden beyond, he made his way to the gate in the high wall that led to the quiet confinement of the knot garden. It was as he stealthily pulled the gate closed behind him that he first caught sight of Jeannette. She was whirling around the moonlit fountain, in perfect time to the ballroom music—partnered not by Francois du Bounnet as he might have expected, but by a garden rake. She was an excellent and courtly dancer, and while her escort was a trifle unbending, she dipped and swayed with fluid grace, so that the dark red bombazine of her livery belled about her legs like a falling flower, and sent the pale petals of her apron whirling.

He stood, his hand still poised upon the gate, his smiling mouth half open, for but an instant, before intercepting the path of this entrancing young woman and her wholly inadequate partner.

"May I cut in?" he asked, with a formal bow, and could not but think of their dance in the orchard. Had it been only yesterday?

She came skidding to a halt with a startled gasp. "*Excusez-moi*! I should not . . ."

He had no desire to hear her apologies. He smiled. "Your reputation will be ruined if you make a habit of dancing so freely with a known rake." Chuckling, for suddenly his heart felt very light, he bent low to whisper in her ear. "He would make a grass widow of you."

The play on words amused her. Her mouth twisted in an uncertain smile.

Gently he slipped the gardening tool from her grasp, leaned it against the wall, and took its place within her arms.

She stiffened, her hand flinching in his as they began to move to the music. "I have no intention of falling prey to such a fate." She spoke fiercely, her gaze direct, as if it were very important he should believe her.

He thought of Francois du Bounnet and found room to doubt her vehemence. Holding her lightly as the music swelled he returned the directness of her gaze. "I know you would not lightly abandon yourself to any man." And yet, even as he spoke, he was imagining she might abandon herself to him as she had so recently abandoned herself to Francois. Such thoughts made him angry. He wanted her, wanted to hold her, warm and willing in his arms, as he had not wanted a woman since Elinor had died. In admitting to himself his desire, his anger intensified. He would have made her a grass widow, himself, right then and there, had she been agreeable.

She blinked, and looked away, as if she read something of what he was feeling in his eyes. She concentrated on her steps and the placement of her hands, anything but his eyes. Despite this break in visual contact, they moved well together, unusually well. Arm in arm, they came together and parted and came together again. Julian was possessed of the feeling that this dance echoed the strange pattern his life had fallen into with this enticing young woman under his roof. They met and whirled in a most intimate fashion whenever they shared conversation, and yet, life, and their positions, pulled them apart again. What had he to offer her, but his passion and a position as grass widow? He could not marry a cook. Could he? To do so would be to insult the memory of Elinor. He wondered what Miss Forbisher would have to say about such conclusions. She seemed a very brave girl to him, to announce to any who would stop her, that she loved her Jonathan, and meant to have him, against all odds, despite his lack of name and connections.

He loved the woman in his arms at this very moment, and yet how could he announce as much, even to her, when he had so recently seen her accept another man's kisses? How was he to go on, yearning for this woman, fighting with his uncouth impulses to touch her, to hold her, to lock his lips with hers, when he knew she went willingly into another man's embrace? She said she was resolved to resist him. He wanted to test that resolve, and yet he could not find it within himself to be happy in that desire. His needs were a threat to her well-being, to her future. Julian was not at all accustomed to being a threat to anyone. It would perhaps be best if he sent her away, as his sister suggested, for both their sakes.

The music ended, the last strains of it faded away, and yet he did not want to let go of her, did not want to stop the whirling footwork that brought them together one last time. She looked at him, confusion clear, and in the meeting of their eyes, there was the charged spark of mutual desire. There was no mistaking its warmth in the widening darkness of the blacks of her eyes, in the sudden rise and fall of her breasts and the breathless parting of her lips.

He closed his eyes, to shut out the pull of that look and yet he swayed toward her as he said, with intense regret. "I greatly fear, my dear, that you have gone from the arms of one rake to those of another. I have the strongest desire to kiss you again, Miss Sound Heart, for I have tasted joy in your lips. I have found happiness in your arms."

She laughed uneasily. "You, sir, are merely happy to have someone to talk to about such things as most people avoid in conversation." She laughed again, uneasily, as if she did not truly believe her own claim.

He was looking at her very carefully. "No," he murmured, shaking his head. "There is much more to the feeling between us than that. You cannot deny it. There is an energy that hums every time we are in proximity to each other. You have felt it. I know you have. I have read your awareness in those lovely hazel eyes of yours, my sweet Sound Heart, or shall I now refer to you as Mademoiselle Bouillé?"

She looked away from him. "You are my master. You may call me what you like."

He drew her to him. "Then I will call you my little bird, and my dearest love, sweet Jeannette, for we are far more to each other than mere master and servant. Will you come to me when I call you thus, I wonder?"

She yielded to the demand of his hands, which slid down the fabric covering her arms, to the bareness of her hands, which he clasped tight—gloved palms hot against hers. Elegantly kid-gloved fingers lifted each work-hardened hand to his lips, and kissed them all along the knuckle. Gently, he drew her closer by caressing them to his cheeks. Then, kissing each palm, his eyes locked seductively on hers, he wrapped her hands about his neck, so that he might slip off his gloves, and run searching palms down along her sides, with caresses so sensual, she moaned. Tightening her hold about his neck, she lifted her mouth to his, that he might kiss her. His mouth came down on hers in a hot, moist rush.

She opened her lips to his heat.

Jeannette was hungry, and would be fed. She longed to be held, and touched, and needed. She longed to end her loneliness. She could not push herself away from the brink of disaster again, in pushing herself away from this man, as she had so many times before. She plunged into his embrace without reservation, and when his hands slid past the curve of her waist to cup the sloping roundness of her derriére, she moaned again, and pressed herself even closer to him, until, responding to her ardor, he increased the heated intimacy of their embrace in pulling her hard against him so that their bodies seemed to kiss as heatedly as did their lips.

And yet, as close as they were, it was not close enough. Burning with a desire to meld herself to him so tightly that they might move as one, flesh against flesh, heated breath upon heated skin, she cravenly nibbled at his lower lip. Never before had she felt the pull of such desire, and yet it seemed that no matter how much she yielded to its tug, it was not enough.

He groaned. It was a pleased sound, and to know it was she who provoked such a sound, pleased her. Just as he had caressed her sides and back, so too, she reached out to caress him, and once again she took his lower lip between her teeth, and tugged. His mouth responded by reaching out for hers in the French fashion, his tongue caressing her lips with liquid fire, then flicking uncertainly between parted lips, and finally plunging provocatively inside.

The heat of her desire, the intensity of her delight, consumed all common sense. She grew faint with this fire, faint with the awful confinement of her clothes, against his searching hands. She wanted to tear every stitch from her body, that he might make all of her as happy as her lips. She pulled her mouth from his, to catch her breath.

One of his hands reached up to caress her neck, and then slid down to cup her breast. His lips, as if they had lost their way in having been separated from hers, sank to her neck as well and trailed downward, following his hand, as it nimbly unbuttoned the bodice of her livery. Her flesh burned against his lips. She sighed, and ran her fingers through his hair as he reverently parted the opened neck of her dress and bent his head to the exposed swell of breast. The coolness of the night air felt wonderful against burning flesh. The cool wonder of his tongue made her shiver, and arch her back, until his seeking mouth nudged against a nipple, and she cried out to feel the knee-weakening shock of such contact. It was he, however, who sank to his knees, the better to caress her breast with his tongue, his hand moving again, stroking her back, her backside, her thighs, sliding down the bunched cloth of her skirt, to reach beneath, to fumble past petticoats, that he might clasp a wool-stockinged ankle and then slide up to cup the roundness of a calf. Gently, but firmly, the hand moved up to part her knees.

And in all this, she relinquished to him freely, like a flower opens itself to the sun, stretching its every fiber toward the heat. It was, at the point that his hands found the bare flesh above her right garter that Jeannette began to have reservations about what she had encouraged to happen. What madness possessed her?

The mesmerizing hand seemed to find some contentment, for it fondled the exposed flesh of her thighs, above all tapes and garters, until her knees buckled with the intensity of her pleasure, and she sank to the grass beside him.

He was not done with her. Abandoning her breast, his lips sought out her mouth again, while his hand, that mischievously wandering hand, moved higher still beneath the fall of her skirts. Jeannette had never thought of her buttocks as a particularly sensitive, or even attractive part of her anatomy, and yet, the attention his wandering hand lavished there caused an abrupt shift in her opinion. Better than before she understood the magic of her own body. Soft, hidden flesh experienced the height of sensual satisfaction in being caressed, and stroked, and fondled.

What Jeannette experienced as Julian worshipped her body with both lips and hands, was the most devastatingly dangerous and wonderful onslaught of emotions and sensations she had ever encountered. Her body sang with the feeling that this was too right an exchange to be the ruin of her, and yet she knew it was just that. There was a knife's edge of peril pressed hard against the yielding flesh of her ecstasy.

But Jeannette's thoughts narrowed. She ignored the precariousness of her position. Nothing apart from the liquid fire of her mouth, and the liquid fire that burned between her legs mattered. The enthralling hand beneath her skirts meant to reach that heat. It moved ever closer, stroking the uneasy juncture of leg and torso, gently teasing the violent curl of her hair. Hand and mouth, they worked a strange sort of teasing, tandem rhythm, a rhythm so erotic, so compelling, so undeniable, that in the end Jeannette opened her legs to him, and pressed herself quite desperately into that searching hand, that it might find the burning wetness that ached so desperately for his touch.

And yet, as if in having reached a sort of culmination, her sanity returned, she jerked away from the burning fulfillment of his touch, pulled completely away from him before he could do or say, or touch anything else.

"No!"

Trembling from head to foot, Jeannette stumbled back from him, trying to fasten her bodice as she went, with fingers that did not want to obey.

He stood, his intention to give chase. She could see that determination in his eyes.

"No, no," she whispered, one hand extended like a shield, the other fumbling desperately with the tiny buttons of her bodice. She was unable to look into his eyes. She knew the danger of losing herself in them. "I will not be your grass widow, monsieur."

"I had no intention . . ." he began, but got no further.

"Lord Endicott! My lord, are you there?" It was the voice of one of the female guests approaching them. Julian was, for the moment, distracted.

Jeannette fled into the shadows. What lunacy! She had just done what she had sworn to herself that she would not do, sacrificing certain happiness as cook to this man, in this wonderful place of plenty, by succumbing to the wonder, the earth-shattering wonder of a tenuous delirium that promised nothing but disaster. Her stomach lurched with the insane stupidity of it.

"Jeannette!" His voice, his features were softly beseeching in the moonlight. He could not see her direction, but his hands reached out into the darkness, as if to draw her back into the mystery he would introduce her to.

But there was no wisdom in such folly, she would not be foolish twice. A good thing, too. The garden gate creaked open.

A second female voice called, louder this time. "Lord Endicott?" There were two who sought Julian.

He would not be following her. The first female voice announced triumphantly, "There you are, my lord."

The voices seemed inclined to gaiety. Every sentence was punctuated with a laugh. "We knew we would find you, did we but look. Will you be so kind as to give us a tour of the glass houses, my lord? Your sister tells us you are producing an excellent crop of melons."

Melons! Jeannette struggled with her bodice buttons as futilely as she struggled to hold back her tears of frustration. What a fool she had proven. Prey to passion, she was no wiser than Penny Fairing. What was to become of her? Surely she could not stay on as cook.

As if in echo of her thoughts, her stumbling flight was interrupted by the unexpected figure of Margaret Crawford, who stood before her, a stone statue in the darkness, blocking her way.

Jeannette shuddered in anticipation of the insults this woman was sure to fling her way.

"You realize you do my brother a disservice in remaining here, do you not, Miss Saincoeur?"

Jeannette tried to sound calm, as if the world were not really upside down and inside out. "A disservice? How so?"

"A man has his needs, Jeannette. May I call you Jeannette?" Margaret plowed onward without waiting an answer. "Surely you understand? Julian suffers the loss of his wife, the loss of his connubial rights. He is a most decent man, my brother, but, he is no saint. You tempt Fate in remaining here, my dear girl, beneath his roof and within his sway."

"'Tis my Fate to tempt." Jeannette hoped the darkness shielded her scarlet face from observation.

"Poor Julian's Fate as well," Margaret did not hesitate to remind her. "But he cannot suffer so much as you might, Jeannette. The rules of ethical and moral certitude with regard to a young woman are far more rigid than those that govern men. You know he cannot make any serious commitment to one such as yourself. A cook! My dear girl, should he so much as think of doing so, he would become the laughingstock of his peers. No, this folly, and folly it is, has the potential of no more than ruining you both, and no less than setting a great many tongues wagging."

Jeannette had no snappy rejoinder. The picture Margaret painted was no more than what she had herself envisioned. What irritated her was that Margaret Crawford should think it her place to remind her of duty and good sense, and that she should insult her with the endearment of dear girl, when it was quite obvious she was anything but dear to this woman.

"You did not think to be Lady Endicott, did you, Jeannette?" Margaret laughed without humor. "'Tis a ridiculous notion. Surely you must agree, give you the matter the least amount of consideration."

Jeannette's heart still pounded furiously with the power of what did lie between her and Julian Endicott. Was it no more than lust? How dare the man's sister presume so much, Jeannette wondered. This matter was between her and Lord Endicott, no one else. The two of them must determine their own Fate. Margaret Crawford's blood ran no bluer than that of the Bouillé family. Her brother's title was no more officious than any Jeannette might have considered had France remained content with division of class and privilege. Jeannette lifted her chin, turned her back on Margaret

Crawford, and walked away, without giving the woman the satisfaction of any response to her snobbery and rudeness.

Julian watched the Burnett sisters approach, while his happiness ran away into the darkness. He wondered if these two irritating young females had any inkling how much he wished them to the devil in that moment.

He had been so close! So close to what? His conscience dared to wonder. The answer bothered him as much as the question. He had come so very close to seducing a young woman he had always meant to conduct himself honorably toward.

She, in turn, had come very close to allowing his seduction to reach culmination!

Gods, what was it these two fribbling females wanted? A tour of the melon house—the very place where he had watched as Jeannette Saincoeur had fallen into another man's arms as willingly as she fell into his tonight? Perhaps it was a good idea after all to refresh his memory on that score.

"Yes, of course, I should be more than happy to escort the two of you through the glass houses," he heard himself say, as though from a distance. His mouth functioned well enough. He even managed to appear interested in their idle chatter as they trailed after him, arm in arm. But, his thoughts were very narrowly focused on nothing other than Jeannette Saincoeur, or Bouillé, or whoever, and whatever she was.

Dear God, she had responded willingly to his overtures of lovemaking! It had thrilled him to evoke responses of an enjoyment that equaled his own. Their moment together had been both wonderful, and frustrating. She had offered him but a tantalizing taste of what he craved of her. That taste left him quite consumed by a hunger for more.

Could it be she was no more than the promiscuous trollop his sister would have him believe? Could it be she readily shared with other men the magic they shared this evening?

He could not believe it was true. Would not believe it. His instincts could not so miserably betray him.

He must speak to her again, touch her again, and soon. He must discover what this connection was she shared with Francois du Bounnet. He would not rest easy until he knew.

They reached the melon house. Mechanically, he performed the role of host, showing the Burnett sisters flowering vines and ripening fruits. The smell of the place sickened him. Here Jeannette had blithely kissed another man. He did not want to be reminded of such a thing, not now while the memory was still fresh of her sweet surrender to his touch. The smell of her lingered in his clothes, and on his hands. Could it be she gave herself freely to another man, perhaps many men? Such thoughts threw dark shrouds of doubt on the sheer joy he felt whenever they were together. He loved her. Could he deny it? But did he really know who she was, and of what she was capable?

"Do you think your cook is indeed a Bouillé?"

It was Adria Burnett who asked, as if so lively were his thoughts, that she was compelled to question him in the matter.

He looked at her blankly.

Her curiosity was not to be denied. She tipped her exquisitely coiffed head to one side, as though the weight of her thoughts were heavy. "I have just been thinking how awful it must be to fall so low. I should never be able to cope, I am certain, for I have no talent for cooking, or housekeeping, and while I suppose I might consider serving as governess to someone else's children, I am by no means a bluestocking, and should feel, beyond a certain age, that I had nothing to teach them."

Her sister laughed. "But, Adria, whyever do you trouble your head with such thoughts? You will make some man an excellent wife, and his children an excellent mother. It is not your lot to trouble over anything else. Is it not so, Lord Endicott?"

Julian regarded the women before him with changed eyes.

As a young man, he would have agreed with such an assessment without blinking. The Burnett sisters were handsome, and amiable young women of suitable parentage, and worthy dowry. They knew how to dress well, and eat politely, and converse. They were both of them fine dancers, doubtless knew some needlework, and either painted with watercolors or played an instrument. They were all that was considered adequate in a wife for a man of title and fortune, and yet, in looking at them, Julian found them wholly lacking in any graces that might convince him to propose to either one of them.

"I am sure the both of you will make some man very happy ... ." he said, and they beamed at his compliment even as he amended it in saying, without true conviction, "as sure as I am, that my French cook is in fact a member of the Bouillé family."

Jeannette had lost her head. For a pivotal moment, she had allowed her heart, and surprisingly, her body, to carry her away from good sense and clear thinking, without for an instant considering consequences. The power of her yearnings astounded her. She shuddered to think what Lord Endicott must think of her. Dear God, what was she to do? She ruined herself tonight, or if not herself, she had most certainly ruined the happiness of her situation. One could not blithely throw oneself into the arms of a man who held one's very future in his hands, and then pretend it had not happened. One could not regain a state of innocence once it was lost.

Matters could not go back to where they had stood before impetuosity led her astray. She could not depend on the sensibility of her heart not to lead her willfully astray again, should opportunity present itself. How could she say, in all honesty, that she would not fall wantonly into Julian Endicott's beckoning arms, given opportunity? Her life was tossed upside down in an instant, her belief in her own strength of purpose, tested. Could she resist the urges of body, heart, and soul, while living under the same roof as Julian Endicott? She thought not. In the end she could not resist him forever, she knew it all too well. Her body sang too happily with the memory of his touch.

He would not set out to ruin her. No, she knew he truly cared for her. He was a kind, sensitive man, but he was drawn to her as strongly as she to him. The power of what they shared would pull them inveritably together again did she stay. Julian Endicott was meant for a union with a young woman of property and title, as his sister said, not with a fallen noblewoman, whose name was regarded with a scorn that surpassed rank, or title. Jeannette knew she had nothing of value to carry into marriage with any man, nothing but a dresser set of silver pieces that bore a crest she dared not exhibit. Julian Endicott cherished dear the memory of his late wife. He could offer Jeannette, in the end, no more position than that of his mistress, a well-kept and pampered grass widow—a female who might be cast aside in a minute, did he one day decide upon a woman he cared to take to wife. Such was a fate she reckoned far more painful to her— body, mind, and soul—than death.

She must not remain, could not remain here in Idylnook, another night. Must not, could not, would not! She would speak to Antoine—tell him she meant to return to France with him after all. He would be pleased, certainly more pleased than she.

Chapter Eighteen

Jeannette and her brother left early the next morning, in a nasty drizzle, as all of the other guests were also leaving. In the bustle of horses and carriages being prepared, and bags trundled about, and bleary-eyed guests toddling out under raised parasols, up too early after having stayed up so late the night before, Antoine and Jeannette wound through a tidal wave of activity without raising a ripple of interest. The carriage door closed on them. The horses were urged to walk on. There was no tearful leave-taking, no handkerchief waving, no sign of anyone either noticing, or caring, one way or the other about their exodus.

It was rather lowering really, but Jeannette made a point of exiting quietly, and without fuss. No one would really know she was gone, until the master's morning claret cup was filled, and the note she had left on his tray, discovered. She and her brother would be a fair piece down the road by then.

Unexpectedly, as the coach turned into the lane, they came upon a mounted man, head bent against the mizzling rain that grayed the countryside around them, leaving everything indistinct and mournful, damp and uncomfortable. It was Lord Endicott, and across the withers of his gray, of all things, a great bunch of wild 'Lady' orchids were tied, their stalks encased in damp burlap. Jeannette supposed he meant to decorate his late wife's grave with flowers, though it was not his usual day for remembrances. Perhaps he was feeling guilty this morning for his transgressions of the night before.

The carriage lurched forward. Lord Endicott disappeared into the mists at their heels.

"Glad to be shut of that place, are you not, Jeannette?" Antoine asked lightly. More of a stranger to her than any of the servants in the house they left behind them, he had no real inkling as to her feelings.

"I am not glad to go, Antoine. I have come to regard Idylnook as my home, and the household there as a surrogate family."

"No! You surprise me."

She surprised herself. Leaving Idylnook behind was much harder than she had ever anticipated. She had come to know this place; house and gardens, orchards and surrounding countryside, almost every inch of it, as intimately as she had once known her childhood home and neighborhood. She had come to regard this place as home, and to wrench herself away, a second time, from such a haven, from people whose affections had taken deep root in her heart, was a wounding experience. She wondered if she could transplant herself again so successfully.

Most of all, no matter how much she might like to deny it, she was going to miss Lord Endicott, with his quiet, gentle voice, sad, knowing gray eyes and the seductive fire in his touch that lit her up from within. Her heart felt stretched as she left so much behind her, and when such a distance was passed that the thread of attachment seemed to reach the breaking point, her heart grew unbearably heavy.

"She has gone off with that Frenchman, the hussy!"

Margaret could sound absolutely pompous in her righteousness at times, Julian decided, rubbing his temple. Lady Crawford eyed the boiled egg that had been set before her, with disfavor. "Wallings saw her, with her own eyes, through the window of the breakfast room, and ran up and told me. Left quite willingly, she said. Well, it is nothing less than disgraceful, if you ask me. I had my mind quite set on eating another of those marvelous baked eggs we had the day before yesterday, and Henri tells me they were her recipe."

Julian did not care about baked eggs, he cared about the fact Jeannette had fled with Francois du Bounnet, without a word to anyone, and after the intimacy they had shared only last night. He had risen from a dream of her, with nothing on his mind but to see her again, so that he might explain his behavior and attest to his genuine feeling for her. As demonstration of his affection, he had ridden far out onto the downs with the first light that he might bring back for her a few of the orchids she found so beautiful. He had spent more than an hour upon his return, carefully planting them, with Mr. Sandford's assistance. He decided, as he stood tucking soil around the tubers from which the orchids bloomed, that he would ask Jeannette Saincoeur to be his wife, before the sun was set. Despite his sister's objections and what was sure to be the censure of his peers, he loved her, wanted her, and could not dishonor her with anything less than marriage.

But she had flown before ever words could be said, or plans put into motion. She was gone and he was desolate. There was nothing but her note now to hold onto, as he paced back and forth in the breakfast room, watching rain run down the windows, with Margaret eyeing his every move.

What did she mean in leaving him so abruptly? She cared for him, he could not so horribly misread her eyes. He had thought she might even love him. Why else would she succumb so readily to his seduction last night? What must his course of action be? Was he to let her go—with an old lover, perhaps—a man who had prior claim to her affections?

The note was in English, and she wrote a beautiful hand, but her words held an awful finality to them. They forced him to recognize just how strong his feelings for Miss Saincoeur, or Bouillé, or whatever her blasted name really was, were become.

Miss Sound Heart was gone, and with her went his peace

of mind, his happiness, his vision of the future. He was stunned, hurt, betrayed.

"Given the opportunity to return to my homeland with Monsieur du Bounnet," it read, "I have decided, for the sake of both our reputations, it would best serve should I do just that. I apologize for leaving you so abruptly, and any inconvenience it may cause you."

She had signed it, With respect and regrets, Mademoiselle Jeannette Bouillé.

There was nothing loverlike in such a note. It was firm and final, and it cut him off as though he meant nothing to her. Was he well rid of Mademoiselle Jeannette Bouillé? Was it for the best that she took herself off with Francois? Julian could not convince himself. He had, despite the Frenchman's prior claim to her, given himself leave to hope. He had gone to dig up orchids in the rain, with that hope to keep him warm.

A tapping on the door stopped his pacing.

"Come," he snapped impatiently. Margaret almost dropped her cup. It was a rare moment indeed that he displayed such pique.

Simms pushed open the door. "My lord, I do hate to disturb you, but if I might have a word, sir, in private?"

Julian looked at him in dismay. What now? He threw a glance at Margaret, who rose from the table, with a look of wounded dignity. "Well, to be sure, Julian, you have but to ask and I will go. Though what you might have to be private about with a butler I cannot imagine."

She passed Simms with her nose in the air.

Simms came in very meekly, and closed the door behind him.

"Out with it!" Julian commanded, his patience worn thin.

"My lord." Simms could not look him in the eye. "It appears your claret cup is gone missing, along with its jug and tray."

Julian frowned. The claret cup gone? Simms would not have come to him if it was to be found anywhere in the house. Who would have taken the thing? Who among the departing guests could be so cruelly callous as to steal from him, after enjoying his hospitality to the fullest extent? Surely not Jeannette. She knew the cup was a gift from Elinor, did she not? If she had needed to take something for money's sake, surely it would not have been the claret cup.

As if he read his thoughts, Simms dared to venture a remark. "I hate to tell you this, my lord, for I do not like to believe the young lady was a thief, but the note from Miss Saincoeur was found in the place that the tray normally sits."

Julian could think of no words. Such a revelation hit him too hard in the lower abdomen. Exhaling heavily with the force of this blow, he lowered himself into a chair and sank head into hands. "It would appear we have both of us been greatly deceived, Simms."

No! His conscience cried. No! He would not believe such a thing. Margaret's consistent belief that he harbored a thief in Jeannette came rushing back to mind. Dammit! He was a softhearted fool! Had he fallen in love with a liar and a thief? Had he come close to marrying someone capable of deception so depraved? Anger filled Julian's heart, anger and the awful weight of betrayal.

He could not let her get away with this! It was not the damned claret cup that had been stolen from him, it was his chance at happiness. He would not lightly abandon that. He rose, but not to pace the room again. This time he moved with an energetic feeling of purpose he had not displayed since Elinor's death. He knew exactly what he must do, and he must do it immediately. There was no time to waste.

"Simms!" he said levelly, "I require my horse!"

Simms had made his way to the door. He was, in fact, in the process of closing it behind himself, but Julian wrenched it from his hand, and passed him into the corridor. Before the butler could recover from the shock of hearing Julian raise his voice, he was forced to scurry to keep up with the pace his master set in making his way along the hallway past Margaret, who stood tearing open a letter that had just been delivered.

"Jules?" Her eyes darted from the letter to Julian as he whisked past her.

"No time, Margaret," he said.

"My lord? You wish the horse to be brought round to the mounting block, sir?"

Julian took the risers at a trot, Simms moving more sedately behind him. "The gray. Saddled and ready with all possible haste."

"Yes, my lord. Right away." Simms reversed his direction, almost crashing into Margaret, who was not watching her path as she both read the letter in her hand and mounted the stairs in Julian's wake.

"Jules?" Her plaintive voice carried up the stairwell.

Julian ignored her as he leaned out over the banister to call out to Simms again. "Inform Alphonse I shall require assistance in packing my valise."

Simms never broke stride. "As you say, my lord."

"Jules!" Margaret was not going to allow him to ignore her this time. She burst through the door to his chambers, waving a bit of paper as he was pulling on his riding boots.

Alphonse sailed through the door on her heels. "Monsieur requires the packing of a bag?" he inquired, snapping open the valise in his hand with prompt efficiency. "How many days accoutrement will be required?" He was already rifling through the wardrobe, selecting what was necessary.

"Two, maybe three days, nothing formal."

"You are going somewhere, Jules?" Margaret seemed dizzied by the alacrity with which Alphonse loaded the bag on the bed. "You are going after her, aren't you? The Bouillé girl." Her voice had an accusative tone, but before she could go on with what he knew must be a tirade meant to stop him,

Alphonse snapped the bag closed, thrust it into his hands, and Julian was brushing past her.

"Yes," he said, between clenched teeth as he cleared the doorway. Margaret fell in at his heels. "I am going after her. Nothing you say or do will stop me. I know you mean to be helpful, Margaret, and for that I thank you, but I am perfectly capable of choosing my own destiny. I loved the girl, I meant to marry her, but I've no intention of letting her get away with this."

She trotted to keep up with him, flapping the paper in her hand. "But, Julian, you must hear me out . . ."

Julian had no desire at all to hear her out. He was not a child in leading strings. "No, Margaret, I must be on my way. They've a two-hour lead. I will not give them a moment more." He descended the stairs at a lope.

"You don't understand . . ." She was having trouble keeping up with him.

"I think I do, my dear." His voice was neither soft nor gentle as it echoed above him in the stairwell. "You do not want me to sully the family name, in marrying a cook, whom you believe also to be a thief. Very sensible, Margaret. I wholeheartedly agree with you."

"But, Jules, you must listen," Margaret gasped, as he strode across the entryway. "A letter has just come . . ." She had fallen far behind him on the stairs. She raised her voice that he might still hear her as he stepped through the door. ". . . from Austria, Jules."

Lord Endicott took up the reins of the gray, and swung into the saddle.

"Julian, wait! You must read it." She was shrieking at him from the door, and again the paper in her hand was flourished. He set heel to the gray, but as they clattered down the drive, he could not help but hear Margaret, whose voice carried quite admirably when she meant to be heard. "She is a Bouillé, after all! The niece of the marquis, no less. They are trying to find her, Julian."

Even with his judgment clouded by anger, Julian felt he

could not leave without knowing the whole. He turned the horse.

Margaret, not yet given up on her powers of persuasion, stood waiting for him in the drizzle, the letter like a flag in her upheld hand. He urged the gray to trot past her, plucked the letter from her fingers, and once more turning the horse, he shouted, "You are a dear, Margaret."

"You must find her, Julian," she encouraged, and once more her voice followed him as he clattered away. "Tell her I am terribly sorry for anything untoward I may have said. I would not have her think me completely devoid of manners."

Julian leaned into the gray's mane. If anyone was in the way of saying sorry, to his way of thinking, it was not Margaret. He would have a profound apology off Jeannette Bouillé's seductively deceitful lips, before he was through with her.

Chapter Nineteen

~

A
ntoine leaned out of the lowered coach window, and
directed the driver to locate a pawn shop of good
repute.

"A pawn shop? Whatever do you need with a pawn
shop?" Jeannette asked wearily, peering out at the miserably
wet houses and shops of Dover.

Antoine was rummaging about in his portmanteau, a look
of pure devilment lighting his increasingly familiar features.
"We shall need the proceeds to be had from these." He
pulled forth Lord Endicott's silver claret cup, its matching
tray, and jug.

Jeannette regarded them with openmouthed disbelief.

"Oh la la, Antoine! Why in the world do you have those,
of all things?" she whispered.

"Well, I would have preferred to have kept the rubies.
They were worth far more, but the alarm was raised too
soon. Having found you, I could not race away without so
much as a how-do-you-do, so I was forced to give them
back again."

Jeannette reached out for the claret cup. She could not
really believe it was here without touching it. The silver felt
warm in her hands. She traced the embossed pattern on the
lip of the cup, the lip that had so recently met Julian
Endicott's mouth. She was horrified. "It was you, took the
rubies from Miss Burnett's room?"

"Yes, the silly girl. She was far too careless with them for
me to resist."

"Oh, but, Antoine, they will think I have stolen these things," she breathed, her horror a crushing weight upon her heart.

"What of it? The man owed you a month's wages, did he not?" Antoine, unsympathetic, had no understanding of what suffering his actions brought her. "Don't worry," he brushed the thing aside, as if their reputations were of no moment whatsoever. "You will never see them again. We shall be long gone before anyone notices. We cannot swim the Channel, you know. The passage home costs money, and I have none."

Home. The very word rang sour. Jeannette was not at all convinced she was going home. She had left the closest thing she had to a home, behind her, and she left in disgrace, as a suspected thief. She could never return now. The situation was mortifying. Julian Endicott had met her with nothing but kindness. To repay him in such a reprehensible way, with lies, and the burglary of objects she knew he held very dear for sentimental reasons, was unforgivable.

Appalled, Jeannette felt as if the years of mind-numbing but honest work she had engaged in, building herself a sound foundation on which to launch her future, was destroyed in an instant, and by her brother, her only remaining flesh and blood!

What perfidy. It was too much to bear.

"Stop the coach," she said, very low. "I am not going with you."

"What?" Antoine laughed. "But of course you are!"

"No! I have no desire to give up the things that are most dear to me, my honesty and decency—in order that I may return to a place I no longer consider home. Stop the coach!"

This time she shouted her request forcefully to the driver, and the horses were pulled in.

Julian drove the gray along the muddy roads at a ground-eating pace. The letter Margaret had held up for him to take along crackled against his chest as the horse moved easily beneath him. His anger kept him warm despite the drizzle of rain that would soon have him damp all over. The anger was strong, fervent. He would catch up to her. There was no doubt in his mind. The interchange between him and Mistress Jeannette Bouillé could not end without one more awful confrontation.

So what if she was a Bouillé? It had meant nothing to him in the past, it meant nothing to him now. The only thing that mattered was the love he had allowed himself to feel for her. Its warmth blazed in a furor of angry disgust. Love! Hah! He did not love her. He hated her. He would gladly throttle her, given opportunity. Why should this deceitful creature live to torment him and ride away with his heart, when his dear, sweet, trustworthy Elinor was taken from him forever? The injustice appalled him. The lengths of his own gullibility made him want to retch. He had been in love with her . . . still was—some small part of his heart cried, as the rain beat upon his set face like tears.

"Damn you," he spat. The gray's ears swiveled. "Damn you," he cried louder. The horse, caught up in the urgency of his cry, broke into a faster lope, his hooves making wet, sucking noises in the mud. "I loved you!" Julian's shout echoed hollowly through the drenched trees on either side of the road. Roosting birds flapped away from damp perches. It was a lonely, futile, angry sound.

"I loved you," Julian whispered brokenly as he touched spur to the gray, and splashed onward, headed for the coast.

"I do not understand your desire to remain here, Jenny."

Jeannette's temper was running short. The pawn shop owner had offered them far less for her silver pieces than Antoine had anticipated. She did not understand how he could have encouraged her to leave her position when he hadn't a sou to his name. Why had he not mentioned the need for money earlier, rather than involve her in such a stupid tangle?

"As it works out, Antoine, I haven't any choice in the matter." She was angry.

Antoine waved aside her response. "You have not wanted to go with me, from the start. You love that silly Englishman more than your own brother."

That he should so easily hit the mark irritated Jeannette almost as much as his flippancy with regard to money.

"It has nothing to do with that," she lied with outraged vehemence. "This England is a pretty country. It is a country rich in many ways, and it has opened up its arms to me and my small talents despite the differences between France and England. Here I earned a place to call my home. And by decent means, not through petty theft."

"But at what cost? Here, you have no standing, no position in society. You spend all of your days in the kitchen, and share a room with a pastry chef. What respect can you command, as cook?"

Her eyes flashed dangerously. "I command respect for what I can do, not for the name I was born into, or the clothes I wear."

He laughed at her, and there was something in the sound of it that made it suddenly clear to Jeannette that the reasons they argued with each other went far deeper than the differences in their opinion over politics and a consciousness of class. They argued because they had only just now found each other, and already they were to be separated.

"There is as much class consciousness here as ever there was in France. You chase after the impossible if you think your English lord will do right by you without benefit of your name."

She sighed. "Oui! You are quite right. I will not argue that point with you, but just as you must do what is best for you, Antoine, so, too, must I do what is best for me. I am very pleased that we had the opportunity to find each other after so many years. I would not see us separated so soon, but no matter what you say, I cannot return to France with you. We have not the money, without selling what you have stolen, and I have not the desire to leave behind me the reputation of having been a thief."

He was frowning in the belligerent manner he always had when things did not go the way he intended them to. "Perhaps, you will change your mind when things are normal again?"

She would give him that much. "Perhaps. Do you think there will be normality in France again? My feeling is that things are forever changed. One cannot stop what is begun in men's hearts and souls with regard to their desire for that change, no matter how brutal."

They had spoken in French so that the pawn shop keeper would not be privy to what they were saying, but there was something in the friendly way he looked at her, as he counted out the money for her silver set and diamond comb, that gave her the impression he might have more of an understanding of her native tongue than he had led them to believe.

She handed her brother the money for his fare, keeping only enough for her own passage back to Kent. She would return to Julian Endicott the things that had been stolen off him. After that? Well, perhaps he would be kind enough to offer her a reference so that she might move on to cook for some other English lord.

The packet to Dunkerque was already underway, cutting waters lit by the afternoon sun as it crossed the Channel by the time Julian reached Dover on his blown and lathered gray. He could see it slipping away into the fog over the Channel from the top of the steep, cobbled street that wound its way through a row of shops to the pier as he pulled the winded horse to a halt.

It was strange how tied Julian felt to that boat, and its cargo. It was as if a piece of him went with it. He tried to convince himself it was the claret cup he missed, a piece of silver and not the girl who took it from him. The idea of something important lost forever left him aching and angry—as bereft as if he stood upon the banks of the River Styxx and watched the passage of a loved one to the other side—as bereft as he had felt the day that Ellnor had been interred into the family crypt, with orchids and white roses to sweeten her passage. He snapped himself out of such dour thought. This was not at all the same. This passage need not be permanent. This passage he had some control over. He had but to discover when the next packet was to leave, and he would be on it.

As he chirruped his spent horse into motion again, the meager light of the sun caught itself up in something bright that was just being placed in the window of a pawn shop he was passing. It was a silver-backed mirror, brush, comb, perfume flask, and salts bottle set, an engraved set that had him off the back of the horse, and peering into the window in a flash. They were hers! There was no mistaking that angry griffin.

That she must sit in the carriage watching her brother's departure, and then head back up the very road she had traveled all morning in order to return alone what Antoine had stolen, was a difficult thing for Jeannette. But it was not the most difficult thing she had ever faced. It was good to know that Antoine was alive, a good thing to clear her name, especially with Julian Endicott. She cared too much what he thought of her, not to clear her name, false though the name might be. She would make it through this fracas, just as she had made it through so many scrapes in the past, with her head up, and her thoughts focused on what good might come out of catastrophe.

She settled back in the coach as it rattled and bucked along the muddy road, Julian Endicott's silver claret cup cradled in her hands. There was a feeling of peace that came from holding the weight of the object. It was, she thought, as if she made a sort of peace at last with the late Lady Endicott in returning these cherished items.

She made peace, too, with her thoughts concerning the

man who had been her employer. She loved him. There were no other words for it. She pressed the cup to her forehead, to cheek, to lip. But the silver held no hint of the heat she had felt from Julian Endicott's lips. She wondered if she would ever feel such a heat again.

"Aye! I remember the couple. Foreigners. French." The shopkeeper nodded, eyeing Julian with keen interest as he agreed to remove the pieces from the window. "A little dab of a woman, and her brother not much bigger."

"Brother?" The word reverberated, sending a chilling spasm down Julian's spine. It had never occurred to him that Francois du Bounnet might be Jeannette's brother, and not her lover. Her brothers were all dead. She had told him as much herself, and neither of them named Francois. Could it be this was just another lie? He had swallowed too many of them already to be anything but skeptical.

The shopkeeper was rattling on.

"What's that?" Julian insisted. "I'm sorry. I've been woolgathering."

Good-naturedly the man repeated himself as he wrapped the silver in the familiar green flannel bag in which Jeannette had carried her precious family heirlooms. "Drove a hard bargain, the little lady did. Might have given her a little more, had I known I would sell these so soon. Said she needed all I could give her, and in the end it still wasn't enough for the two of them to get to where they were going. He kept trying to make her sell me a pretty silver cup and flask. She would have none of it. Told him they must be returned to their rightful owner. Got the feeling they was nabbed goods."

"What are you saying, man? Did one of them stay behind then?"

"And who are these people to you, sir, if you don't mind me asking?"

How to answer that one. Julian sighed. "The young

woman has been part of my household for the past few months."

"Umm, then you'd be the gent the brother was warning her against. He said you would never do honest by the girl. Begging your pardon, sir, but I'll be knowing your intentions before I tells you any more."

Julian swallowed what threatened to be a much misunderstood laugh. This gentleman was very serious about the subject matter they discussed, and yet Julian could not think of a more preposterous situation. That he must answer for his intentions to a shopkeeper he had no more than just met, struck him very funny. Yet, the man waited an answer. He must give it.

He leaned in over the counter. "Have you ever been in love, my good man? Really in love? The kind of bond that outlives death?"

The shopkeeper nodded, his jaw softening and eyes misting with memories. "Aye. Her name were Abby. A grand girl. I were heels over head in love with the lass. Her father, may he burn in Hell, would not let us wed. Poor girl. He should have let us be. She died of smallpox within the year."

Julian frowned, reminded of his own lost love.

"I lost my wife, last year, in childbirth. She was everything to me. I wanted nothing but to follow her. Do you understand? So, I locked myself away in the country, and stopped eating. I would have died for that love, except for the dab of a woman you have met. She reminded me that there are reasons to keep on living, and loving."

"Ah!" The man nodded.

"She is the most important of those reasons, man. Do you understand? Of course I mean to do right by her."

The shopkeeper seemed satisfied. "That's what I wanted to hear, lad. Best after her."

"You know where she meant to go?"

The old man looked him keenly in the eye, and seemed satisfied with what he saw. "Said she meant to go home again, lad. Do you know where that might be?"

"Home?" Julian frowned. "Her home was in France."

The old man winked at him. "A lovely place she said. Called it Idol's Nook, or something very like. Do you know where that be?"

Julian closed his eyes, and let loose a shaky laugh. "Yes, as it happens, I do."

Chapter Twenty

~

Jeannette went in by way of the servants' entrance when she returned to Idylnook. She went first to the place she felt the most secure—to the warm bustle of the kitchen, where for a moment, unnoticed, she stood and savored the familiar smells and sounds and the comforting sight of Polly rolling dough, and Danny basting a fowl.

It was Polly who lay eyes on her first. Polly who put down her pin with a startled, "Coo, girl! Is it really you standing there? Danial, only look who has just pranced in, as casual as you please."

She opened wide her floury arms as she said it, and Jeannette fell into them willingly, despite the dust, for she was in dire need of a good squeeze.

Danny stepped back from the oven, his face ruddy with the heat, his mouth twisted in a knowing grin, "Cor! Does her ladyship know you snuck in, lass? She's been dyin' to get her hands on you, she has."

Jeannette had no doubt that was true. Margaret Crawford had probably let everyone in hearing know how much she would like to have her clapped into irons, when the theft of Julian's claret cup had been discovered.

"Is the master in?" she asked self-consciously. It was time to get on with what she had come to do. "There is something I would return to him."

"The master?" Polly's eyes widened. "He came not with you?"

"With me? Whatever do you mean?"

Danny laughed. "You must have passed each other on the road, girl. He's gone off after you."

"Gone! Oh dear. Well then, I must speak with Simms, before I go."

Mrs. Gary walked into the kitchen in that instant, and let out a little shriek when she set eyes on Jeannette. "Goodness me," she mumbled, exiting the room as swiftly as she had entered. "Simms!" They could hear her calling. "Simms! Come at once. You will never guess who is standing in the kitchen."

With a trifle more dignity, Simms pushed through the door.

"Miss Saincoeur, you are returned," he said with his customary severity. "Or should we now address you as Mademoiselle Bouillé?"

Jeannette, who had bent to pull the claret cup, tray, and jug from her valise, looked up at him, face flushed, stolen silver in either hand. "Either name will do, Simms. I was born a Bouillé, but Saincoeur has served to keep me alive on more than one occasion."

Behind him, the door to the kitchen swung wide again. This time it was Lady Crawford who pushed her way in. "But where is Julian?" she insisted. "And whatever do you do here, in the kitchen, Mademoiselle Bouillé?"

Jeannette rose, nervously arranging the silver cup and flask on their matching tray as she did so. "I came to return these things to your brother, Lady Crawford, but I understand he is not in. Perhaps you will give them to him for me, when he returns?"

Margaret blinked at the silver that was held out to her, momentarily speechless, and then she reached out to lift the silver cup so that it no longer rattled in agitation against the glass flask. "How very clever of you. You have found Julian's silver cup. We were wondering where it had gotten itself off to. Simms, you will be so good as to relieve mademoiselle of that tray, take her bag up to the green guest room, and show her to the little drawing room. Polly, we shall require a pot of tea, and some of your lovely currant tarts, if you please."

Feeling very much as if she had been swept up in a tempest, Jeannette handed the tray to Simms, and allowed herself to be led away.

Julian felt as if his heart wore wings as he headed away from the coastline, back toward the apple orchards and cobb-nut trees of home. He was happy and relieved, and filled with expectation. Jeannette was not a thief! She had not meant to hurt him. She did not love another! Muddy and wet, and road-weary though he was, he felt light, almost buoyant, as if he could rise above the saddle, and fly home faster than the tired gray could carry him.

The future looked clear to him now. It held promise. He had but to explain to Jeannette his feelings for her, and present her with the gift of her sacrificed silver, and the day would be a perfect one, brought to perfect conclusion. Nothing stood in his way now, not even his own misunderstanding.

Nothing stood in his way but a masked horseman, who rode out of the wet hedge along the side of the road, and blocked his path, with a hoarse, "Stand, and deliver!"

Unarmed, Julian was not about to challenge a masked man with a four-barreled pistol leveled at his chest. He did as the man suggested.

"Please sit down," Margaret Crawford waved Jeannette toward one of the comfortable chairs that graced the drawing room.

Jeannette chose an ornately carved cherry-wood chair. It had the least amount of padding to sink into. She had no desire to flounder about in goose feathers should she feel required to rise with any haste. Warily, she eyed Lady Crawford. What dreadful accusations did this woman mean to hurl at her head this time? Perhaps nothing more than she deserved. Jeannette felt terribly self-conscious of her circumstances. The weight of guilt weighed heavy on her soul. How did one go about explaining the fact that one's identity was a lie, that one's brother had also fabricated his identity, and that same brother had stolen valuables from this very house? This promised to be a most uncomfortable interview.

Oddly enough, Margaret would not allow their exchange to be uncomfortable in the way that Jeannette expected it to be. In fact, she did her utmost to make Jeannette feel very much as though she were an honored guest, and not a thieving French cook. That in itself was rather uncomfortable.

"Miss Saincoeur," she said, with a stiff smile, "or would you prefer that I call you Miss Bouillé? I am so glad you have returned to us, and can only hope that my brother comes close behind. He did leave in a dreadful temper this morning."

He was angry with her. Well, it was no more than she had expected, but that he would go chasing after her, in that anger, surprised her. She thought about the claret cup, and could not but feel dreadful.

"He has a letter for you from them," Margaret was saying with an expectant look.

She had not been attending. What letter? Who was the he that had it, and who were the them she referred to, with such expectation? "Excuse me, what did you just say?"

Margaret laughed uneasily. "I daresay you are just as surprised as we were to receive such a letter. We had no idea your relatives were in Austria, and longing to have you come and live amongst them."

"Tante Natalie has written? When? Where?"

"The letter, from a Claude Bouillé, was delivered only this morning, my dear," Lady Crawford cleared her throat. "Within a half hour or so of your having left us."

There was something about Margaret's eyes that reminded Jeannette of Julian. Was it sorrow she read there, or perhaps pity?

"I am very sorry, Miss Bouillé, that we did not know earlier of your connections. I am also sorry to say I cannot immediately press this letter into your hands. Julian took it with him, so that he might give it to you himself. It was our understanding that you meant to return to your homeland." Her polite and careful distance was rife with question.

Jeannette thought it only fair to satisfy her curiosity. "Yes, that was my original intention, but I changed my mind. My brother has gone on without me."

"Brother? Monsieur du Bounnet is your brother?" Margaret's expression remained calm, but her voice soared in surprise.

Jeannette was too dizzied by the unexpected revelation of a letter to pay undue attention to Margaret's reaction. She was unbalanced by the woman, so suddenly had she reversed her tack. That there was a letter . . . that she should discover herself with family, not only Antoine, but an aunt and cousins as well . . . It was too much.

She tried to explain. "Yes, but of course his name is no more du Bounnet, than mine is Saincoeur. We have each of us chosen to hide from the brand of being a Bouillé, you see. It was much easier . . ."

"Oh, but you have no need to explain, my dear." Margaret's spirits seemed to be rising. Her voice, at any rate, rose. "These are most troubling times for you and your countrymen, to be sure. I can only hope you will be equally forgiving . . ." she paused, genuine concern pulling strangely at her lips, "of any slights or disparaging remarks that may have come your way during your sojourn at Idylnook. I believe my brother is truly quite fond of you, and would not have you leave us, if you mean to leave us, with hard feelings."

She seemed genuinely contrite. Jeannette found her solicitousness almost harder to bear than her former antagonism.

"I bear you no ill will, my lady," she said honestly. How could she bear the woman ill will when she so lightly brushed aside the temporary disappearance of heirlooms from her brother's house?

"And Julian? You do not hold him in any contempt, do you?" Margaret was regarding Jeannette with a most searching look. "I had, I must admit, almost begun to think that you and my brother . . . that he . . ."

Fortunately for the suddenly tongue-tied Margaret, tea was brought in to them, at that moment, by a round-eyed Mrs. Gary.

"Here you are, my dears," she said, her eyes darting with great curiosity from one face to the other. "A nice, hot cup of Darjeeling, and some of Polly's currant buns. Is there anything else I can get you? I am sorry to say we are all out of lemons at the moment." She knew Jeannette favored a slice of lemon in her tea. And yet, the concern in her gaze had more to do with a desire to convey support than bother over missing lemons.

Jeannette managed to smile at her. "You need not be concerned," she said, and she referred to more than lemons in saying as much.

Mrs. Gary's eyebrows rose. She went away mollified, but little wiser than when she had come into the drawing room.

Margaret poured them each a cup of tea, and having taken a sip of her own concoction of milky brew, she put the cup down in a rather decisive manner, and said, without a trace of embarrassment, "What I was trying to say earlier, before our little interruption, is that I believe my brother loves you, and I would have you know, despite past indications to the contrary, that I currently have no objection to the match, should he decide to ask for your hand."

Jeannette dropped her spoon into her cup with a splashy clatter.

"I'll be having all your valuables, gov'nor, if you don't mind." The masked man waved the end of his heavy, four-barreled pistol under Julian's nose.

"But of course you will," Julian agreed, for he was not about to argue with the armed rogue. Sighing, he handed over his purse, gold pocket watch and fob, and grimacing, slid an emerald ring from his finger that had once belonged to his father. He was about to slide his wedding band off as well, when the robber shook his head.

"I'll not be taking your wedding band, guv. I've not fallen so low as I'll be party to breaking up a cull's marriage. What have ye got in the peter?" He prodded the green flannel bag Julian had strung, along with his valise, across the gray's withers.

Julian frowned. "Of all the things I must give up to you, my good man, this is the hardest," he admitted. "It is nothing much, really . . ."

The robber would see for himself, and so he yanked the bag free, and unfolded the fabric.

"Oiy. I'll not sneer at this lot. 'Twill not fetch much on the black market right enough. These markings will have to be burnished off, don't you know, but 'tis pretty enough to my eye, and worth a coachwheel or two. I'm thinking I'll have it off you anyway." He folded the flannel up again, and stuffed the bundle under his coat.

"Wait!" Julian dared try to negotiate. "Perhaps we can strike a bargain. It means far more to me on a sentimental level than you can ever expect to get off it in your line of work."

"A bargain?" The highwayman laughed behind his mask. "I mean to take anything of value off of you anyway. What have you to bargain with? We are not in the High Street haggling over wares, my brave fellow. This is a robbery."

"I know, I know. I am not in the habit of shopping the High Street with my hands in the air. Had these things no value but that of money, I would gladly give them to you and send you on your way. But there is a most moving story connected with them. . . ."

"Go on. You've piqued me interest. It's not often a cove will wrangle over the least valuable thing I takes off of him."

"Well, you see, these things are not mine at all."

"What? Nicked 'em, did you?"

"If, by that, you mean did I steal them, no. The silver belongs to a young lady I know. They are the last of her worldly possessions of any value, though she was once possessed of great wealth. Rather than turn to a life of crime, herself, which I am sure you will agree, is not an easy life for a girl . . ."

"Ain't the easy life for no one, gov'nor."

"Yes, well, she pawned them, that her brother might return to France."

"Now why should I care one whit about where the girl's brother's off to?"

"Well, you see, that brave young man means to see what he can do about getting rid of Bonaparte for us."

The highwayman cocked his head. "Oh yeah? Go on. You may be able to ransom the goods off me yet if it means the end of old Bony and will serve to keep some sweet, young mort out of my kind of trouble."

Chapter Twenty-one

~

Jeannette was in a state of shock and confusion. Once again, her life was tipped upside down. She had been shown to a guest room, and her bag had been unpacked by the upstairs maid, who had not dared to so much as ask her how she was. She had changed out of the dress she had traveled in. With no other clothes to speak of, not even the new, wine-colored livery which she had left in her old room in the attic, she was forced to don the blue-sprigged muslin in which she had departed France. Margaret had come in, remarked favorably on the dress, and politely suggested that her hairdresser was at Jeannette's disposal should she require her services. For the first time in years, Jeannette's hair was taken down out of the neat chignon she had grown so accustomed to, and properly dressed in curls.

The dresser and Margaret both seemed highly pleased by the results, but Jeannette felt as though she regarded a stranger in the mirror. Was this what would win her the promise of marriage from Julian Endicott? Proof of connections, a pretty dress, and curled hair? Was she not worthy without such trivialities? Her raised status, rather than cheering her, threw her into a most melancholy state. What was she to do with herself now? She longed to disappear into the kitchen, but knew she could not.

She went down to dinner with Margaret at her side, feeling decidedly odd and useless. She no longer fit comfortably into this place called Idylnook. Most of the servants threw long, sideways glances at her when they thought she was not looking, and refused to meet her eyes, when she was.

Mrs. Gary was willing enough to look her in the eye, but she seemed a little less sure of herself, nonetheless. "You look very pretty this evening, my dear. Ever so fine."

Jeannette thanked her, and smiled widely when Williams threw her a wink in serving up the main course. Dear, comfortable Polly stood in the doorway off the dining room, and waved a trifle uncertainly. Simms, and Simms alone, showed no change of attitude. The stiff-necked butler regarded her with the same high-nosed sort of snobbery he always had. But then he observed everyone with equal hauteur down the length of that remarkable nose.

It was after dinner was cleared away that he begged leave to inform her that Mr. Sandford wished to speak to her. "Would you mind going out to the garden to chat with him?" he inquired regally.

Jeannette did not mind at all an escape into the garden. It was still misting rain, but she had always felt most comfortable in the gardens here at Idylnook. She pulled on her traveling cloak, and a bonnet, to shield dress and hair from the rain, and walked out to the head gardener's house.

He opened the door promptly when she knocked, but rather than ask her in, out of the rain, he said only, "Come. There's something I would show you, miss."

Through the growing darkness they went, to the largest of the glass houses, the one where Mr. Sandford grew rare blooms.

"Here!" he trudged swiftly down one of the aisles, lighting a lantern as he went. "You'll want to see this."

He stopped in front of a large tray of freshly turned soil and chalky stone, and hung the lantern from a nail above their heads. In the circle of light it threw, four sad-looking orchids were carefully staked in the soil.

"Wild 'Lady' orchids," Jeannette breathed. "You are trying to grow them here? Why, they're lovely!"

"They are that, but you could have knocked me down

with a feather when his lordship come in, all soaked from the rain, saying as how he meant to plant these flowers, of all the flowers he might have chosen, because you found them beautiful."

"Because I found them beautiful?" Jeannette was shaken by a sudden chill.

"Aye, that's what he told me."

Jeannette was silent a moment. It touched her, more than she could find words to express, learning that Julian Endicott had been planting flowers for her, flowers that saddened him, even as she and her brother had left Idylnook behind them, his silver packed away in Antoine's bag. There was a fullness within her heart, a sweet pain, to have been given the gift of knowledge that might otherwise have completely slipped her awareness, in learning of Julian's intentions.

"Thank you for telling me." She reached out swiftly to touch Mr. Sandford's arm.

He nodded, and cleared his throat uncomfortably. "I thought you might like to know."

She strove to make him easy, with less emotionally charged conversation. "Can they thrive here, so far from the downs?"

"Can't say." Mr. Sandford peered at the orchids with knowing eyes. "The truth lies within. They are none too happy about being moved, but the soil is akin to what they like, and they have excellent light and water. I've a feeling they'll perk right up after a little bout of homesickness. Plants are a good deal like people in some ways. Who can say just why one person can transplant themselves to a new place, and be happy—while another, given the same circumstances, pines away for what is left behind."

Jeannette smiled, and thought of herself and her brother. "I think there is a good chance they will be happy here."

Sandford eyed her with his wise and weathered blue eyes. "And yourself, miss? Can you be happy here?"

She was surprised he should ask. "I have been very happy here."

"And yet, you went away, did you not?" He seemed uncomfortable in having said so.

"Yes, I did. And, I came back again."

"There be good reason for my prying ways, miss. You see, Master Julian did ask me, when he came here this morning with the 'ladies' here, did I think the servants would care to have you as mistress of Idylnook."

"Mistress of Idylnook?" Jeannette gasped.

"Right. Said he meant to have you, would you but have him."

Jeannette gasped, and shook her head, and felt a sudden need to sit down. "He said this to you this morning? Before he knew I was gone?"

"Aye, and I answered him easily enough." Sandford eyed her calmly, waiting for some sign that she collected herself.

Round-eyed she regarded him, her mind turning on the information she had received. Julian had stated his intention to marry her, this morning, before he knew for certain she was a Bouillé, before he knew by anyone's word but hers that she was anything but a cook.

Mr. Sandford stood calmly watching her.

"How did you respond, Mr. Sandford? Will you tell me? Do you think I would make a good mistress for Idylnook?"

He smiled at her, his expression earnest. "Told him, miss, that most of us knew from the beginning that you was no garden-variety cook. You succeeded in making the master eat again when we was all but half convinced that he might waste away from his sadness. I have seen him smile again; and have watched the whole house freed of its mourning. I told him how I was thinking there was none better suited to the role, miss."

Jeannette beamed at him. "Thank you very much, Mr. Sandford."

It was nearing dawn by the time Julian reached the road that would lead him home. He was covered in mud, wet to the skin, and weary to the bone, but the green flannel bag was tucked under one arm, and despite the fact that he had been forced to walk the past ten miles, he was feeling quite pleased with himself. He had managed to convince the masked robber to give him back Jeannette's silver in exchange for three things of far greater value—his horse, the bag of clothing that Alphonse had so carefully packed for him, and the gold wedding band that had once tied him irrevocably to Elinor.

It had been remarkably easy to slide the gold band from his finger, far easier than he ever would have guessed. Elinor was gone. One could not remain forever married to memories. He would miss the gray far more than the ring. The ring bound him to the past, to sorrow, to the dust of dreams that would never come true. The gray, on the other hand, would have carried him into the future much faster, and in a far more comfortable fashion.

The highwayman had been happy to oblige in such a lucrative trade, and yet, there had been some spark of humanity in him that made him turn in the saddle, when he might just as easily have gigged the horse and disappeared into the night without another word. "You're a lucky bloke, guv'nor," he said, in all seriousness, though it was he who sat the horse, and carried away all of Julian's valuables.

Julian smiled, rain trickling down his face. "I am, am I?

"Aye! To have found two loves in one lifetime. You would seem to live a charmed life, guv."

Julian had laughed, and given the man a wet bow. "May your life be equally charmed, sir, for your charity today. You are a decent fellow."

The highway man chuckled. "Ta, guv. You'll not find many as will agree with you, but I thank you for the compliment, as well as all of the lovely goods, all the same. 'Night, now."

With a touch of his hand to the hat that held his mask in place, and a touch of his heels to the gray, he had disappeared into the night.

Julian had not paused to watch as he and the horse disappeared into the mist that hung over the road. He set off walking the sodden road immediately, anxious to be home.

Hours later, all that Julian could think of as he broke into a stumbling, mud-hampered run toward the few lights that still burned in the windows at Idylnook, was how anxious he was to be done with this journey, how glad he would be to see Jeannette, and what drastic changes his mind and mood had been through, since he had set out the previous morning.

Chapter Twenty-two

~

Julian opened the front door with the furtive quiet of a burglar. A lamp was shining in the library, and another in the spare bedroom above it. He had no desire to rouse Simms, who would feel it his duty to attend to him. Alphonse, too, was sure to come and fuss over the condition of his clothes, did he make any noise. Mud-caked boots and drenched overcoat he removed at the door. His coat he abandoned as well, that he might sneak quietly about in damp shirtsleeves and stockinged feet. The precious flannel bag of silver he could not so cavalierly leave behind him. He kept the damp parcel tucked beneath his arm.

The house slumbered around him, curiously quiet but for the ticking of the clocks that graced almost every one of the downstairs rooms as he crept into the library. The lamp from the window would see himself safely up the stairs.

In the circle of golden light on his desk, his claret cup sat filled and waiting for him, with two blue flowers floating on the surface, and a wilting cucumber fan drooping over the lip. Prettily arranged at its base, there were a selection of crisp water biscuits, in case he should come in hungry, which indeed he was.

He smiled. The claret cup's presence made certain Jeannette Saincoeur—no, he must get used to calling her Bouillé—was returned. He crossed to the tray, took up a biscuit, and wondered how kindly Jeannette had been met by Margaret. Where in his house did she now rest her pretty head? Could it be his love was in the attic with Polly, as in the past? He wished more than anything to take her in his arms, and carry her to his bed. His feet were cold on the marble floors, and he could think of nothing he would rather warmed them than this woman he meant to take to wife.

He picked up the claret, to wash down the biscuit, and thought he heard a sound. So familiar was the room to him, though he peered into abject darkness, he knew at once that he was not alone. Someone slumped in the wide, leather sofa in the darkest corner of the room—probably Alphonse, who prided himself on always seeing the master safely to bed.

Julian picked up the lamp, with the intention of leaving his faithful valet undisturbed. As he turned to go, throwing light at odd angles through the darkness, he was stopped in his tracks by a muffled sigh. There was a decidedly feminine quality to that sigh. It did not sound at all like a noise Alphonse would make. His heart raced a little faster.

Whoever it was, he would not wake her, and so he approached with the lamp held low. A female, he could tell by the cascading fabric that made up her skirts, was lost in sleep's embrace upon the sofa.

"Margaret?" he whispered. Deep within, he had hoped it might be Jeannette, but this female wore not the new livery in which he had grown accustomed to seeing her. She stirred a little as he approached with the light, and so he put down the lamp, and stepped in front of it, that he might shake his sister awake and relieve her fears that some harm had come to him in the night.

He stopped breathing when the face in the shadows was revealed to him, for it was not Margaret at all. The woman who awaited his arrival was Jeannette, her hair and dress unfamiliar to him, her face very dear in sleep.

His thoughts flew back to the day on the downs when he had found her likewise sleeping. There was a sweetness about her face, at rest—a softened peacefulness, that lent her dark features a childlike vulnerability. Hair and skin, she was burnished by the golden glow of his lamp. There was a curious richness to this vision of a loved one's face, rising up out of the darkness that surrounded her. She looked like a painting by one of the Dutch masters, come to life.

Feelings that had warred within Julian all the way home were gentled by the sight of Jeannette's face in slumber. His heart filled to overflowing from the tender, protective well-spring of love. This frail creature seemed so strong in daylight, so invincible. And yet, he saw, in her sleeping state, qualities exposed to him that reminded him of Elinor, who had been bright, and cheerful and childlike, and anything but strong.

He could not stop his mind from comparing the two women, though there seemed some disrespect to both of them in doing so. He loved them both. They had that in common. They were each of them bright, intelligent young women. They both had the cherishable capacity to make him feel loved, and worthy of love. And they both seemed to bring out the most positive characteristics within his nature.

Beyond that, there was no comparing them, really. They were not in the least alike in form or figure. The one was possessed of an enormous energy, flexibility, self-posses-sion, and strength, the other had been cheerful and artistic, and thoroughly content, even graceful, with everything life brought her way, even death. Untested by hardship, she had snapped like a twig when the winds of time and Fate had turned against her. Bent and swayed though Jeannette had been by trials and tribulation, she yet grew strong and thrived.

The love Julian held in his heart and soul for Elinor was a complete and separate thing from the love he felt for Jeannette Bouillé. There was, within his heart, room for both, a vast capacity of room. Knowing as much, truly knowing it within the core of his being, made him a happy man as he knelt beside Jeannette.

Her lips, slightly parted and softly kissable as her breasts rose and fell with the gentle rhythm of sleep, roused a hunger within Julian, a hunger he had long kept at bay.

Unable to resist the lure of it any longer, he leaned in close to her face, until he felt her breath upon his lips. The warm, sleepy smell of her filled his nostrils. Smiling, his joy profound, he kissed her gently awake.

She roused slowly, responding weakly at first, to his searching lips, and then awareness returning, with a sleepy fervor that equaled his own. She tried at one point to speak. He silenced her with his mouth, and with a sweet, capitulating sigh, she allowed herself to be silenced, and satisfied herself with kissing, and being kissed.

When at last they were the both of them surfeited with the sensation of mouth against mouth, he leaned back to find her smiling at him, the soft, childlike quality of her expression still intact. Her hazel eyes glowed with an irresistible warmth, a blazing admission of her love and trust in him, that required no words to be understood. Julian lost himself in those eyes.

"You are come home," she murmured, the words unseemly sensuous in their sleepy warmth.

"As you are, my love," he whispered, and he kissed her again.

"Home," she admitted happily, and the word held an especially magical lilt. "You found the claret cup. I taste it on your lips."

He nodded, "Thank you for returning it to me. I know that you did so at great cost." He held up the familiar green flannel bag that held her silver. She would never know at what cost he brought it back to her.

Her eyes got very big. She let loose a gusty little noise of surprise and sat up. "Mon dieu! However did you find that!" Her loving eyes regarded him again. "How very clever you are." She reached out, but not for her green bag. Her hands, her arms, sought his. Her beautiful eyes drank him in, starring with unshed tears.

He sank onto the sofa beside her, and enfolded her in his embrace, and stroked her hair, and clasped her to his chest.

"You are so very kind, monsieur." Her voice came muffled from his neck, where she nestled her head and warmed him with both her breath and her words. "I have seen the orchids."

His hands were irresistibly drawn to the curls that clustered along the nape of her neck. "Yes, my love. I decided you were right. I could not forever hold grudge against flowers for their part in past sorrows."

She sighed, and squeezed herself closer to his chest. "I was much moved."

"Was it only yesterday I planted flowers for you, my love?" He pulled back a little that he might look into her shining eyes, and caress her cheek. "It has been a very eventful day, Jeannette."

"Oui, monsieur." She lifted her mouth to be kissed, and his heart sang at this open expression of her feelings for him. He quite happily obliged her, and then took her chin in his hand, and regarded her with a most serious expression.

"You must learn to call me, Julian, Jeannette."

She nestled closer, and tipped her chin that she might kiss his hand. "Oui, Julian." Her accent gave the name new cadence. "I will call you whatever you wish, mon ami."

"Will you call me husband then, my love?"

For the first time that evening, Jeannette pushed herself, as much as she could, out of his embrace. "Oh, but, monsieur, I would not answer such a question until I am certain you meant to ask it of me, for I am not Jeannette Saincoeur, but truly a Bouillé, after all."

He pulled her close to him, and kissed away the worried look that had taken possession of both mouth and eyes, and as he lavished a trail of soft kisses down her neck, and enjoyed the fact that this dress was cut fashionably low, he said, "Shh, shh, shh, my dear Sound Heart. I know who you are. I've a letter for you, from your relatives. But, no matter what the name may or may not be, I know who you are."

"Who am I then?" She sounded very curious, and more than a little bit aroused by the havoc his gentle hands swiftly wreaked upon the carefully tucked muslin fichu he would have out of his way, exposing the warm, white, scented flesh of her bosom.

"You are, my love, the borage flower in my claret cup . . ." He kissed the swell of one breast. "The sweetest sauce upon my lips . . ." She moaned, deep in her throat, and he sought out the softness of the other so that it might not feel neglected. "You are the lightness in my heart and eyes, and soul." She traced a spine-tingling pattern with her fingertips along his jaw, and earlobe, and across his shoulders, until he made her dizzy with kisses, and the stroking, seeking, teasing play of his hands on her breasts and back and neck.

Gently he pressed her back onto the sofa, and slid himself into the soft, creaking embrace of leather beside her. "You are the woman whom I love to watch sleeping . . ." He stretched himself into the curve of her, one elbow bent to support his head. "By your side I wish to lie every night for the rest of my life." He leaned very close, that he might whisper in her ear. "You are the voice I listen for, the steps I would follow, the arms that I cling to." He lifted her arms as he spoke, to wrap them around his neck, and then ran his palms hotly down her sides, that he might clasp her hips hard against him as he kissed her breathless. "You are a hunger in me that will not be sated. I could eat you up right here, so starved am I for you, my darling . . ."

"But, no, no, monsieur," she protested, her breath coming hard and fast as she tried to push him away. "I am overwhelmed."

"Ah, my sweet Jeannette, my dearest Sound Heart, one should be overwhelmed by love. It is an overwhelming emotion. You love me, do you not?"

She stopped pushing him away. "With every fiber of my being, monsieur."

"Then, why do you push me away, my dear, when all I have in mind at this moment is loving you, with every fiber of my being?"

"I am frightened, Julian."

He fell back, to read her face carefully as he asked in disbelief. "You fear me, sweetness?"

"No, no." She clasped a palm across her low-cut bodice, as though to hold back something that would spill out of her. "I fear this strange, consuming wildness within my heart, that would abandon me to you."

"So that two halves might make a whole," he whispered, smiling the sweet, exultant smile of the conqueror whose most important battle has been won. "You need not fear such feelings." He took the hand from her breast, and held it snug against his own that she might feel the uneven pounding within.

"Such carefully restrained urges beat within my own breast, my dear. They are a beautiful thing, really, and should not be forever caged. I love you, my dear, hazel-eyed girl. What wells up in my heart and soul and loins is love for you. Can it be that what you fear within your own heart is love as well?"

She sighed heavily, and closed her eyes, and clung to him, her whole body trembling with the emotions she held carefully in check.

He kissed her nose, and touched her lips, and smiled when she opened her eyes smiling, and lightly kissed upon his fingers. "You have not answered me, Jeannette. Will you abandon yourself to the love that rises within you? Will you marry me, my sweet?"

She opened her eyes, her expression no longer troubled and pensive. "I love you, Julian. I should be happy to marry you," she said with conviction.

"That settles it, then." He rose from the sofa, and handed her the lamp. "Hold this in the one hand, and wrap the other about my neck." She did as he directed without question. He took her sparrow-fine body into his arms, and as she lit the way, carried her out of the study and into the hallway.

"Where do you take me, monsieur, that I cannot carry myself there, on my own two feet?" she whispered in his ear.

"To our room, Jeannette," he said, with a soft, suggestive

chuckle. "I refuse to let you go again, now that you have given yourself up to me, and I hold you safely in my arms."

"But, monsieur!"

"Julian. Please, call me Julian. I would hear my name fall sweetly from your lips again."

"Julian. This is neither right, nor proper."

"It would be even more improper, Jeannette, were I to allow another night to pass away without the wonder of your soft warmth in my arms. We should not wake to another morning lonely in our beds, when our hearts are so in tune. There are things I would do and say to you, wonders that we should share, that ought not be delayed, for life is short, time against us, and Fate all too inconsistent to depend upon. You know it is so. All of these things have worked against your happiness in the past, have they not?"

"But, in the eyes of the Lord, we are not yet husband and wife. This will be sin, we are committing. Will it not?"

"Nay! I will not allow it that God might be so heartless as to keep us apart but for the words of a vicar. My dear Jeannette, if you are to lie beside me for all eternity, what can one more night upon this earth matter? Time and love are precious gifts. They must not be squandered. I vow to you, upon my heart, with God alone my witness, that we are, in my mind, from this moment forward husband and wife, do you but deem it so. Body, mind, heart, and soul, do I come open and willing to you, and no other. Would you refuse me, if only for a few hours?"

They were come to the bottom of the stairs. Without any evidence of strain, he began to mount them. She rested comfortably in his arms.

"I think it would be best, monsieur, if I returned to my room for the remainder of the night."

"And will you sleep, my love, returned to your room? Or will you, all unhappy in our separation, pace the night away, until morning, when we may be together again? I shall surely pass the hours in such a misery."

She smiled fondly up at him as the light moved with them

up the wall. "I do not think my heart will still its pounding long enough for me to sleep a wink, 'tis true."

"And shall I ride now, and wake the vicar, and insist upon his attendance? Banns have yet to be posted. The delay might go on for weeks, and I burn for you now, with a flame that would consume me, body and soul. Would you refuse me the heaven of your arms, in the name of propriety alone?"

"You would have me as your mistress then, until I might be your wife, in the eyes of all that is Holy?"

"I would have you, Jeannette, in any way you will give yourself to me, for I have within me a deep pining hunger that would be fed. The flavor of your passion, offered to me in the smallest of tastes . . ."—he bent his head to nibble gently her earlobe—"has plumped the shrunken, withered melancholy of my soul to such an extent, that I am grown greedy for more. But . . ." he sighed, "not so greedy that I would take you unwilling to my bed. If you would hold onto chastity, then I give it you as a wedding gift, and take you, with vehement protest, to the maidenly privacy of your own little room."

It was not until he had said as much, that Julian looked up to see a ghostlike, female figure, all draped in white, head to toe, standing at the head of the stairs, in front of the shadowed portrait of Elinor.

Any other words he might have said, died upon his lips.

Jeannette had never felt happier than she did at this moment, in the close haven of Julian Endicott's arms. What a dilemma he posed. He meant to marry her. She knew him to be sincere, and yet it was a dreadful thing to deny him the love she longed so earnestly to express. He was completely correct in assuming she would sleep not a wink.

How did one tell a man that one wished to capitulate to the earthiest of needs? How did one give in to desire without losing all self-respect? Did her very thoughts damn her? They were dangerous thoughts indeed.

She was about to answer him, about to tell him he need not bother to carry her any further, for whatever she decided, she must, herself, walk bravely into, or away from such temptation—when he stopped dead on the stairs, and looked up, his face frozen with what looked like fear.

Her gaze followed the direction of his. A white shape slid past the portrait of the late Lady Endicott, a ghostly female figure, advancing on them, bound for the stairs.

"Mon dieu!" she exclaimed.

The figure paused, as though halted by her voice.

Hands shaking, Julian put her down and stepped up a riser, so that his body blocked hers from perceived danger. He loosed the lamp from her fingers, and held it high.

Margaret Crawford squinted at them in the sudden glare. "Hallo, Jules. Glad to see you are safely home."

Margaret's voice was wonderfully, abrasively human. Jeannette felt weak with relief. She had, for a frightening moment, believed it was a ghost they encountered, the ghost of Elinor Endicott, come back to claim for herself a husband who would stray.

"Is that Miss Bouillé who follows you up?" Lady Crawford inquired with studied politeness. "I was afraid she did fall asleep waiting for you, and was just about to go down and see she got safely to bed."

"I shall see her safely to bed," Julian's voice was shaking with what Jeannette was sure must be both amusement and relief, for she was sure, he had, as readily as she, believed they confronted the shade of poor Elinor, in the bobbing white shape that had advanced on them out of the darkness.

"Excellent," Margaret agreed, with perhaps a trifle too much enthusiasm. "I am off to bed, then." She turned her back on them, and made her white-muslined way back toward her room.

Julian turned to Jeannette with an almost hysterical glee. "Dear God," he admitted, suppressing laughter. "I thought she was a ghost."

"I did, too," Jeannette confessed, choking back a giggle.

"Oh, Jules, dear." The voice of Margaret wafted down the corridor to them as they attained the height of the stair landing.

"Mmmm?" Julian responded, still trying not to laugh.

She came floating back toward them, her hands and feet and face, not so visible as the billowing white of her gown. "I intended to ask the vicar to share breakfast with us tomorrow morning . . ."—her gaze roved between them—"but I begin to think it would perhaps be wiser to put him off till nuncheon, for with such a late night . . ."—her voice was almost suggestive, though her expression might be considered politely indifferent—"we shall surely stay abed till all hours in the morning. Do you not agree?"

Julian smiled. "Very sensible, Margaret. I am sure you have the right of it."

She turned again toward her chambers. "Well then, a good night to you both, my dears. Do get some sleep."

Jeannette, embarrassed to be discovered skulking about in the middle of the night, and amused that she had mistaken Margaret for the ghost of Julian's first wife, did not understand the extent of Julian's mirth as he fell back against the wall, hand over mouth, choking back gusts of laughter.

"What?" she insisted, lifting the lamp to stare at him in confusion as he wheezed through his fingers, his face gone pink. "What is so very amusing?"

"Which room has she put you in?" he asked, between breathless outbursts of stifled laughter.

"That one," she said, pointing.

He stopped laughing, long enough to lift eyebrows in amazement. "That one? Directly across from my chambers?" He stared back down the hallway into which his sister had disappeared. "Changed her tune entirely, has she?"

He began to laugh again, and Jeannette found his lightheartedness a delightful thing. It was not until they stood beside the door to her room that Julian leaned very casually against the door frame and told her with a rueful grin, "She believes we mean to spend the night together, you know."

Jeannette regarded him with surprise. "No! I did not know!"

"Yes, and it is no mistake that the vicar has been invited to lunch tomorrow." His smile deepened. "It would appear that your being a Bouillé has distinct advantages."

"Has it?" Jeannette gazed up at him as he looked down at her so warmly, his eyes glowing with mirth, and love and desire. This man she gazed upon was much changed from the first time she had laid eyes on him. His pallor was gone. There was healthy color in his cheeks and lips. His eyes glowed with a vibrant light. Every inch of him radiated a vitality that had once been dimmed almost to extinction.

"Indeed." He opened the door for her, and pushed it back against the wall. The room loomed like a dark and empty cave beyond the lamplight. A lonely place, she thought. She regarded the prospect of a long night in this room with trepidation.

"I shall wish you good night then, dearest."

He meant to leave her.

"Monsieur?" A thought occurred to her, but so audacious was this idea that she was afraid to look at him in voicing it.

"Mmmm?" He drew her into his arms so that both of them stood in the doorway. His mouth looked ready to be amused, his eyes filled with his pleasure in examining her face. His gaze darted over every portion of her aspect, and as he looked, his mouth softened, and his eyes seemed in some strange way to melt in the heat of his feeling for her. He kissed her very softly before she could go on, and said, his voice gruff with emotion, "Ask me anything, my love, and I will do my best to answer you forthrightly."

She raised her eyes to his, and licked her lips, for this was a very dangerous thing she meant to suggest. "Do you think, Julian, that we might sleep together . . ."

His eyes rounded, astounded at what she began to suggest, and a wonderful smile touched his lips, as though, like some fairy godmother, she saw fit to grant his fondest wish.

The door across the hall opened up, and a bleary-eyed

Alphonse stumbled out of Julian's room, yawning hugely. "Monsieur?" He opened his eyes from the yawn, and blinked at Jeannette in consternation "Mademoiselle." He thumped his shoeless heels together, trying valiantly to recover himself, and urbanely face them as if it were a common thing to find the master and the cook who was accused of having run off with heirloom silver whispering intimately in the darkness of the hallway in the wee hours of the morning.

Jeannette was mortified, but Julian looked as if he were inclined to laugh again. He was smiling rather foolishly as he said softly, "You may go to bed, Alphonse. It was very good of you to wait up for me, but I shall see myself unclothed."

"As you wish, milord," Alphonse gave the two of them an admirably cool, business-as-usual nod, before trotting off down the corridor on the way to his room.

Julian was grinning rather wickedly as he turned to Jeannette. Her cheeks felt as if they roared with flame.

"You were saying," he pressed.

She dropped her gaze, flustered and unable to witness his blooming anticipation, for she did not think he would be so thrilled when she was done with what she had to say. "I was just wondering... Might we sleep, just sleep, in each other's arms? In that manner I might go to bed a maid, and rise up on our wedding day a maid, in my own eyes, if no one else's?"

He exhaled heavily, and she dared to peek up at his expression. He had bit down upon his lower lip, and studied the floor. Swiftly, as though he felt her eyes upon him, he raised his regard, gave his fair head a wistful shake and smiled at her with a sadness that made no sense to her. "In all honesty, my dear Jeannette, you ask too much of me."

"Oh." She shrank from him, disappointed beyond measure.

He touched upon her shoulder, stroked her back, her hair, the line of her neck. His voice was low, almost gruff as he said, "I do not think I could restrain myself from seeking to take from you, what you would keep, despite the best of intentions and every ounce of my willpower." He traced the rise of her cheekbone with the tip of a finger. "You are too beautiful, my love, too delicious by far."

"Oh!" she said again, not quite so disappointed.

"I am touched by your suggestion. . . ." He withdrew his hands from their explorations. "To be fair, I must refuse. I bid you good night." He handed her the lamp, and kissed her chastely on the forehead. "Until morning, my love."

Wistfully, she watched him cross to the door of his room. Blinking back stupid tears, she watched the door close. With a deep sigh, she closed the door to her own room, and leaned against it, wondering if she were a fool to prefer another night alone. Mentally she shook herself, for she was profoundly exhausted, both by the hour, and the gamut that her emotions had run. She set down the lamp, and dejectedly began to undress herself.

Julian was breathing heavily when he shut the door to his room. He leaned against the door a moment, closed his eyes, and listened to the heated rush of his pulse. "Damn!" he breathed into the silence of the room. "Damn, damn, damn!"

He began to undress himself with an energy that had buttons flying and bits of clothing wadded up in balls about the room. "Gods!" How could he refuse her? Was he completely devoid of all sense? To lie with a woman, just lie curled about her, the smell of her hair in his face, the sound of her gentle breathing like a caress to his ears—was that not enough? Could he not restrain himself, hands and mouth and loins, just for one night? But, even as he raged about the room, he knew it would be torture, acute, bliss-filled torture. Rare was the man whose self-restraint could withstand such a test.

Jeannette paced the guest room like a caged cat, her arms thrust in a plain white muslin wrapper. Impatiently, she let down her hair, and began to comb the curls with a vigor that left the dark strands crackling with energy. She had wanted so desperately for him to say yes. She had imagined lying next to him, imagined the rich masculine heat of him blanketing her loneliness. To be refused was difficult indeed. She wondered if she fell in his estimation in any way, for proposing such a thing. How could she ever get to sleep now? Was she too prudish in refusing the full extent of his lovemaking, when he meant to marry her? Would God really frown upon them? She threw herself down upon the comfortable bed, and found no comfort there. She punched at the pillow, and set her head upon it, and could think of nothing but Julian, and how much she yearned for his touch to set her on fire, as it had the night he had fondled her so intimately in the garden.

She stared at the wall, and she stared at the ceiling, and she punched the goose-down pillow again, and stared at the lamp on the table by the door. She would never get to sleep with the lamp still glowing, but she was feeling too frustrated to get up and dim the wick.

Julian paced to the door of his room, and then away from it. The candle he had lit flickered in the wake of his movement. He was still clad in breeches and stockings, if nothing else, and yet he could not bring himself to strip them off and don nightshirt and cap, for that would be admitting there was no possibility of sleeping other than alone this night, when he had been offered quite a different opportunity indeed. He paced to the door, and stared at it. Did he mean to cross the hall and take her by force? Did he mean to sweep her into his arms and cajole her into following him back to his bed? Did he mean to beg her forgiveness and tell her that of course he would sleep with her, under any conditions? He turned away from the door, and sat upon the chest at the foot of the bed, and removed his stockings. Could he refrain from touching her? Could he lie beside her for hour upon hour, and not lay a finger on her? Gods! The very thought made his blood race. It was too much to expect of any man, far too much to ask of a man who had been so long without sexual connection.

He got up, barefoot, and paced to the door, unlacing his breeches as he went. It was too much to ask, too much to refuse. He strode to the door, lay hand upon the latch, and took a deep breath.

Jeannette flew across the room in an agitation to douse the light. She burned with a heat, with an inner brilliance that rivaled the glow of the lamp. She would get no rest tonight. Her desire was too strong, her imagination too vivid. She stood, one hand upon the door, gazing at the burning wick in the lamp. As she did, she thought she heard a noise, and leaned her head against the door panel. Footsteps paced the floor of the room opposite her own. Julian Endicott rested no easier than she. She clung to the door, and listened, wishing with all her heart she had the courage either to go to him, or to go to bed, and not be torn asunder in this limbo of dreadful indecision.

The footsteps receded, would seem to have stopped, and her heart suffered to think he was easy while she was not.

She lifted the glass chimney on the lamp, and as she drew breath to blow out the wick, she heard the pacing start up again, advancing, receding, and advancing yet again, only this time the steps paused only long enough that he might wrench open the door, and pace to the middle of the hall, where she waited, in an anticipation of fear and delight, for his knock upon the door, for surely he meant to knock.

But the footsteps halted, and with an oath that made her gasp with enough breath to douse the lamp, she heard him turn, the steps taking him away from her again. The latch on his door turned, even as she, blinded by the sudden onset of darkness grappled with her own. By the time she had rattled the thing open, he was across the hall again, and almost on top of her. His voice, breathless and pinched, was announcing his intention to sleep with her as chaste as any child, did she but desire it, while, she, her words stumbling over his, was bravely announcing her intention to spend the night in his arms, maid or mistress, married or no.

He stopped her from finishing her declaration with his mouth hungrily on hers. Lifting her in his arms, he swept her into his room, and very quietly kicked the door shut behind them.